SPECULATIVE JAPAN

Outstanding Tales of Japanese Science Fiction and Fantasy

To Shige-san,
Best wishes!

Gene van Troyer

ジーン・ヴァン・トロイヤー

Grania Davis

SPECULATIVE JAPAN

Outstanding Tales of Japanese Science Fiction and Fantasy

Edited by Gene van Troyer
and Grania Davis

Kurodahan Press
2007

IN MEMORIAM

JUDITH MERRIL
1923–1997

AND

YANO TETSU
1923–2004

Printed in Japan

FG-J0021-S1
ISBN 4-902075-26-1

KURODAHAN PRESS
KURODAHAN PRESS IS A DIVISION OF INTERCOM LTD.
#403 TENJIN 3-9-10, CHUO-KU, FUKUOKA 810-0001 JAPAN

CONTENTS

CONTENTS

JUDY-SAN

Judith Merril, 1923–1997
By Grania Davis

Known as "the little mother of science fiction" and "the demon-grandmother of Japanese science fiction," Judith Merril was a ground-breaking intellectual pioneer throughout her rich and fascinating life.

Judith Josephine Grossman was born in Boston in January, 1923. After the death of her father in 1929, she lived with her mother in Boston and New York, where she was drawn to the counter-culture movements of that time – Zionism and socialism. Although those movements eventually lost their appeal, the free-thinking idealism and futurism of the counter-culture remained essential for the rest of her life.

In 1940, she married her first husband, Trotskyist Dan Zissman, and their daughter Merril was born in 1942. Merril's name was adopted as Judy's pen name by 1946, when she separated from Dan, and became involved with the New York Futurians and the science fiction community.

Her first acclaimed science fiction story "That Only a Mother" was published in *Astounding Science Fiction* in 1948, and her first notable novel *Shadow on the Hearth* was published in 1950.

In 1948 she married science fiction writer Frederik Pohl, and their daughter, Ann, was born in 1950. She and Fred Pohl divorced in 1953.

Her first *SF: The Year's Greatest* anthology was published in 1956, and she became increasingly noted as an anthologist. During 1956 she helped organize the first Milford (Pennsylvania) Science Fiction

Writers' Conference, which drew many of the finest writers in the field, and she remained active in Milford into the 1960s. It was in Milford that I first met Judy and her family, in 1961, where she encouraged me as a young mother and aspiring writer.

In 1967 she moved to England for a year, and edited the new wave anthology *England Swings SF*. Her reputation as an anthologist grew. I met up with Judy again in London and Paris, and our friendship also grew.

By 1969, Judy was fed up with the Vietnam war and the political mood in the U.S., and immigrated with daughter Ann to Toronto, Canada, where she became a leading member of the Canadian science fiction community. In 1970 she donated her extensive science fiction collection to the Toronto Public Library, and founded the Spaced Out Library, now the prestigious Merril Collection of Science Fiction, Speculation and Fantasy. Judy preferred the term "Speculative Fiction," and we have tried to honor that preference in the title of this anthology, *Speculative Japan*.

Her first visit to Japan was in 1970, when she was invited to join an international group of SF writers and scholars at the International Science Fiction Symposium. During 1972 she was invited to spend six months in Japan, working with Yano Tetsu and many others, where she initiated the Japanese SF Translation Project. The translations moved slowly, and she never lived to see the anthology that she envisioned, but her pioneering work led to the publication of a number of Japanese SF stories in English. Some of these were reprinted by Martin Greenberg and John Apostolou in a 1989 collection *The Best Japanese Science Fiction Stories*. After many decades, her work has led to the publication of this anthology.

Her sojourn also led to the founding of Honyaku Benkyō-kai, the Japanese SF translators' group, which was a major force in translating English language SF into Japanese. Thus her visits to Japan had a major cross-cultural impact. I met Judy-san again in Japan in 1972, where we shopped for rice bowls and discussed the meaning of "love." This was my first introduction to the mysteries of translation, and Judy later invited me to work on her proposed anthology.

She returned to Toronto, and became a Canadian citizen in 1976. She remained very active in writing, publishing, lecturing, TV, and the Merril SF Collection. She spent the grey winter months in Montego Bay, Jamaica.

I last saw Judy in 1988 at Boreal 10, a small Francophone con in northern Quebec. Afterward we kept in touch occasionally by phone, especially during the 1994 "Visions of Mars" project, which attempted to send a CD-ROM of international Mars-themed SF, including some Japanese stories, to Mars.

By 1991 her energy and health began to decline, and she required heart surgery. She died of heart failure on September 12, 1997. Judy-san is still missed, and this anthology is dedicated in part to her memory.

For further information about Judy Merril's life and work, I refer you to her granddaughter's excellent biography, *Better to Have Loved* by Judith Merril and Emily Pohl-Weary (Toronto: Between The Lines Press, 2002), which is the source of much of this information.

Preface

Sᴘᴇᴄᴜʟᴀᴛɪᴠᴇ ᴊᴀᴘᴀɴ is an important contribution to a conversation that spans the globe, provoked by the question of human destiny. Where are we going and how should we adjust our perceptions in a rapidly changing world?

This conversation has been going on for a long time, though at times it seemed all too one-sided. In now bringing these Japanese literary treasures before a new generation of English-speaking readers, the editors, translators and authors of this volume have provided a valuable service.

As Gene van Troyer explains in his fine introduction, both history and national character played important roles in shaping Science Fiction, across every ocean and around the planet. This diversity is strength. But the shared underlying notion – that writers and readers can broaden their horizons by exploring space, time and reality, using thought-experiments that stretch the mind – this is an essential common element, one that bridges every culture brave enough to embrace the spirit of SF.

This core willingness to question our own assumptions is the same one that underlies both art and science. Whatever your nation of origin, you will not find it more richly expressed than in SF. In much the same way that Hokusai offered us thirty-six views of Mount Fuji, the stories that you'll find collected here will broaden your view of what is possible or imaginable, provoking unusual – and sometimes uncomfortable – thoughts. That is as it should be.

Yamano Kōichi's "three phases of Japanese SF" suggest that this is an especially valuable time for Occidentals to lift their heads, paying heed to storytelling excitement in the East. Capable, confident and boundlessly imaginative, Japanese authors are busy blending the traditions of Murasaki and Yano with the very latest tech-rich imagery of a cybernetic future. They are posing challenges that we had better get busy answering. All of us.

INTRODUCTION

Phase Shifting
By Gene van Troyer

THE QUESTION will inevitably be asked: what is the difference between Anglo-American and Japanese science fiction? We'll get back to that.

Speculative Japan represents the third major collection of Japanese science fiction and fantasy short stories in English translation ever published. The first two were *The Best Japanese Science Fiction Stories*, edited by John L. Apostolou and Martin H. Greenberg (with a lot of behind the scenes help from Grania Davis and Judith Merril), published by Dembner Books in 1989 and now long out of print. The second was *New Japanese Fiction*, edited by Tatsumi Takayuki and Larry McCaffery, published as a special issue of *The Review of Contemporary Fiction* in 2002.

About half of the stories in the present volume appear here in English for the first time: Hirai's "A Time for Revolution," Toyota's "Another *Prince of Wales*," Fukushima's "The Flower's Life is Short," Kajio's "Reiko's Universe Box," Mayumura's "I'll Get Rid of Your Discontent," Kōno's "Hikari" and Yamano's "Where Do the Birds Fly Now?" All of the other stories are reprinted from various magazines, journals, and general story collections. Well-informed readers may also notice that several of the reprinted stories were first collected in Apostolou & Greenberg's collection. They are collected again here for a couple of reasons other than that they are good stories that deserve yet another reprinting.

In his afterword, Asakura Hisashi mentions Judith Merril's translating efforts on behalf of Japanese SF and her desire to promote an awareness of it in the English-speaking part of our universe. She and her co-translators had gathered about fifteen stories for a projected anthology – "The Book," as she referred to it – along the lines of her successful *England Swings SF* anthology. A confluence of problems – other contract commitments, the time involved in translation, and North American publishing industry mergers, editorial firings, and contract cancellations – put the dream represented by The Book on indefinite hold. When the 1989 Dembner collection came about, not all (fewer than half) of the stories Merril had collected and translated could be included. *Speculative Japan* has given us the opportunity to recombine as many as possible of the original Merril translations and translations that others had done for her with those that had yet to see print, and present them together as had originally been intended by Merril and her Japanese partners in the SF Writers of Japan's Honyaku Benkyō-kai (Translation Study Meeting). Of course, as the years passed and Grania Davis worked with others on the project, more stories were added to the list.

Japan's history of technology and mythology play a role in the history of its science fiction. Its earliest major literary works, the *Kojiki, Nihongi* (or *Nihon Shoki*, Chronicles of Earliest Japan) and Lady Murasaki's *Genji Monogatari* (arguably the world's first novel) are replete with fantastic imagery that has influenced the course of Japanese literature to the present day; and the opening of Japan to the outside world in the latter half of the nineteenth century started the wholesale importation from the West of all technological ideas that would serve to assist the Japanese effort to become an industrialized nation, one that could stand as an equal to the European and American nations that dominated the world. That said, science fiction in the standard sense did not begin until the Meiji Restoration and the importation of Western ideas.

The first "science fiction writer" of any influence to be translated into Japanese was Jules Verne. His influence led to novels by Japanese authors about inventions they imagined. Oshikawa Shunrō's

Kaitei Gunkan (Undersea Warship) is a popular example from 1900. The novel dealt with submarines and the coincidentally accurate prediction of a coming Russo-Japanese war. The period between the world wars was more influenced by American science fiction. A popular writer in this era was Unno Jūza, who is sometimes deemed "the father of Japanese science fiction." Science fiction has been in Japan for well over a century, perhaps for as much as 120–150 years, and World War II, of course, ended with Japan in the unenviable science fictional position of being the only nation at the receiving end of atomic warfare.

The literary standards for SF in this, and the previous, era tended to be low (not unlike much of what passed for fiction in American pulp magazines), and Japanese readers and literary critics before World War II rarely, if ever, saw science fiction as serious literature. Instead it was a form of entertainment or amusement for children. Prior to WWII and in the early postwar years, arguably SF was not even recognized as being a genre in its own right, and was classified as belonging with mystery and ghost stories – in other words, just one area of tales about the strange, the weird, and the unreal.

We don't make any claim that the stories in this collection present a definitive picture of Japanese science fiction. Definitive collections are not, we think, really possible for any literature that is alive and thriving. If it's alive, it's always changing, and in the changing it eludes fixed definitions. At the very least, however, *Speculative Japan* represents an idiosyncratic cross section of the history of Japanese SF over the last fifty years, when Japanese SF emerged as a distinct genre in Japanese literature, and they cover the three major phases of the genre as it has developed.

Yamano Kōichi (Yamano 1994) has identified these as outlined below.

The *Pre-Fabricated House Phase* (or "infiltration and diffusion"): Japanese SF writers who made their debuts in the early 1950s and were deeply influenced by traditional Western definitions of SF. Instead of creating their own worlds, they immersed themselves in and emulated the translated major works of Anglo-American authors like Asimov, Heinlein, Brown, and Bradbury. Somewhat like living in a "ready-built" home, the SF genre in Japan thus grew into Japanese culture regardless of whether there was a place for it.

Remodeling the Ready-Built Home Phase (or "adaptation and acquisition"): The second phase, in the 1960s, was characterized by an attempt to "remodel" the prefabricated house through the works of writers like Komatsu Sakyō and Tsutsui Yasutaka who expanded the world-view of Japanese SF to include socio-political and multi-temporal themes, evolutionary and information theory, and new (and sometimes quite existential) patterns of reader-text interaction. But, in so doing, they often distanced themselves from traditional Japanese cultural perspectives, foregrounding a Western-style "rationalistic" and objectively macroscopic world-view.

Putting Up a New House Phase (or "creative departure"): The third phase in the evolution of Japanese SF was meeting the need for Japanese SF to develop its own cultural identity, to move away from imitating Anglo-American models, to focus on questions of the human – ideology and metaphysics instead of rockets and robots – and to present actuality informed by the writer's own consistent subjectivity in the context of the Japanese civilization. The SF works of Abe Kōbō reflect many of these aspects, as do the SF stories by writers like Mayumura Taku, Hirai Kazumasa, Ishikawa Takashi, and Yamano Kōichi. Such authors paved the way for Japanese SF to find its own originality and voice.

In this historical sense, the stories collected in *Speculative Japan* reflect this journey from the borrowed to the reinvented and, finally, the uniquely Japanese, as reflected in works by authors like

Ōhara Mariko, Kōno Tensei, and Kawakami Hiromi. It's a voice and perspective that are still in the process of developing. Japanese SF seems to have moved from hyper-rationalized attempts to present the world in tidy little packages that "explain" it all, rather like classical physicists mapping out the clockworks of a finite universe, to a literature that maps the universe as a place of often indeterminate mental states, rather like quantum physicists describing a universe that is solid and particulate from one perspective, and at the same time hazy and fluid from another perspective.

The stories in *Speculative Japan* that could be said to fall primarily into the first phase would be Komatsu's "The Savage Mouth," Ishikawa's "The Road to the Sea," Fukushima's "The Flower's Life is Short," Yano's "The Legend of the Paper Spaceship," Toyota's "Another *Prince of Wales*," Kajio's "Reiko's Universe Box," and Mayumura's "I'll Get Rid of Your Discontent." All of these stories in some way seem to express a rational, reductive view of an explainable universe. Phase two stories – easily examples of the Japanese New Wave's beginnings – would be Hirai's "A Time for Revolution," Yamano's "Where Do the Birds Fly Now?", Tensei's "Hikari," Hanmura's "Cardboard Box," and Tsutsui's "Standing Woman." Thematically, these stories in some way reject a totally rationalistic view of the world as being completely explainable. Ōhara's "Girl" and Kawakami's "Mogera Wogura" fall into phase three as stories that reflect the universe as a mental or cybernetic state of existence. The universe may be moored to a physical reality, but the equally if not more important parameters are in some way metaphysical. The final offering in this collection, Yoshimasu Gōzō's poem "Adrenalin," is beyond the scope of genre. It flows like a steady bath of encouraging energy from the heart of the heart of Storyland, a creative anthem.

JAPANESE science fiction in English translation involves, at least at one level, a complex process of importation, reverse-importation, and exchange that has occurred between Japanese and western

SF since the beginning of the 1950s. Judith Merril experienced this directly in the early 1970s when she embarked on her translation project with her Japanese collaborators. Merril had taken a hiatus from her role in American SF as a premier anthologist and reviewer during much of the 1960s, and her journey into Japanese SF served to reconnect her to SF, helping her to overcome a growing sense of skepticism about SF's relevance to contemporary world problems (Newell and Tallentire 2005). As a writer and editor, she believed it was a SF author's obligation to imagine probable or alternative futures, and the field seemed to be failing this expectation. It was when she was asked to write an essay about translation for *Hayakawa SF Magazine* that she realized an important connection: for much of her career she had always been a translator of one kind or another – between Canadians and American political refugees in Canada, the "counter-culture" and the "establishment," and between the different science fictional visions of North America, the U.K., and Japan.

"In the broad sense," she wrote, "the idioms and images of science fiction have proved one of the best means of translation, between traditional and emergent cultures in North America. In the specific sense, I suspect SF can now provide the best opening channel for meaningful values-and-concept exchanges between Japan and North America" (in Newell and Tallentire).

Merril could not speak, read, or write Japanese, so she had to work with a team of Japanese. They would meet, laboriously go through a story phrase by phrase and sentence by sentence, navigating a landscape marked by Japanese SF neologisms, typically seeking through evocation and suggestion to capture meaning in English equivalents that would sound like what a Japanese author *would* write if they wrote in English.

Japanese SF critic and cypberpunk philosopher Tatsumi Takayuki characterizes the process of exchange as the ultimate arrival at "soft translation." He writes, "Japanese culture inspired English-speaking cyberpunk writers, but the transaction was not a one-way street" (Tatsumi 2002):

> For cyberpunk fiction also provided the Japanese with a chance to reinvestigate their own cyborgian identity. Aramaki Yoshio's New Wave short story "Soft Clocks"... foregrounds the contrast between the imperialist gluttony of "Dali of Mars" and the anorexia of his granddaughter Vivi. In the heyday of the cyberpunk movement, this text was translated by Kazuko Behrens and Lewis Shiner for the January-February 1989 issue of *Interzone*. While Aramaki in his own way digested and cannibalized outer space-oriented American SF of the 1950s, Lewis Shiner in turn digested and softly transfigured "Soft Clocks" for a later generation and another culture. This kind of "soft translation" or transaction between cultures is becoming more and more significant for the future of global SF.

This process of translation is also perhaps most evident in the pervasive international presence and popularity of Japanese manga and anime, and of video games, which on the one hand are derived from manga and anime and on the other inspire spin-off manga and anime series of their own (a theme addressed in Suga Hiroe's "Freckled Figure," which we hope to publish in a later volume of the *Speculative Japan* series. Clearly the explosion in anime, manga, and video games that are pervaded with SF themes and story lines has created a new generation of audience that does not necessarily see itself as SF-oriented. If the prestigious literary awards like the Akutagawa Prize, the Tanizaki Prize, and the Naoki Prize going these days to authors of science fictional works are an indicator, it may be that SF in Japan is in the process of morphing into a standard for Japanese literature in general. In a sense, the modern mythos reflected in Japanese science fiction almost seems to be circling Japanese literature back to something akin to its mythopoetic origins.

And we circle back to the opening of this introduction: what is the difference between Anglo-American and Japanese science fiction? We can't say definitively, but can only point to trends and tendencies. Viewed through one facet of the jewel, we can say, as Tatsumi (2002) does, that "what with the imperative of American democratization and the effect of indigenous adaptability, the postwar Japanese had simultaneously to transform and naturalize themselves as a new tribe of cyborgs" as reflected in the images from manga and anime. Japanese SF leans (or has leaned) more on robots and cyborgs than on stars and planets. Readers love, for instance, Asimov's robot stories much more than his *Foundation* novels, as something that can be emblematic of the country's historical quest to redefine and reinvent itself – especially in the radioactive wake of 6th August 1945, the day the Imperial Sun God fell and a new Sun God rose.

From another facet, that which looks back to the past, we might have said that the overall preoccupation of Japanese SF was to discover how the Japanese got to where they are by reflecting the past against the mirror of imagined futures or alternate worlds, a view that would be in keeping with a nationwide obsession of the Japanese to discover, or perhaps redefine, who they were in the post-WWII half of the twentieth century by comparing themselves to America, the only country to have vanquished them in war in over a thousand years. The future pointed the way back to who they once were. Anglo-American SF, on the other hand, might have been said to use the future to understand the present and plot a course forward. That's one simple way of looking at a convenient answer. Another convenient answer might be that Anglo-American SF is still about hypothesis formation, testing, and reporting the results of the experiment with a tidy conclusion that announces "problem solved;" while Japanese SF is more about the on-going experiment and less about, or even absent, a tidy conclusion. Beginnings and endings are less important than the middle. Japanese genre SF stories leaned more on softer sciences (for instance, psychology and biology) rather than hard science; but recently many hard SF stories have begun to appear. One more characteristic is that Olaf Stapledon-like philosophical, transcendental stories – stories that explore the meaning of humanity and the individual – seem to be more common in Japanese SF than in U.S. or British. This may be a reflection of culture in general, with the social concerns of Japanese with regard to matters of group, hierarchy, and where one fits into the equation, as opposed to the Anglo-American culture of the independent self-reliant, problem-solving rugged individual.

A less tidy answer is that if as a literature science fiction in Japan is doing what good literature seems to be about, any differences between SF produced in Japan and elsewhere in the world will be matters of costuming and cosmetics. The stages will be different, as will the casts of characters, but the stories will be the metonymic Ur stories of Storyland, the stories shared by everyone, and the science fictions of Japan, North America, and the U.K. still share a core of identity. All of them posit a rational world counter-pointed by an irrational fantasy. Likewise, the science fiction and fantasy imagery shared across the borders of language and culture in movies, manga, anime, and video games has become a common property of global SF. This further blurs meaningful distinctions beyond the obvious features of language and local settings.

In this first decade of the twenty-first century, in which the vastness of geospace has collapsed into various rooms in the house of cyberspace, it might not even be sensible to keep thinking in terms of differences. In a world where the remotest places on earth are just a screen's view away on a computer connected to the internet, where images and hastily (if often badly) translated text quickly lose their exotic textures and become absorbed into local consciousness, it may make more sense to think in terms of the coincidentally similar and globally shared – as suggested above by movies, television, videos, and online gaming and role-playing adventures shared between players in St. Louis, Missouri, Ishikawa

City, Japan, and Mumbai, India. In the scope of this global cyber reality, literature loses its locality and becomes parallel and synchronistic (Tatsumi and McCaffery 2002). Even as we write this, even as you read it, storytellers in Vancouver, New York, Moscow, Johannesburg, and Osaka may be setting the scene for a tale to unfold in Rick's Casablanca nightclub. Rick, or many parallel Ricks, might even be a character in each alternative tale.

That, of course, is a question for literary critics and theorists with far greater insight than we humble SF editors possess, with our simpler effort to present interesting stories to readers who just want a few good stories to pass the time with, like good conversations. If we've managed to do anything with this collection, we're sure we've accomplished this. Let's sit back and enjoy this first fifteen-stop leg of our journey, and thanks for coming along for the ride.

Finally, a few acknowledgements are in order. We are indebted to the assistance given to us in compiling this anthology by Asakura Hisashi, Itō Norio, Kobayashi Yoshiō, Maki Shinji, Ōshiro Makoto van Troyer, Ōshiro Tomoko van Troyer, Shibano Takumi, Shimada Yōichi, Tatsumi Takayuki, and Yamagishi Makoto; as well as the interest and encouragement of the Science Fiction and Fantasy Writers Association of Japan. Any errors of fact, omissions, or misinterpretations are, of course, our own.

References

Newell, Dianne, and Jenea Tallentire. 2005. Translating Science Fiction: Judith Merril in Japan. *Science Fiction Foundation: Academic Track Essays.* 22 March 2007 <http://www.sf-foundation.org/publications/academictrack/newell.php>.

Tatsumi, Takayuki. 2002. A Soft Time Machine: From Translation to Transfiguration. *Science Fiction Studies* #88 (29.3).

Tatsumi, Takayuki, and Larry McCaffery, eds. 2002. *New Japanese Fiction.* Special issue of *The Review of Contemporary Fiction* 22.2 (Summer).

Yamano, Kōichi. 1994). Japanese SF, Its Originality and Orientation (1969). Translated by Kazuko Behrens. Edited by Darko Suvin and Tatsumi Takayuki. *Science Fiction Studies* #62 (21.1).

SHIBANO TAKUMI

"Collective Reason": A Proposal

(1971, rev. 2000)
Translated by Xavier Bensky
Introduced by Tatsumi Takayuki

SHIBANO TAKUMI (1926–) has been called the father of Japanese SF because, as the founder of Japanese science fiction's first fanzine, *Uchūjin* (Cosmic Dust), it was he who discovered and nurtured so many of the genre's authors. Under the pen name Kozumi Rei, he authored *Hokkyoku shitii no hanran* (1959, rev. 1977, Revolt in Polar City) as well as many short stories, and he translated numerous works of hard science fiction, from Larry Niven's *Ringworld* (1970) to John Cramer's *Twistor* (1989). As "C.R." he also authored two monthly columns in Cosmic Dust: "Fanzine Review" and "Eye of Space."

Shibano's idea that "a professional SF author should be a fan as well" necessarily brought him into conflict with *SF Magajin* (SF Magazine) editor Fukushima Masami over the constitution of fandom and "prodom." But in discussing the motives for the formation of the Science Fiction and Fantasy Writers of Japan (SFWJ), Fukushima wrote this about their relationship:

> Those who can see this only as a petty, short-sighted turf battle for the leadership of Japanese SF have no appreciation for the bone-breaking struggle Shibano and I have both waged to establish this genre. In fact the two of us have worked to accomplish a common goal, he in his way and I in mine (*Mitō no jidai* [The Untrodden Age])

Interested readers can discover further details in Shibano's memoir *Chiri mo tsumoreba – Uchūjin no yonjū nen shi* (1997, When the Dust Settled: Forty years of Cosmic Dust). In the 1960s, the friction between Shibano and Fukushima, like the debate between Yamano Kōichi and Aramaki Yoshio, was an inevitable conflict in pursuit of this "common goal," promoting SF.

Shibano's view of SF unfolds from his definition of the genre as "a literature recognizing that the products of human reason separate themselves from reason and become self-sufficient." What Shibano identified as "the idea of SF" was a posthumanist theory constructed from a vantage point after modernism, and his position resonates with contemporary ideas of poststructuralism and chaos theory. Shibano applied these theories in the columns he wrote as "C.R.," asking a fundamental question: whether the fans who read SF were medial forms leading to the posthuman, or perhaps already posthuman themselves. A being who could grasp the failure of individual reason by means of individual reason itself would be a mediator *à la* Arthur C. Clarke – i.e., an Overmind. But the ability to shed that skin of reason by oneself is a quality, he argued, that belongs to the posthuman as conceived by authors like A.E. van Vogt and Robert Heinlein. The idea at the heart of Shibano's theory was this: young people are naturally receptive to SF; but those who continue to read SF as adults are people who suffer the weight of the individual self in the real world as they reduce that self to something infinitesimal. Considered in light of Shibano's ideas, Fukushima Masami's confession four years earlier is even more interesting. Fukushima wrote: "I feel a helplessness at the fact that while I have been so wrapped up in SF's bold efforts to remake reality, half my life has slipped by." That is why, Fukushima said, "I feel an affinity for stories about other dimensions, about time travel, about immortality" (*SF Magazine*, Feb. 1966).

Shibano first set down his vision systematically in 1970, in a *Cosmic Dust* column "SF no shisō" ("The Ideas of SF") that he signed

Kozumi Rei. But no sooner was the first installment published than its Renaissance humanist position was opposed in print by SF author Aramaki Yoshio, then a recent arrival on the literary scene. The debate seemed as if it might end with a simple acknowledgment of these different understandings of the concept of humanism, but it stretched on unexpectedly in monthly installments from October 1971 through December 1972. In 1992, twenty years after the debate, Shibano revised and reedited that (initial) essay for republication in my volume *Nippon SF ronsōshi* (2000, Science Fiction Controversies in Japan). This is the version translated below.

Tatsumi Takayuki

SHIBANO TAKUMI

"Collective Reason": A Proposal
(1971, rev. 2000)

0. FOR NOW, let's call it human "collective reason." Although it is thought to consist of the combined reason of many different individuals, it actually has an autonomous life of its own, something beyond the scope of individual control and understanding, like a child that no longer obeys its parents. It is a function of the phenomenon of collective thought that emerges in human groups, following the same pattern as individual reason. The development of civilizations and the formation of cultures depend on it. (Jung's "collective unconscious" could also be seen as one of its expressions).

Needless to say, the product of individual reason attaining a kind of autonomy is not particularly novel in itself. Science and technology, of course, and even laws and works of art, develop of their own accord, detached from the intentions of those who established or created them.[1]* Collective reason may be the generalized case of such phenomena. Furthermore, there is nothing that necessarily limits its site of emergence to human groups, but to deal with too many different cases right at the outset would probably only create confusion.

I would like to state beforehand that "collective reason" is still just a working hypothesis for interpreting reality from a different angle. The purpose of this essay is not to prove the existence of "collec-

The notes for this essay begin on page 37.

23

tive reason," but rather to construct the concept by considering a number of things in the history of human groups as illustrations of its appearance.

1. Let us begin our explanation at the very beginning. Long ago, it is said, when human beings were trying to gain a footing on the earth as an emerging species, the first step in the cerebral process that gave birth to "civilization" was the recognition of temporal patterns stemming from the experience of keeping the fire lit. A fire dies out if it is not fed, but you can't disregard the fire's intensity and feed it too much either. From such experiences, the human cerebrum learned to take a set of consecutive phenomena from what was at hand, and to identify the first event as the "cause" and the second as the "effect." One could consider conditioned reflexes in animals as an example of this in its primal phase, but within human groups such correlations established themselves in the form of superstitions as the basis of social behavior, and went even beyond what was originally required. Early humans thus came to live surrounded by innumerable taboos, good and evil augury, and proofs of divine retribution, all mixed together whether they were useful or not.

For the group overall, these probably served to protect early humans from the outside world, create stable lifestyles, and lead them to prosperity. However, individual members undoubtedly saw many of these superstitions as meaningless, burdensome, or even harmful restrictions on their lives. Based on the premise that there was a system governing these superstitions, a process of analysis began that split and developed in two different directions. The first was "religion," which attempts to square everything away by hypothesizing a transcendental being at the root of all things, and the second was "science," which attempts to persuade by investigating the regularity of various phenomena and connecting them together with evidence. I apologize for the terribly rough treatment of the matter, but schematically speaking, this should be correct.

24

God → human centrality

The observations that follow are based on the history of the West, in which these two positions developed with an intensity that made them irreconcilable. In the modern age, the absolute quality of the transcendental "god" faded, and in response, the absolute quality of the image of "humankind" came to the fore. It was a shift in consciousness that obeyed the same collective motivation as before. Thus appeared "modern humanism." Simply put, for the more advanced human groups of the day, threats caused by problems within human society now outweighed threats from the outside world, so rather than a "religion" that sought the grace of god, it was humanist "ideology" (a term I use here as the largest common denominator) that provided the most effective tools to deal with the situation. (Of course, considered more closely, this represents the correlation between religion and ideology on the one hand, and science on the other. That is not the focus of this essay, however. Moreover, while it is true that religion and superstition's roles were dwarfed as a result of this process, their influence has not weakened in the least, even today. This probably demonstrates that, as members of the collective, our everyday thoughts and actions are still governed less by rational ideas than by intuitive beliefs and even taboos akin to conditioned reflexes.)

The crux of this long introduction is that this series of developments was not born from the minds of individual contributors within the collective – at least not in the sense that each one consciously headed in that direction. Rather, this was the emergence of an effect unwilled by and unrelated to any individual consciousness.

Moreover, while the religion and science (and, in some respects, superstition and ideology) born from this autonomous reason played an important role in making human beings more human, they also created a variety of harmful influences, as everyone knows. One of my justifications for giving the title of "reason" to a mere working hypothesis is that its products are such double-edged swords. Each of the cases considered below exhibits this same pattern.

2. In the last ten years or so, Japan has seen tremendous changes in its social values. It has readily assimilated many antecedent traditions from the West, and is trying to go beyond them in some fields. Consider, for example, the declining value of leadership positions: job titles with the word "head" in them have begun to lose their former appeal, the number of salaried workers who shun executive positions is on the rise, and the notion of managerial posts as rewards has lost its meaning. What could possibly be the reason for this?

Actually, to raise that issue, we need to begin by asking why positions with the word "head" in them rank so high in the first place. What is the origin of the notion that leaders should be respected by their subordinates as "superior" beings, and why should obtaining such a position turn into a lifetime goal?

Resuming our account of origins, early humans (like some herd animals) required leaders with outstanding wisdom and experience in order to protect the collective from foreign enemies. Even if it meant sacrificing some constituent members, protecting and preserving the leader served to ensure the safety and prosperity of the whole. The rise of a primitive sense of "hierarchy" [*jōge*] can probably be explained through power relations. The "strongest" individuals (not only physically but overall) obtained the right to slack off their work, give orders to other members of the group, or monopolize the attention of the opposite sex. Although they came to shoulder unexpected "leadership responsibilities" as a result, strong individuals wielded the power to bend rules as well, though there were probably also many cases where a sense of responsibility came first. But here too, this value system necessarily began to develop independently of its origins [*jisō o hajimeta*]. As a result, the leadership's protective structure became exaggeratedly formal, inflated beyond necessity, and laden with what some considered ridiculous rituals, peculiar mores, and a variety of other supplementary elements that proceed from a sense of hierarchy. Finally, this led to the formation of the larger "surface" or behavior pattern represented by the collective's particular customs – in other words, its "culture."

Humanism, which was to become the foundation for all of modern ideology, originally rejected such blindly hierarchical relations. It seems that such things don't happen all at once, however: much of humanistic thought has not discarded "god," and there were even some early cases in which the existence of a slave class was sanctioned.

"god" in modern age

One vision of what would happen if humanism's original sense of equality were carried forward in a linear fashion can be found, for example, in Robert Heinlein's *Beyond This Horizon* (1948). That is indeed a world in which each and every citizen is forced to become a leader, and I think it is truly an excellent forecast. In reality, though, it turns out that Heinlein's honorable "armed citizens" are those who ride in automobiles and spew exhaust fumes on the pedestrians who correspond to the "unarmed citizens" in the novel. It seems that science fiction predictions cannot help but be apocalyptic.

It appears, in any case, that humanism is quickly eroding in turn. I find it very hard to believe that a future such as Heinlein's world, strictly based on modern individualism, will ever really come to pass. In our current circumstances, it appears that progress toward universal equality is proceeding less quickly than the disintegration of culture resulting from changes in the correlation between "responsibility," "honor," and "reward" – the things that had heretofore constituted a *raison d'être* for all members of the collective. The decline in the status of leaders is, in the final analysis, just one aspect of this trend.

I think it safe to say that what has sustained this development until now is a contemporary humanism – I call it "indulgent humanism" – that has gone through broad changes since humanism's strict early phase when it confronted God. But what about the future?

What awaits us on the road ahead is not merely the loss of hierarchical relations but rather their very reversal, is it not? That is the trend, at least. I would like to consider this matter in the following pages.

3. There was an incident at a certain American university last year [1971] in which a group of students took university office computers "hostage" and issued demands to the administration. Since respect for computer life was not the absolute priority it would have been with human hostages, the incident was promptly concluded by police forces who stormed the office. Still, for its suggestion that we may now live in a world where computers are recognized as having "personalities," this incident stirs up deep emotions. While the ringleaders didn't seriously equate humans with machines, in their own minds at least they did not clearly perceive the truth of modern humanism's hypocritical demand for the absolute priority of human life.

In due course, our own common beliefs about man-machine equivalence are bound to reach to the level of these students and go beyond it. In fact, the sense of "hierarchy reversal" that I mentioned earlier may be humanity's preliminary effort to adapt to the age that most likely awaits us, in which machines will dominate humans. [2]

Future computers will probably one day surpass human beings in all abilities, take complete control of all industrial activity, and eventually make advances into the fields of politics, art, and culture in general. When an advanced machine attains the position of supreme being – or even just leader – people will go about their business under its control (a control probably exercised from within their bodies and without), just as naturally as people go around looking at their watches today. This would truly be the advent of a full-scale computopia, but humans won't stand for it if they perceive this state of affairs as "servitude" to machines. Therefore, we have begun in advance the operation of clearing away the old notion of hierarchy. Couldn't we think of it that way? [3]

28

So how could human beings rationalize such a system? I'll share with you an amusing allegory pertaining to this. It was in a round-table discussion published in a computer trade journal:

Once upon a time, human beings could not stand bearing the burden of responsibility for their own actions and tried to comfort themselves by finding something to rely on. They chose the dog as their model, an animal that lives a carefree life and entrusts its owner with the power of life and death. In imitation, humans contrived the existence of "GOD," which was "DOG" written backwards, and made everyone its slave, shifting all responsibilities onto it. Eventually, however, the existence of God came to be a nuisance. Humans became sick and tired of always praying to God and swearing allegiance, like dogs wagging their tails to show obedience to their masters. Eventually, however, they found a more suitable model. That was the cat, an animal that lets itself be taken care of without ever fawning on humans. Convinced of their choice, humans are now excitedly trying to invent "TAC," which is "CAT" spelled backwards.

This "TAC," of course, is something that supposes an omnipotent machine system. Come to think of it, many early computers such as ENIAC had names ending in "AC." Joking aside, though, this story paints a frank picture of future society. In the end, human beings are destined to settle into their roles as pets of the machine system. That is the storyteller's parting shot.

Then again, the reversal of hierarchies may already be established by that time, so these machines that settle into the role of humans' owners will probably be considered "slaves entrusted with plenary power" rather than "despots." With that caveat, it is not a bad prediction. Nevertheless, if society were to actually turn out that way, its appearance would most likely surpass anything forecast in science fiction.

One work of fiction that paints a full and accurate picture of such a computopia is "The Evitable Conflict" in Isaac Asimov's *I, Robot* (1950). Here again, however, it seems that a science fiction prediction ends up as a kind of apocalyptic statement. Considering how times change, I think it is unreasonable to hope for a future penetrated by a scientific reason so similar to the brand we have today. [4]

4. So far, I have frequently mentioned "the erosion of humanism" and, in contrast to strict modern humanism, I have used expressions like "hypocritical contemporary humanism" and "indulgent humanism." In fact, it seems as if the word "humanism," along with the term "democratic," has already turned into an all-purpose pardon of sorts. Needless to say, a surplus of slogans represents a decay of meaningful substance. (If I'm not careful, someone might argue that "collective reason" itself is an expression of humanism. Well, obviously, I'm kidding again, since my argument means denying the conclusiveness of this thing we call the individual.)

At any rate, just as the basic structures of thought once changed from "religion" to "ideology," as the machine system advances, another turn will surely follow. So then, from the human point of view, what will be the fundamental principle to emerge in the wake of the ideology called humanism?

Of course, even I don't have a clear image of it, but the one thing I can say is that it will probably be a concept akin to "methodology." This will be of a completely different order from so-called scientific methodology, however. Like the structures that preceded it, it will have to be something that can provide a standard for the actions of individuals within the collective. [5]

When the substance of this "methodology" becomes visible, we will probably also be able to grasp the now ambiguous mechanism by which "collective reason" manifests itself. This process could likely start off with the machine system acquiring a position as a thinking entity external to humans. At the risk of oversimplifying, I'll illustrate this with a familiar situation: imagine a futuristic computer, serving as moderator at a symposium for humans, able to synthesize all the participants' statements and state a conclusion.

Remarks like this may come across as abrupt, irresponsible, and careless. Therefore, I would like to state the following, just in case. The future computer I am talking about is not some new gadget that will suddenly appear one day. It is an entity that will come into being after the computer society sustaining human society goes through many generations, automatically building up a system by interconnecting and by generating ever more sophisticated programs and subprograms, until all this progressive development converges on a single course. Right now, we can only predict the direction of this development, not its ultimate outcome. So to address an issue much closer to hand: in the eyes of humans, will this entity be seen as a step in the right direction?

Since the criteria for what is considered "favorable" will probably change between now and that time, we simply cannot make any definite statements. Nor does it seem likely that our individual wishes will be reflected in the process of determining the course of developments – this will be decided by the flow of circumstances surrounding the various computer companies' programming and networking as they continue to evolve. No single individuals – not politicians, religious leaders, philosophers or even the computer scientists and software developers directly engaged in the system's operation – can subjectively interfere with its evolution. As the considerations and intentions of developers, the requests and responses from users, and countless other short-sighted ideas and feedback become haphazardly assimilated, without any larger vision or judgment whatsoever, an enormous complex of software steadily accumulates. In this way, the collective reason of the so-called "First World countries" that rule our globe is already in the process of achieving autonomy today.

This is the setup for what Aldous Huxley described in *Brave New World* (1932). Details aside, the strange atmosphere of the future society portrayed in that classic work may be surprisingly on target.

5. In my student days, I believed that all metaphysical arguments could be reduced to a physical level. I also thought that no "truth" was absolute, and that any truth was a relative concept that might lose its status as truth, depending on the standpoint of the person advocating it. If someone pointed out to me that I was a rationalist, I would boast in retort: "I'm not so irrational as to let myself be bound by an ideology like rationalism." That in itself is just a play on words. But one false step, and this can lead to the loss of one's standards of behavior. Anyone who would reject the "absolute" must remember the ineluctable dilemma that making all things relative is, in itself, an absolute position. This is a paradox that beleaguers all the forms of logic that don't resort to dogma.

As you have probably noticed by now, this very essay has, from the beginning, contained such a paradox. To think that an individual like myself, relying on my own diminutive faculties of reason, is arguing for a collective reason that transcends individual reason – what could possibly be more contradictory?

Nevertheless, now that I have begun, I intend to follow this through to its conclusion. As with Schrödinger's cat, a single paradox surely doesn't render the entire system meaningless. Moreover, it might seem that I'm flirting with paradox once again, but this very argument has the effect of shaking the foundations of collective reason, at least in some small way.

What is clear is that reality has already advanced to the stage at which the simple law of excluded middle no longer applies.[6] The seeds from which such paradoxes began to gain recognition and assert themselves as facts were sown early in the natural sciences. To cite an example that falls within my own limited understanding, physics dealt with the opposition between the particle and the wave theories of light. And, moving into the twentieth century, it was able to pull off the fusion of materialism and idealism by making Einstein's relativity and Heisenberg's uncertainty the foundation of all its theories. This was a process in which both the "object" and "subject" established by materialism and idealism were removed from consideration, and the relationship between subject and object – "observation" – was given a new reality. Of course, qualifying it as such does not solve the actual mysteries of nature, so from a scientist's point of view, such naming is probably just wasted motion, a meaningless redundancy. The only thing I have accomplished with this reasoning is to indirectly persuade myself. I don't pretend to have reached a true understanding of real circumstances.

Actually, "observation" in physics is shifting its attention away from this new reality and back towards the object. In contrast to this, let us call orientation toward the subject "recognition," in the narrow sense of a phenomenon that still does not make the subject entirely clear. We could mention Zeno's paradoxes (again, something even my own individual reason can grasp) as an early investigation of this. Finally, the physicist Gödel's "incompleteness" revealed a paradox at the foundations of mathematics, and investigated the structure of "cognition" – or rather, rendered strict investigation meaningless. As we all know, Gödel proved logically that within a given branch of mathematics, a system of deductive logic that includes the idea of infinity can never constitute a closed system, as had been thought.

What would happen if this were applied to all systems of deductive logic? What if all extant logic (except in a few cases where the object of discussion is finite) were ultimately impossible to close and perfect? [7]

6. To tell the truth, I first began to take an interest in the existence of autonomous ideas when I entered junior high school and learned algebra. Until then, I had strained my small brain trying to solve arithmetic exercises, but now I could translate them into the numerical formulae that are the language of mathematics – setting up an equation with x as an unknown quantity, and then solving it by applying an algorithm. There was no longer any need to go through all the steps of a procedure, always keeping in mind something like a computer's "internal state." All this permitted a partial lapse in the comprehension of circumstances through reason – in a sense, a partial suspension of thought. This is because on the route from superstition to science (if not on the path from superstition to religion), collective reason left behind evidence of its passage in the form of these formulae.

It is quite a leap, but as a more developed version of this query, I could mention an example well known to science fiction fans, the "twin paradox." I will not question the conclusion provided by the formulae, but neither can I truly comprehend it with my faculties of reason. As I have been arguing, since formulae are independent of the reasoning minds that create them, any development in our reason that hinges on those equations also represents something that deviates autonomously from individual reason. And it is far more convincing than single-engined individual reason because it constitutes a verified system (meaning a system whose usefulness we can see first hand).[8]

To take another more familiar example, textbooks use conservation of momentum and transfer of energy to explain the moon's retreat from the earth and the child's top that flips upside down when you spin it. True, the former can be accounted for by differences in the gravitational pull that different parts of the earth exert on the moon, and the latter can be explained by the build-up of friction on the floor. However, as all these elementary analyses become bothersome, we resort to higher-level principles, which appear from the lay person's perspective to be arbitrary laws.

By now, it should be clear what I'm getting at. My hypothesis of collective reason follows the same pattern as these examples. Regrettably, in this sphere it is hard to discern any equivalents to the corroborating formulae or elementary analyses of physics. It goes without saying that, in former times, the systematization of superstition and the protection of the leadership were rooted in the efforts of some individuals to seek profits for themselves, just as society's present march towards computopia is probably driven by the plans of individuals and companies positioned at strategic points inside and outside the system. But even if it were not clearly impossible to quantify the mechanisms involved, I don't believe that the actions of these figures are having the effect that they intended.

Ultimately, this is why I have only been able to offer a small number of predictions here. I look forward to a time in the future when we will have a slightly clearer sense of the direction computers are advancing in, and we will be able to list a greater number of examples. (It is also possible that one single counterexample will cause my entire system to collapse, but this would also resolve the question.)

With that, my efforts to construct an idea of collective reason have completed their full circuit, and if my ideas have gained general acceptance thus far, I suppose my efforts have borne fruit. But letting the argument run a little further, it might be said that my efforts themselves could be regarded as a manifestation of collective reason. If that is the case, though, all of this has been no more than a game of language. What then is the purpose of debating the fine points? If individual reason can never cope with collective reason, isn't my individual proposal itself meaningless?

Yet one cannot condemn this as a necessarily fruitless endeavor. Judgments about the relevance of debate, or whether individual reason can cope with collective reason, cannot possibly be made from an individual standpoint, either. Thus, only one single criterion of evaluation remains – namely, the fairly utilitarian criterion of whether or not this debate can give us some standard of behavior.

- de-centered subject
- (not in an observer or controller individual) of the world

In other words, from this point on, the focus of our discussion will move beyond logic and enter the realm of practice.

7. So, while I don't like superfluous additions, I would like to talk generally about practical aspects. What each of us can do now is focus our conscious attention on the human condition – by means of the idea of "collective reason" or other individually invented criteria – and decide how we will deal with that condition as individuals. Given two judgments based on the same reasoning, the one made with a clear consciousness of that reason is bound to be different from the one that lacks such an awareness. Perhaps as a general result of that act of choice, we may be able to change slightly our level of comfort with the future computopia. (Of course, we will not be able to judge the results right away, and we might discover our choice was entirely meaningless, but what of it?)

Needless to say, from here on, it comes down to an issue of each person's morality. Now this may come as a surprise, given the earlier tone of this essay, but currently the most reliable foundation for such morals continues to be humanism. It may erode, or become just a hypocritical slogan; it may represent a mere indulgence for the masses. But this doesn't matter in the least. In fact, isn't that kind of broad, diffused humanism actually preferable to rash ideology? Strict modern humanism is an exaggerated position situated between domination from the top and domination from below, compared to which worldly present-day humanism seems to have persevered through a longer history. In any case, at our current stage of consciousness, every decision-making "individual" is still a flesh-and-blood human being, so I suppose it is only natural that people should seize on this body that is so intimately connected to the interpreting subject. That which experiences pleasure or pain, that which lives or dies, is still none other than the self, right? Indeed, but only until the eventual domination of the machine system is complete.

It is when I am faced with humanism as an act of faith, something accepted like an infant accepts baptism, that I want to turn away. What is important is this: instead of clinging to humanism as an article of faith and forcing it on others as the One Truth, one should accept it as an ethical standard whose present necessity is proven by experience, and adhere to it until something better is discovered. (If you will pardon a rough analogy, getting the knack of this is much like choosing democracy as a mode of politics.)

I'm sorry but somehow this seems to have turned into a morality lecture. At any rate, even without saying all this out loud, I think in the consciousness of those who love and read science fiction, a common understanding is developing along these lines. Besides, as I've indicated, one function of the SF we love is surely to provide a point of departure for this questioning consciousness and these kinds of judgments. Of course, I don't think such an understanding is the exclusive property of science fiction fans, nor can I say that all science fiction fans are that way, but at the very least, this may explain why among themselves fans are able to enjoy a different kind of conversation.

My proposed definition of science fiction is this: "Science fiction is the general term for a sphere of literature (and its related genres) that embraces the concept of a 'collective reason' that is autonomous and removed from individual control." [9]

NOTES

1. The term translated throughout the essay as "autonomy" is *jisō*. Written with the Japanese characters for "running by oneself," it literally means something like "self propelled." It suggests not only independence from external control but also dynamic motion – something that literally "gets away" from us. This seems to be in keeping with the essay's idea that not only is collective reason

free from individual control, but that it may follow an unexpected trajectory that takes it far away from individual reason.

2. In order to avoid misunderstandings, I would like to state that the prediction I have outlined here is a vision of mankind's future situated at the extreme of optimism. That is because it is entirely based on the idea that war will not exterminate mankind early on, that pollution and overpopulation will not wipe out civilization, and that today's pace of development will continue as it has. Furthermore, I don't want to give the impression that I'm looking forward to the age of machine domination. It is merely inevitable, regardless of what we may or may not hope for.

3. There is nothing outrageous about this concept of "domination from below." It is a system that has appeared throughout Japanese history and persists to the present day. In other words, it is not inevitably the stronger individual who occupies the position of leadership. This probably arose as a necessary compromise with the emperor system. It might be one of the Japanese people's most valuable inventions.

4. It goes without saying that the machine system's domination of human beings is still far away and that those currently ruling the collective are flesh-and-blood human beings. So this reversal will be inconvenient for those individuals presently occupying positions of authority (and not only executives, I should add), but for the sake of mankind's future, we will have to ask them to put up with it. For example, a former Alexander or Moses will cut a lowly figure as a group tour guide, while an Admiral Nelson or Tōgō will find himself overseeing departures and landings from an airport control tower; in other words, although the nature of the job will remain the same, there will be a demotion in rank. To take an extreme case, the slave driver who formerly lashed oarsmen below deck will end up sitting in the driver's seat of a bus. I'm sorry for entertaining myself with free associations, but however you look at it, the picture of passengers in seats arranged just like a galley, each pushing a button to get

off the bus, is far removed from images of the elegant ship's passengers of yore. The slaves, now freed from their toil by the machine's control over energy, are still controlled by bus timetables and service routes.

5. In its form, I wonder if this isn't a type of model theory. That's what it seems to be. Moreover, there are in fact clues allowing us to speculate about its internal properties. For example, consider the statement: "Christ taught people to love and Marx taught people to hate" (I read this in an essay by Umehara Takeshi). Of course, this is not a comparative theory pitting religion against ideology but rather an expression of the dual nature of our interest in the world around us, as seen from a point between these two paradigms. It is important to consider this question apart from the image of "good" and "evil" that accompanies the words "love" and "hate." To illustrate, what would someone teach us who represented an age between religion and the superstitions that preceded it? If such a person existed, he or she would teach "awe and suspicion." And just what would a person representing the transition to the coming "methodology" have to teach us? I still don't know exactly how such investigations pertain to the problem at hand, but perhaps examining the problem from this angle will give us a glimpse of humanity's future.

6. The law of excluded middle states that for every proposition P, either P is true or NOT P is true. (*Trans.*)

7. I confess that this concept of observationism is not my original idea. It is something I arrived at by reinterpreting the idea of "pure experience" (*junsui keiken*) in Nishida Kitarō's *Zen no kenkyū* (1911, An Inquiry into the Good). Those who are poor at natural sciences but well versed in Eastern thought may find this discussion easier to understand if they replace the technical terms "observation" and "cognition" with the well-known Zen koan "the sound of one hand clapping." Yet it is not at all my intention to praise Eastern wisdom. It seems to me that as a Japanese person, so-called "existential"

thought is something innately self-evident to me. The important thing isn't attaining a state, but rather understanding what it means when a result one pursued through individual reason and individual logic ends up connected to something that contradicts both these things.

8. In other words, no matter how it may contradict individual common sense, conclusions obtained through the application of such mathematical methods are "correct" and automatically tend toward the next phase of development. Of course, in actuality, I don't think there are too many cases in which scientific research has followed that exact procedure, but that doesn't change the fact that this is the fundamental pattern. In advanced fields of physics, one can see any number of exemplary cases. Such elements are rare in humanistic fields of research such as sociology or psychology, where no matter how rigorous one's theory may be, one is not supposed to confront people with facts that violate common sense. This probably helps to explain why early works of science fiction were essentially "natural science novels" [*shizen kagaku shōsetsu*].

9. This is accompanied by a series of definitional systems. If we follow David Hilbert, who pioneered the study of logic and the foundation of mathematics, we must establish a system of axioms before constructing any definitions. But for an argument consisting of natural language [*kotoba*], the resulting assertions might be too vague to be understandable. So we need at least some indication or index of the nature of the axioms. As a result, the definitions, which are one step removed from the logical system, become a declaration of the theorist's position. Some may doubt that, but when we debate the nature of science fiction in our everyday lives, each one of us has our own preferred models of the genre in mind, so my own definition of SF is nothing more than an expression that integrates these models. But if, in this process, I can discover some commonality with the models that others have embraced, we can go beyond swapping our favorite SF stories and hope to start developing an effective theory.

Furthermore, in my own case, I cannot help trying to analyze why I am so taken with science fiction as well, and as a result of that analysis I have necessarily arrived at a definitional system.

Leaving the details aside for another occasion, what I have attempted with this system is something like "an explanation for our non-human observers." I admit that the task has been beyond my abilities, but if I were to say that I was prompted by the description in the beginning of Stanislaw Lem's *The Astronauts* (1950), perhaps my readers will understand.

Others may ask why I bother at this point. One could cite Abe Kōbō's objection: "As soon as it is given the name 'lion,' the lion is changed from a legendary being into a mere beast." I don't think science fiction is something that can be named or defined quite so easily, however; and it is for that very reason that I cannot help but be interested in its definition.

Reprinted from Science Fiction Studies *#88*
(Volume 29, Part 3, November 2002)

KOMATSU SAKYŌ

The Savage Mouth
Translated by Yano Tetsu and Judith Merril

NO REASON *at all.*

Why should there be a reason? People want to find reasons for everything, but the truth of things can never be explained. All of existence: why *is* it as it is? Why just this way and no other?

That kind of reason, no one would ever be able to explain...

SEETHING with anger, he stood looking out of the window, gritting his teeth. Some days, suddenly, this fury overwhelmed him, suffusing the very center of his being: a violent irrational urge to destruction, which could never be explained to anyone. He jerked the curtain closed: breathing hard he stiffened his shoulders and moved back to the inner room.

The world we live in is worthless, absurd. Staying alive is an absurdly worthless thing. Above all, this worthless character – myself – is quite intolerably absurd.

Why so absurd – ?

"Why?" There it was again.

Worthless, absurd, simply *because* absurd and worthless. Everything – prosperity, science, love, sex, livelihood, sophisticated people – nature, earth, the universe – all disgustingly filthy, frustratingly foolish. Therefore –

No. Not "therefore" at all, but *anyhow, I'm actually going to do it.*

I will do it. Rubbing a kink out of his shoulder, he cried out silently: *I really will.*

Of course, this would be just as idiotic as anything else – indeed, among assorted stupidities, maybe the stupidest of all? But at least there was a bit of *bite* to it – a taste of sharpness. Perhaps the result of a touch of madness at the core of the meticulously detailed scheme? Maybe so, but at least –

What I'm going to do now has certainly never been attempted by anyone in his right mind!

Destroy the world? How many tens of thousands of people throughout history must have cherished *that* fantasy! This was nothing so banal. His anger would never be quenched by anything so absurd. *The flames within me are fanned by a truly noble desperation...*

ENTERING the inner room, he locked the door, turned on the light. *Now* – the thought brought a glitter to his eye – *now it begins.*

The room shone in cool light. In one corner were an electric range and oven; a gas burner; a slicer; large and small frying pans; an assortment of kitchen knives; and a kitchen cabinet stocked with all kinds of sauces and relishes and vegetables. Next to them was an automated operating table, fully programmed and equipped to perform any kind of surgery ever done on the human body – even in the biggest hospitals, no matter how complex or difficult. And next to that, a supply of prosthetics: arms, legs, every available variety of ultra-modern artificial organ.

Everything was ready. It had taken him a full month to work out the plans in detail, another month to get all the necessary equipment set up. By his reckoning, it would take a little more than one additional month until he was all done.

Right, then – let's get started.

Removing his trousers, he mounted the operating table, attached monitoring electrodes at several points on his body, and switched on the videotape.

It begins –

With a dramatic gesture he picked up the syringe lying on the stand next to the operating table, checked the pressure gauge, adjusted the setting – a little high, since this was the first shot – and injected a local anesthetic into his right thigh.

In about five minutes, all sensation was gone from the leg, and he switched on the automatic operating machine. Buzzing and humming of machinery; telltale lights blinking on and off; his body jerked back reflexively as several extensions emerged from an arm of the shining black machine.

Clamps projecting from the table secured the leg at the shank and ankle. A steel claw holding a disinfectant gauze pad came slowly down onto the thigh joint.

The electric scalpel sliced silkily through the skin, cauterizing as it went; there was hardly any blood. Cutting the muscle tissue... exposing the large artery... clamping-off with forceps... ligation... cutting and treating the contracting muscle surface... The buzzing rotary saw was soon whirring toward the exposed femur. It hit the bone; his eyes blinked shut at the shock.

There was almost no vibration. The diamond embedded in the ultra-high-speed saw made only the faintest rubbing noise as it sliced through bone, simultaneously treating the cut surface with a mixture of potent enzymes. In exactly six minutes his right leg had been cleanly severed from the joint.

Wiping his sweat-soaked face gently with gauze, the machine handed him a glass of medicine. He drank it down in a single gulp and drew a deep breath. His pulse was racing; more and more sweat came pouring out. But there was almost no blood lost, and no sensation of anything like pain. The nerve treatments had worked very well. No blood transfusion would be needed. He inhaled a bit of oxygen to ease his dizziness.

His right leg, separated from his body, lay sprawled on the table where it had dropped. A contracted circle of pink muscle tissue surrounded by yellow fat, with red-black marrow at the center of the white bone, was visible through a tightly wrapped clear plastic dressing. There was almost no bleeding. He stared at the hairy *thing* with its protruding kneecap, and was almost overcome with a fit of hysterical laughter. But there was no time now for laughing: there was more still to be done.

He rested only long enough to recover his energy, then issued instructions for the next part of the job.

The machine extruded a steel arm, picked up an artificial leg and set it in place against the cut surface; the unbandaged treated flesh was already healing. The signal terminal of the artificial synapse center was connected to a nerve sheath drawn out from the cut surface. Finally, the structural support was firmly attached to the remaining thighbone with straps and a special bonding agent. *Finished.* He cautiously tried bending the new leg.

So far, so good. He stood up gingerly: It made him dizzy and shaky but he was able to stand and walk slowly. The artificial leg was made out of some kind of lightweight metal that produced a tinny sound when it moved. *All right – good enough –* He'd be using a wheelchair most of the time.

He lifted his own right leg off the top of the table. It was so heavy he was almost staggering. Inside himself, he was once again seized with a paroxysm of savage laughter. *All my life I've been dragging all this weight around.* How many kilos had he liberated himself from by cutting off this support?

"All right," he muttered to himself, still giggling. "Enough. Now to drain the blood…"

Carrying the heavy joint over to the workbench he stripped off the plastic wrap and hung the leg from the ceiling by the ankle, squeezing it through his hands to start the blood dripping from the cut end.

Later, washing it in the sink, with the hairs plastered down by the water, it looked more like the leg of a giant frog than any other kind of animal. He stared at the sole of the foot poking grotesquely over the edge of the stainless steel sink.

My leg. Protruding kneecap, hard-to-fit high instep, toes infested with athlete's foot – *That's my leg!* And he was finally completely carried away, bent double in an uncontrollable spasm of poisonous laughter. *At last there will be an end to that damned persistent athlete's foot...*

Time to get ready for the cooking.

He used the big slicer to cut the leg in two at the knee, then began stripping off the skin with a sharp butcher's knife. The thighbone was thick with delicious-looking meat. *Of course: it's the ham.* The tendons were stiff; he was covered with sweat as he worked the hand-slicer, quickly piling up large chunks of meat surrounded by muscle membrane. He put chunks of shin meat to simmer in a big pot filled with boiling hot water, bay leaf, cloves, celery, onions, fennel, saffron, peppercorns and other spices and savory vegetables. The foot he threw out, keeping only the meat scraped out of the arch. The ham he sliced up for steak, rubbing in salt and pepper and plenty of tenderizer.

Will I have the courage to eat it? he asked himself suddenly. Tough lumps always stuck in that spot in his throat. Would he really be able to stomach it?

He clenched his teeth, oozing oily sweat. *I will eat.* It was no different from the way human beings had always cooked and eaten other intelligent mammals: cows and sheep, those gentle, innocent, sad-eyed grass eaters. Primitive man even ate his own kind; some groups had practiced cannibalism right up to modern times. Killing an animal *in order to eat* – perhaps there was some justification for that. Other carnivores had to kill to live too. But human beings...

Since the day they came into existence, through all of human history, how many billions of their fellows had people killed *without even eating them?* Compared to that, this was positively innocent! *I'm not going to kill anyone else. I'm not going to slaughter miserable animals. This way, what I myself eat is my own meat.* What other food could be so guiltless?

The oil in the frying pan was beginning to crackle. With shaking hands he grasped a great piece of meat, hesitated, hurled it in. Crackling fat began to flood the air with savory smells. Still trembling, he was gripping the arms of his wheelchair so hard he almost snapped them.

All right. I am a pig. Or rather, human beings are much worse than pigs: filthier, nastier. *Inside myself there is a part that is less-than-pig, and a "noble" part endlessly angry and ashamed at being less-than-pig.* That "noble" part was going to eat the "less-than-pig" part. What was there to fear in that?

The crisply browned slice of meat sizzled on the plate. He smeared mustard over it, applied lemon and butter, poured gravy on top of that. When he made to use the knife, his hand was dancing so that it set the plate to clattering. Streaming with sweat, he jabbed in the fork, gripped the knife with all his strength, sliced, and then carried *It* fearfully into his mouth.

On the third day, he amputated the left leg. This one, just as it was, shinbone and all, he skewered and smeared liberally with butter, then roasted it on the rotisserie in the big oven. He was fearless by now. He had discovered himself to be surprisingly delicious: with that discovery, a mixture of anger and madness rooted itself firmly in his heart.

AFTER the first week, things got more difficult. He had to amputate the lower half of his body.

On the toilet installed in the wheelchair, he experienced the delights of defecation for the last time in this world. As he ejected, he guffawed.

Look at this mess! What I am now excreting is my own self, stored up in my own bowels and turned to shit! Perhaps this was the ultimate act of self-contempt – or might it have been the utmost in self-glorification?

The gluteus maximus was the most delicious of all.

With everything from the hips down gone, the point of the artificial legs was also gone, but he left them in place for the time being. Now that it was time for the internal organs, he consulted the machine's electronic brain: "When I have eaten the intestines, will I still have an appetite?"

"It will be quite all right," was the reply.

He discarded the large intestines, put the small intestines into a stew with vegetables, and used the duodenum to make sausages. He replaced the liver and kidneys with artificial organs, then ate the originals in a sauté. The stomach he set aside until later, preserved in a plastic container filled with nutritive fluids.

AT THE end of the third week, he exchanged his heart and lungs for artificial organs, and at last ate his own once-pulsing heart, fried in thin slices: a deed even beyond the imagination of a priest at the Aztec sacrificial rituals.

By the time he made a meal of his own stomach – soaked in soy sauce, with garlic and cayenne pepper – he had come to understand clearly that *people are quite capable of eating, even if they have no need of food.*

In the wide range of varied and exotic products people have used for food, how many had been discovered out of curiosity, and not from hunger at all? Even when their curiosity is satisfied, humans will eat the most unimaginable things, *as long as there is anger.* In a fit of fury, eating the flesh of your own kind can be like crushing a glass with your teeth...

The wellsprings of appetite lie in the savage aggressive impulses: killing-and-eating, crushing-and-crunching, swallowing-and-absorbing – *that is the savage mouth.*

By now, the end of his throat was only connected to a disposal tube. Nourishment for his remaining tissues was poured directly into the blood from a container of nutritive fluids; endocrine functions were maintained with the help of artificial organs.

By the end of the month, both arms had been completely eaten; the only part that remained was from the neck up. And by the fortieth day, almost all the muscles of the face had been eaten as well: the lips alone were left to chew with the assistance of attached springs. Only one eyeball remained; the other had been sucked and chewed.

What sat there now, mounted on a labyrinthine mechanism of pipes and tubes, was the living skull alone: in that skull, only mouth and brain survived.

No...

Even now, an arm of the machine was peeling off the scalp, taking a saw to the top of the skull and removing it cleanly.

Sprinkling salt and pepper and lemon on the trembling exposed cerebrum, in the act of scooping up a great spoonful – *My brain,* thought the cerebrum-that-was-he. *How can I taste such a thing? Can a man live to savor the taste of his own brain-jelly?*

The spoon punctured the ashy-hued brain. No pain – there is no sensation in the cerebral cortex. But by the time the arm of the machine scooped up that pale mushy paste and carried it to the skull's mouth, and the mouth lapped it up to swallow, "taste" was no longer recognizable.

"HOMICIDE," the Inspector told the reporters crowded into the entrance as he came out of the room. "And what's more, a brutal and degenerate crime, most likely unprecedented. The criminal is probably a medically knowledgeable psychopath. Looks like an attempt at some sort of insane experiment – the body was taken apart limb from limb, and hooked up to all kinds of artificial organs..."

The Inspector disposed of the press and went back into the room, wiping his face from exhaustion.

A detective came over from the incinerator and eyed him questioningly. "The tapes are burned," he said, "but – why are you calling it murder?"

"For the sake of maintaining peace and order." The Inspector took a deep breath. "Declare it murder – conduct an official investigation – and leave it shrouded in mystery. This case – releasing the facts as they are in this case – it goes against all reason! You can't make ordinary decent citizens look into the pits of madness and self-destruction hidden away at the bottom of some people's minds. If we did such a thing – if we carelessly exposed people to a glimpse of the savage beast lurking inside – well, you can be sure someone else would try to follow this guy's example. These kinds of people – *there's no way to know what they're capable of...*

"If the general public were suddenly made aware of something like this, people would begin to lose confidence in their own behavior – they'd start probing and peering at the blackness inside their own souls. They'd get entirely out of their depths – completely out of control!

"You see, what is at the root of human existence is *madness* – the blind aggressive compulsion that lies in wait at the heart of all animals. If people become conscious of this – if really large numbers of people start expressing that madness under slogans like *existential liberation* and *do your own thing* – we're done for! It's the end of human civilization. No matter what kind of law or force or order we try to work with, it'll get completely out of control!

"People tearing themselves apart, killing each other, wrecking, destroying – the symptoms are already beginning to show up – this one commits suicide by swallowing fused dynamite – that one pours gasoline and sets himself on fire – another starts screwing in the middle of the city in broad daylight. When there is nothing more reasonable left to attack, the caged animal starts to destroy his own sanity – "

"Yaa-a-a!"

The young detective screamed and jumped back from the rotting skull. He had been about to remove the foul-smelling spoon still held between the lips when the skull sank its teeth into his finger, nipping off a pinch of meat from the tip.

"Be careful," said the Inspector wearily. "The foundation of all animal life is a great starving swallowing savage mouth... "

The skull, with its naked brain, its one remaining eye beginning to come loose, and strong springs replacing its vanished muscles, was now slowly crumpling and chewing the scrap of meat between its swollen tongue and sturdy teeth.

– First published in Hayakawa Mystery Magazine, *July 1969*

HIRAI KAZUMASA

A Time For Revolution
Translated by David Aylward

T{HEY} stood huddled at the bottom of the atmosphere, shivering in the cold. The rough wind stabbed through
their thin flesh, and the dim sunlight no longer had enough energy
to warm their bodies. Being raised in nursing machines had so lowered their vitality that the raw presence of nature was almost a death
sentence, but there wasn't one of them who wanted to go back to the
temperature-controlled comfort of the Pit.

"No trees for birds to rest... no fields where animals can run. We
can't live here."

"Are you saying we should go back to the Pit?"

"See for yourself! It's obviously a dead world. Radioactivity has destroyed all life. We were rejected before we even arrived. Time has
run out for us."

Since the human race had long ago contaminated the surface of
the Earth, humans now lived beneath it, in the Pit, their minds so
paralyzed by their terrible mistake that it was an effort even to go
on breathing. This giant underground hothouse held them in an un-
relenting embrace from the moment they were born until the time
they died. Like a faithful nurse sticking to her single task, the Pit was
a strict, untiring supervisor, not for an instant lifting her eyes or letting her charges stray into the savage outside world. It was a great
steel prison that pinned humans down under lacquer-hard layers of
sympathy and benevolence.

While humans had become a sort of domestic pig, kept in a state of
whimpering dependency, machines were masters of the world, ab-

solute despots. To breathe, to laugh, to be happy: everything was decision, command, and execution. They had dismissed the scientists who created them, trampled down the politicians, and sent away the lovers forever, down into the sewers like so much garbage.

Outside, on the surface, unseen by any eye, the sun might slowly sicken, the moon might perish, the phantom sea forget its anger and a blue slate sky stop its crying forever. But the human race slept on, buried in a hole dug in the corpse of the world.

"So you think we made a mistake?"

"No! Why should we fear death? Here, we can sing our death songs in peace. If we had taken up our pens and brushes and instruments before, we would have been forced into brainwashing machines. We had no choice but to try and escape, whatever may happen to us now. Our existence has become precious, irreplaceable. Humankind is failing, but we have inherited its spirit."

They were artists, all of them, of multiple kinds. At one time, each had been a poet, a writer, a musician or a painter. There were not many left to carry the torch of humanity. In the Pit it was about to go out, but these few – who still had images in their eyes and songs on their lips, whose spirits still flowed through their hands – were struggling to keep it alight.

But they had been born in the darkest age since history began. Their first baby tears were shed in plastic incubators, for in their world, men no longer lusted after women, nor did women bear children. Having no real birthplace, they were exiles before they were born.

In the Pit, artists had been thrown aside like dust by a single number on the dial of a Probability Statistics Machine. What was the use of them? There was no longer an audience for their productions. They were disowned, and their vocations prohibited.

They had escaped that harsh oppression through an abandoned conduit, sealed off many centuries before, climbing ten thousand feet to the surface in headlong flight. But when, after great hardships, they emerged, the scene that greeted them was a wilderness of sand and rock, without a tree or a blade of grass.

"What are we going to do now?" They gazed around them with despairing eyes.

"Look there!" one of them shouted.

"It's them!" another groaned, his voice thick with a complex of fears.

They were suddenly enveloped by a low humming sound as if a great hand of fire were wrapping itself around them. There was no way their puny bodies, as fragile as butterfly wings, could breach the impregnable wall that surrounded them. In their fear and despair, they became confused.

"We're trapped!"

"We can't run any farther!"

"Don't panic. Don't give them a chance to take you. We must get away at any cost."

"But how can we?"

"Gather yourselves together, and try to merge your minds into one!"

Like a grove of trees lashed by a storm, they huddled close to each other, refusing to be blown away. The encirclement drew tighter as the weird humming continued.

"Concentrate your minds. Squeeze out all the power you can. We must do the impossible. Don't forget we have a mission. We have to get away!"

After their joined minds had all melted into a chaotic mass, they got ready to use the rising pressure to project themselves outward.

"All right! Now!"

Like a shower of blinding sparks from a crack in a red-hot blast furnace, they escaped.

EARLIER in the evening, just enough rain had fallen to wash away the dust, making the colors of the neon signs sparkle with renewed

brilliance. The many welling and twisting, stretching and contracting lights played like the instruments of an orchestra against the
jet-black fabric of the night.

In the green-tinted darkness at the bottom of the city, every side-
walk was giving the same performance on a smaller scale, in pools of
water that glittered like the shards of a broken mirror, and in the pupils of each passer-by, it was distilled into minute, twinkling points
of light that might have come from distant stars.

It was only rarely that people could see these scenes so clearly. But
now, undisturbed by the honking and screeching of cars, and free of
dust and heat, the air had the cool, sweet taste of a natural spring.

The lovers were even happier than usual as they paced and murmured along the dark streets, feeling the night fill their minds with
tiny soda-water bubbles of silence. And when they laughed, their
teeth were wonderfully white, their voices like pieces of ice clinking
against the sides of a glass of lemon squash.

Then the crowd parted abruptly, like a school of timid fish frightened by a shark, and the figure of a lone man came into view.

From under the straw hat tilted back on his head, the man glared
around him with a strange, watchful expression, thrusting out a
razor-sharp lip as if he could slash an enemy with it, instead of the
switchblade in his coat pocket. He was dapperly clad in a boldly patterned shirt left open to show his bare chest and a pure white sash
wrapped tightly around his stomach. As he strutted along, swinging
his shoulders from side to side, the clatter of his wooden sandals
was like a loudspeaker, warning of danger; people shuddered as if
they'd heard a rattlesnake and made a wide detour around him.

He was just another cheap hood, still a youngster, but he could do
a lot of damage. The only schooling he'd ever had was in reforma-
tories, where he learned nothing except how to talk tough and use
a knife. This kind of practical training had been fiercer and more
thorough than he would have gotten in the army, and he had spent
more time at it.

After graduating from this apprenticeship with several broken teeth and one half-amputated ear, he had become one of the leaders of a gang of thugs who were roosting in the neighborhood.

Here and there, garishly dressed young men stood in front of alleyways and pinball parlors, waiting to buy prizes from people coming off the machines. They called respectful greetings to him through the noise and confusion.

In reply he gave each a brief, condescending nod and shouted back, "Keep it up, boys!"

Or, spitting from the corner of his mouth, "Don't slack off, you guys. Keep your eyes out for those winners!"

While he was inspecting his kow-towing minions, he threw out his chest and felt very important. Then after he had finished, he pushed his hat even farther back on his head and walked on in high spirits, the night wind teasing his bare chest.

A little problem had come up tonight, just the kind of thing it was his special job to handle. It seemed that two of his prize-buyers had quarreled with some customers.

After taking them into a back alley, his men had had to back down because there were four of them, and they were tough. When he reached the place, he beckoned to some of his men hanging around outside a pool hall and marched into the alley where the standoff was. His two prize-buyers had only been circling around and making threats, like bobcats on a fence rail. They were glad to see him.

"Boss, these guys..."

They started to tell him all about it, but he checked them, and glared around at their four opponents. They looked like dressed-up factory workers, with bright pink twill shirts and worn but stylish jeans. They wavered a little when he appeared, but they could handle themselves in a fight and faced him defiantly enough. But they were obviously rank amateurs, being too reckless for their own good.

"Here comes another one," scoffed the toughest-looking one,

standing a little apart from the others. "I'm starting to get mad. If I start on 'em, they won't know what hit 'em!"

He thrust his jaw out belligerently, to show he was someone to be reckoned with.

"You better get outta here, buddy, while you're still in one piece. We're not just a bunch of your boot-licking prize-buyers, so don't try and push us around. Bugger off, or we'll kick the shit out of you!"

The man in the straw hat kept his face expressionless, like a turtle's, not even blinking his eyes. But he wasn't a gang leader for nothing. In a situation like this, he knew exactly what to do.

"Put the stuff down and beat it. But you'll have to learn some manners first."

"Screw you!" the tough one said, and swiftly plunged his hand into his shirt.

His response was a series of actions that came from many years' practice. His knees and fists worked quickly, with machine-like precision. He disabled his adversary easily, with a final thrust of his knee, then turned and took a pool cue from one of his men who was standing behind him.

"This is what happens to punks who try and muscle in on my turf!"

The cue sliced through the air with a vicious whirring sound. The other three yelled and tried to shield their faces from the whirling tip, all the fight suddenly gone out of them.

Licking his lips, he turned to the one crouched on the ground and began beating him savagely, lashing his back and shoulders and head till the blood ran. He only stopped when the cue snapped neatly in two, like a piece of chalk.

His victim had fainted. He turned a cold eye on the remaining three.

"You guys want the same?"

Their knees were shaking like reeds in the wind. He gave one of them a contemptuous kick in the ass, and finished up by shoving their faces into a can of rotten garbage.

AFTERWARDS, he swaggered along the street more exhilarated than ever, feeling like a cruiser that had just sunk a submarine. He was so pleased with himself at doing a skillful job that he almost forgot to go on his rounds.

His main business as a mighty gang boss was collecting a so-called "protection fee" from a group of bars in the neighborhood. In return, he supposedly kept any vandals from breaking into their places and wrecking them, but of course it was just a scam.

The first bar he came to was a tiny place. He flipped open one of the door panels and rolled in like a Western gunslinger. The bartender and the hostesses flinched inwardly, as if they had seen a poisonous spider, but they didn't dare show their reactions in their faces.

He showed up several times a month to collect his protection fee. When they saw him, the customers would all leave as fast as they could, and anybody who came in afterwards would turn right around and go back out.

He never even paid for his drinks. But if he got even a hint that he was a nuisance, he would swear at them and start kicking chairs around, ready to break that hole-in-the-wall bar into even smaller pieces.

There was always something ominous in his manner, as if, at a signal from him, a squad of his men would charge in, rampage around like the Foreign Legion, and leave the place in a shambles. So the bartender and the girls had to welcome him with hypocritical smiles, hoping to find some way to get rid of him quickly.

"Say, business looks pretty good here, today!"

At the sound of his voice, the customers at the counter quickly thinned.

"Why it's Shin! Come in, come in. I'm terribly sorry, darling, but Mama-San is out just now."

At this, he gave the hostess a sharp look, but keeping his voice friendly, he said, "That's OK. No hurry. Mind if I wait?"

To relieve the chilly atmosphere, the bartender began to beam and smile for all he was worth. "Yes, sir! What'll you have? A highball? Coke and whisky?"

"The usual," he said coldly.

"Ah. And what would that be?"

"Of all the stupid...! What do they keep you here for?" he said, in a tone of poisonous contempt. "Can't you even remember what the customers like?"

The bartender's face twisted into a forced smile.

"Whisky straight, and don't you forget it!"

He hunched his shoulders and pushed his elbows down on the counter. A nervous atmosphere pervaded the near-empty bar.

Suddenly, something stirred in the depths of his heart, like the murmur of the sea, and the blood churned in his body.

Funny! he thought, and shook his head. A strange feeling of intoxication came over him, filling his body with a numbing fire.

Funny! his mind muttered to itself. Then, shrewder and sharper than a fox, without any warning, the feeling launched out into his body from inside him, probing into the subtle change.

Look out! it whispered to him. *Something very strange is going to happen to you!*

His vision seemed to pass through the walls, coming to rest in a place very far away from the painfully cramped bar. A beam of light was aimed directly at him across a vast expanse of space. When it reached him, it filled his organs, and flowed up into his brain.

You're changing! his mind whispered in terror.

Had time suddenly been reversed? A dazzling red flash of light bathed every corner of the little bar, then flared into soundless explosions of color. Wave after wave of orange, yellow and green, blue and violet swept through the room like a tornado, then sank to a flicker, leaving the bar the same as it was before.

"I'm here!" somebody whispered.

He closed his eyes, then opened them and stared steadily around him, as if at a completely new world.

The whisper came again. "I'm here! At last!"

"Aren't you drinking?" the bartender said nervously.

"I'm drinking, I'm drinking!"

He took a cautious sip of his whisky, as if testing the water of a strange country.

The drink burned in his stomach, and soon the fever of ancient festivals was throbbing in his veins.

"Gimme another." This time he gulped it boldly.

Without any warning, words came to his mouth.

"The isles of Greece, the isles of Greece..."

The bartender stared at him. The hostesses looked over in surprise.

"What did you say?"

He was even more bewildered than they were.

"Where burning Sappho loved and sung..." the voice recited, while he shrank back from it.

What the hell was going on?

"Where grew the arts of war and peace..."

"Eh?"

"Where Deles rose, and Phoebus sprung!" The words kept pouring out, without his even thinking of them.

"Eternal summer gilds them yet..." – came out like hiccups – *"... But all, except their sun, is set."*

The mouths of the onlookers were gaping with astonishment, while he stared back at them with panic-stricken eyes.

"The Scian and the Teian muse,
 The hero's harp, the lover's lute,
Have found the fame your shores refuse;
 Their place of birth alone is mute

To sounds which echo further west
  Than your sires' 'Islands of the Blest.'"

His tongue had rebelled against him. Disregarding his frantic orders, it threw out an unending stream of poetry.

"The mountains look on Marathon –
  And Marathon looks on the sea;
  And musing there an hour alone,
  I dream'd that Greece might still be free."

Finally, he gave up trying to wrestle with his own tongue, and rushed out of the bar, still declaiming:

"For, standing on the Persian's grave,
  I could not deem myself a slave."

Normally, this ignorant bully was the personification of violence who would go off like a shotgun if you so much as looked at him. He was more likely to slug people than talk to them, or kick them than bother to keep his temper, and if he did open his mouth, it would close on you like a tiger trap. But now the tough gang leader was helpless, so confused he was on the verge of crying.

I'm done for, he thought to himself. *This damn heat's got to me. I've gone crazy!*

Even to himself, he was ridiculous. Who would take orders from a boss who blabbered like a prissy idiot?

The voice in his mouth was still spouting out stuff he had never heard before:

"Adieu, adieu! my native shore
  Fades o'er the waters blue..."

And:

"Tambourgi! Tambourgi! thy 'larum afar
Gives hope to the valiant, and promise of war..."

He went blundering around in dark alleyways, shivering, in a re-lentlessly rising panic.

Then he had an idea.

"Maybe some brainy guy can tell me what's going on... pull me out of this mess and prove I'm not crazy... if he does, I don't care who he is, he'll be my best friend... I'll even give him my woman!"

Just then, he came across some of his henchmen. They had pushed two people into the same back alley he was in and were in the middle of harassing them. Their victims were an unlucky student and his clean-looking girlfriend, obviously very frightened. The girl looked ready to burst into tears.

"Hey, watching you two smooching has made us real hot. 'Give me a kiss,' she says! If you want to do that, you have to ask our permis-sion, understand? If you haven't got any money, kid, we'll just bor-row your girl for a while."

Sweating in the heat, the boss impatiently muttered, *"I have not loved the world, nor the world me..."* and went up to where they were talking.

At the sound of his approach, his men turned their heads sharply and stopped to greet him one by one.

"We didn't like the looks of these two, boss, so we were just having a little chat," said one of them.

Without even looking at them, he spoke to the student.

"Say there, sonny..."

He was so surprised he could say it properly, he went almost weak with relief. Apparently, the unpredictable voice in his mouth was going to be quiet for a minute. This kid looked like somebody he could ask about it.

63

"You're a student, aren't you?" he said, looking hopefully at the boy's pale, bloodless face.

"Y-yes, I am, but..." was the stammering reply.

"Studying hard? You're going to college right now?"

"That's r-right," the student stuttered, his face uncomprehending.

"I guess you know about a lot of things, eh? Well, there's something I want you to explain to me. OK?"

"Explain?"

"Wait a minute. I'm going to show you."

The student nodded, still plainly baffled.

Well. Let's go, he thought, waiting. Then the voice that controlled his mouth began again:

> *"So, we'll go no more a-roving*
> *So late into the night,*
> *Though the heart be still as loving,*
> *And the moon be still as bright."*

The voice flowed into every corner of the limpid darkness of the alley. It made no impression on the stupid faces of his men, but the student and the girl were listening intently.

> *"For the sword outwears its sheath,*
> *And the soul wears out the breast,*
> *And the heart must pause to breathe,*
> *And Love itself have rest."*

The voice went on reciting in a calm but penetrating tone:

> *"Though the night was made for loving,*
> *And the day returns too soon,*
> *Yet we'll go no more a-roving*
> *By the light of the moon."*

64

When he was finished, nobody said anything. He took a deep breath.

"What d'you think?"

"It's a lovely poem," the boy said. "It's Byron, isn't it?"

The girl opened her eyes wide. "Yes, it's definitely Byron."

"Byron, you say?"

"Yes. Lord Byron. He was a nineteenth-century English poet."

"Byron..."

He held the name like a pearl between his teeth, savoring it with the tip of his tongue. All at once, understanding leapt into his mind, and the name seemed perfectly familiar to him. The parasitic entity in his head had begun to penetrate into his subconscious.

"Of course: Byron!" he said, excitedly.

"You know him?" the student asked, surprised.

"I just heard of him now, but I know all about him..."

His personality had become multiplex: on one level a ruthless gangster, and on the other, a man who could recite Byron from memory.

The student was bursting with questions. He gave the kid's shoulder a friendly push.

"All right, you can go now. You've been a big help to me."

"Me? Did I do something?"

"Sure you did, you saved my life! I'm still confused, but I'll soon clear it up."

"So is it all right if we go, then?"

"Sure, sure, like I said. Go right ahead!" he said expansively, trying to show how grateful he was.

At this, his henchmen, who had been standing around absent-mindedly, abruptly woke up and protested.

"But, boss...!"

"What's the matter?"

They stirred discontentedly. He had obviously violated the rules. They didn't know why he had, but they felt that somehow or other it was unfair.

"We don't get it!"

They whispered together, then one of them summoned up his courage, and demanded, "Why are you letting them go?"

He was confused for a minute.

"Why, you say?"

In one corner of his mind, he knew their anger was justified, and sympathized with them. But the old consciousness was fighting with the new one, and he forgot why he had let their victims go. Always quick to anger, he exploded at his men.

"Shut up!" he roared. "It's none of your damn business!"

The student and the girl hurried away, still not understanding.

He glared aggressively at his sullen-faced followers.

"They're my friends, see? Don't gimme any lip!"

"Sorry, boss." His simple-minded followers submitted, and after apologizing, went off to hunt for their next victims.

OUT in the street, people were still enjoying the beautiful night filled with sparkling lights.

He wandered through the dark streets until he was exhausted, sprinkling poems like grains of silver sand, and smiling at everyone who went past.

A rapid chemical change was taking place. Two irreconcilable personalities were confronting each other in one body, each trying to push the other out. The mind that controlled his mouth still lay dormant in his subconscious, but when it took hold of his consciousness, the gangster's mind would be completely expelled.

At midnight, he was standing in front of an apartment door; the face under the straw hat had not changed, but it was now that of a totally different person.

A woman was waiting by herself in the room.

"You're a little early, aren't you, baby?" she said languidly. The man stared at her, frowning.

"It's *soo—oo* hot, isn't it? I can't even sleep," the woman com-

66

plained. She wore only her panties, and her bare breasts and arms, as white as bacon fat, were soaked with sweat.

"Hot? On a beautiful night like this?" he said, wondering, his head tilted to one side.

"What do you mean, silly?" She turned over on the bed and looked at him with eyes clouded over by the heat. "Come over here."

She seemed to be trying to forget the heat by making him do what he usually did with her. She sidled up to him and her white arms, coiling like snakes, wound themselves around his body.

He pushed her hands firmly away.

"There's something I have to do."

She looked at him in surprise.

"Go ahead, then! What is it you have to do?" she snorted discontentedly.

Without answering, he looked around the room until his eye came to a table where the radio was blaring away. It had been extorted from the owner of an appliance shop.

"I'll start with this."

He grabbed the radio and lifted it. Its volume rose to a shriek, as if it knew it was in danger. He threw it on the floor and smashed it, stilling its noise forever. Then, calmly, with no other sign of malice, he trod on it with his heel and ground it down as hard as he could.

The woman's jaw dropped, and her hands beat the air.

"What—what are you doing!"

He smiled at her.

"These little monstrosities are still in a primitive stage, but in time, they'll grow larger. Then they'll even begin to move by themselves and dominate the men who made them. Before that can happen, I'll put an end to all of them!"

And he took hold of an electric fan that was within reach and twisted the life out of it. It beat its wings like a great moth and breathed its last. Next his eye fell on the television set. This too had been obtained by squeezing a false debt out of someone.

67

The woman screamed.

Disregarding her, he went up to the television and steadily continued his attack. He disposed of it with utterly merciless precision. While the woman screamed more and more loudly, he smashed the screen into tiny splinters. Then after hurling the set against the wall, he pounded and kicked it repeatedly. Finally, he split the wooden console and bent all the machine parts, the vacuum tube making a sound like grinding teeth as it broke.

"Stop it, Shin! Stop it!" the woman said in a weeping, trembling voice.

"No, you're mistaken. It's not Shin you see," he laughed loudly. "I'm the one who's here now!"

The woman looked at him with eyes frozen in terror. Then she realized the truth. This man was not her lover. She had never met this stranger.

She jumped to her feet and snatched up her brassiere. Her white body disappeared out the door like a rocket fading into the night sky. He didn't even notice her, but merely continued the relentless destruction. Then, looking around the shattered room, he noticed the calendar on the wall: *July, 1967.*

I'm an exile, he thought. *But I've always been an exile. Now I can be a revolutionary, too.*

How can we say when the insane reversal of nature really started? Already, man has stopped living by himself, and has even entrusted his thinking to machines.

...But there are some things machines cannot do. They had trapped us, but when our desire to escape danger reached a limit, secret powers were released from the hidden places in our minds, sending us along the axis of time, to these glorious days that cannot be reached by the hands of the monstrous commanding machines, back to their childhood when they have not yet specialized.

In this time, men still have courage. They are filled with a savage energy, and if we use this energy in our hosts, we can stifle these future despotic tyrants, the machines, while they are still in their cradles. Then we can totally rebuild the future!

All the artists are coming from the future. At first, only fifty of us, then several hundred, then probably several thousands, will follow. A wave of revolution is surging through time. And we are all working for a single purpose!

He smiled to himself.

There are many things to be done. But this is the beginning of the revolution!

"Now then, to work!" he said aloud.

– First published in Hayakawa SF Magazine *(January 1963)*

KŌNO TENSEI

Hikari
Translated by Dana Lewis

Hikari – light, lumière, Licht

Traveling by night train, I awoke from a light slumber and looked drowsily out the window.

Perhaps the low-hanging clouds had closed in. There were no stars, only an endless darkness. Far away in the black I could see something shining, a faint glow.

The lights of a town? Perhaps.

I thought I could make out houses, buildings, trees.

But could that really be a town? The light did not seem to spill from homes so much as cover the whole village in a faint luminescence, flinging up houses and trees in black silhouette. That was all.

"It's one of their towns."

I turned at the voice. A man had slipped into the empty seat opposite mine. His staring eyes were fixed on the faint and distant glow. He was stocky. He asserted his presence with an almost ponderous force. He was that kind of man.

He was not perspiring, yet his cheeks and neck had a greasy sheen. That kind of man.

Their town?

Again I looked out the window.

It must have been a considerable distance to the light. The train ran on, but the glowing town did not move.

"Strange town," I said.

The man looked at me for the first time.

"Yeah," he said. "It's a strange town. Strange folk live there. It's a strange town."

There was anger in the man's eyes, and thorns in his voice.

"It's odd how it shines like that," I said.

The man nodded silently, and now he stared at me steadily. His eyes were bloodshot. I could see the veins like a net.

"It's like a distant nebula," I ventured.

The man nodded again, wordless.

"Who are they?"

"Them?" the man muttered. He nodded to himself once, twice. Then he took out a cigarette and lit it. He narrowed his eyes. Inhaled deeply. Puffing out a misty cloud of smoke, he began to talk. About them.

"THE FIRST was a kid. One kid," the man said.

"The first what?"

"The first what? Yeah. Good question, that." He wiped sweat off his forehead with his fist. "The first – what would you call it? – the first sign of the change."

"Change? You mean in that town? The shining town?"

"Right. That's how it ends up. In the end. But first I met this kid. In the middle of the night. It was well past midnight, already pushing one. It was that late at night, and there was this kid beside the road."

"How old was he?"

"Six, seven, something like that. A boy, sure, but even so, no kid should be out like that. Fact is, fact was, I was drunk. So at first I didn't believe my eyes. Just couldn't believe it. 'Cause there was something weird about this kid, you see? I ran up against his eyes at a kind of awkward moment."

"You ran up against his eyes?"

"Can't really say that, can you. But that's how it felt. Fact is, I was pissing."

The man's laughter held a distant, lonely ring.

"Yeah, I was pissing against a lamp post like a dog. You know, it's strange. When you're drunk and you piss it seems to take forever, don't it? Standing there, the wind blowing on you, looking up at the stars in the sky, not all of them so pretty, and letting it come out bit by bit. That's not so bad, you know. Not when you're drunk."

I laughed with him. It may have been a foolish thing to talk about, but I felt myself liking this man.

"But just then I got this strange feeling," he continued. "And when I looked over into the shadow of the lamp post I, well, like I said, I ran up against this kid's eyes."

"He'd been watching you?"

"Yeah, he'd been watching me." The man quickly wiped his face with his hand. "He'd watched his fill, he had. The kid'd been watching the whole time. All that stuff dribbling out."

Again I laughed despite myself.

"Ah, now that's a disaster. What's got to come out won't come out."

"Right, it won't."

He laughed bitterly. "How about a drink," he offered. Taking a pocket flask from the windowsill, he poured some of the liquid into a plastic cup, then intently filled the small metal cap for himself.

"But about the kid's eyes," he continued. "They had this weird light. It wasn't like they were shining or anything like that. It was like they shone through to somewhere else. It was like some light inside was leaking through."

"Pretty creepy."

"You'd think so, wouldn't you, hearing me talk. Fact is, it wasn't. For some reason, it felt sad, like he'd been blinking away tears. Just staring at me behaving like that. If it had been daytime I would have said something, would have told him, you know, 'Sorry, kid.' Something like that. Even if I didn't think I'd done anything bad, I'd of said it. Anyway, that kind of feeling."

I nodded.

"I see," I said.

"But it wasn't daytime. It was past midnight. So what I really said wasn't like that at all. What I said was, 'What do you think you're doing! What're you doing out at this time of night!?' But the kid just stared me in the face. Just stood there not saying a word.

"'Do your parents know you're out now? Do you live near here?'

"The kid doesn't say a word. Just the same clear eyes. He wasn't deaf. He jumped when I spoke to him. Soft in the head, maybe? I thought about that. But one look at his eyes and I couldn't buy that, either.

"I tried all kinds of things. 'Children shouldn't be out this late.' 'Hurry home.' You know the drill. But all he did was stare. So I got angry. It was weird how angry I got. The damn brat looks at my face the same way he looks at my dick! That kind of angry. I got really mad. Well, hell. Maybe because I was drunk."

The man gulped down the liquid in the small metal cap, and smiled sourly to himself as he carefully poured another slug.

"So that was all?"

"That night it was," he said. "The kid suddenly turned his back on me and walked off. Some of the street lights were out, but it didn't seem to bother him, not even where it was pitch black."

"Strange story," I said.

The man snorted.

"If you think that's strange, then heaven help you. That was just the first time I met them."

"Them?"

"That's right. Those disgusting, goddamn..."

The man tossed down another thimbleful.

"The next time was the next morning. I had a bit of a hangover, drank some miso soup for breakfast, that's all. Left for work at the last possible minute. But when I turned the corner to the station, I got the shock of my life. There were three of the brats. A boy about

74

fifteen, a girl about eleven, and the kid from the night before. Can you guess, can you imagine, what they were doing?"

"No," I admitted.

"The little brats were cleaning! The girl was sweeping the road, the older boy was erasing the graffiti, and the kid, that six- or seven-year-old kid? He'd plopped a bucket down in the street and was scrubbing away with a washcloth. Around the bottom of the lamp post."

"The problem lamp post."

"Yeah, that's the one." The man laughed desolately. "That would get to anybody, right? They looked like a family – their faces were the same, anyway – but more than that, their eyes were all full of the morning sunlight and were incredibly clear."

"Even the boy who'd been up so late?"

"Yeah. I know it's hard to believe, but damned if his eyes weren't shining. Their clothes were shabby, but they were all clean, all fresh."

"Did you say anything?"

"No, I just walked by as fast as I could. I felt like a fool."

"I can imagine."

"You do understand, don't you? The situation, at least? After I'd gone a little way I looked back. They were still at it. It wasn't as if they were watching me or anything. So in the end it was like I'd decided to run away, over nothing."

The man stopped talking, and for a few minutes stared out the window. The blackness had closed in again, without any lights even vaguely suggesting a town. The first one had long since vanished. But the man continued to peer this way and that, as if something was flitting around outside the glass.

"So what I'm saying is, they were the germs."

"The germs?"

"That's right. They brought it."

"You mean the children."

"Yeah. The children… and their parents. It was that family."

The man suddenly sighed, then covered his mouth as if his breath stank.

"IT WAS the next day."

The man continued his story.

"It was the day after I met the kids cleaning up. I got up that morning and my family was gone.

"Now, I have some kids. Or maybe I should say I used to. My daughter was eleven and my son was nine. We had a small house, and every morning I'd wake up to fights over the TV and the smell of miso soup boiling for breakfast. But that morning it was God-awful quiet. Something felt wrong.

"After a while I sensed somebody moving around outside. Then I heard my family's voices.

"I went out the front door.

"Every family in the neighborhood – the women and children, anyway, I didn't see many guys – every family was out washing the gutters and scrubbing the street. They were polishing the concrete block fences, and some were even polishing the nails on their houses.

"It was very weird.

"I knew that once a month, the first of the month, I think it was, all the wives in the neighborhood would get together to sweep out the gutters. But to have every family in town skip breakfast and plunge into a frenzy of cleaning, even the wainscoting? You can't tell me that's normal.

"'What are you doing,' I asked my daughter. She looked at me like she was dazzled.

"'What?'

"'I can see you're cleaning up. But why now? Have you had breakfast?'

"My daughter looked at me serenely for a second, then shook her head.

76

"'Then what do you think you're doing! Isn't anyone making breakfast?'

"'But, this is more important.'

"Suddenly she smiled. Exactly like those kids.

"'Who told you to do this?'

"'Nobody,' she said, slowly shaking her head.

"'Then what –' I couldn't go on. I looked around, feeling strangely flustered. Far away, down at the corner, those children were helping some of our neighbors. A man and a woman were with them, their parents apparently. The couple were skinny, but they worked with annoying energy.

"'Did those people tell you to?'

"'No-o.'

My daughter shook her head again.

"'Then why are you doing it?'

"'It's a good thing to do.'

"'I don't care if it's good or not! There's a time and place for everything. Get your mother and brother over here and quick!'

"My daughter went to where her mother was working, and the two of them and my son talked together for a minute. Then all three of them looked at me with a pitying expression on their faces. That's it. It was that expression. The same expression as that kid I'd met in the middle of the night, the same as his brothers and sisters in the street the next morning. It's the expression they use when they look at us."

The man said the last in a fury. Snatching the pocket flask, he drained the remaining quarter of whiskey in a single gulp. As he finished, a hairy hand, stinking of sweat, suddenly stretched over my shoulder and handed him a bottle. A heavy-set man was leaning on the back of my seat. Something about him reminded me of my companion. He nodded at me, and I looked around the car.

There were more than a dozen passengers, and most of the ones near us were clearly interested in the man's story. They were leaning half into the aisle to listen.

77

Most were men in the prime of life, but a few women clustered in a corner of the coach.

"They didn't particularly oppose me," the man said. "I mean, my family. On the surface at least, they went meekly into the house, made the soup, and sat down at the table, same as always.

"But something was different. My son and daughter didn't turn on the television. When I flicked it on they just smiled and didn't give it a glance.

"'What's wrong?' I asked. And why shouldn't I? These were the same kids who always fought like savages over what channel to watch. My wife and I had to shout to make them stop.

"'What's wrong?' I demanded again. But my kids, and even my wife, just smiled. The same pitying look. And my son and daughter, who had always dug into their food, were barely putting anything in their mouths.

"'Are you sick? Are you angry with me about something?'

"They looked at each other and smiled together, and shook their heads in unison. You can imagine how infuriated I was. It was like overnight my family had turned into people from another dimension, into aliens. It was the only way I could explain it.

"'OK! I get it! So you don't want to talk! Fine, I'm leaving!'

"I leaped to my feet. My knee caught the edge of the table and heaved it up, spilling the soup and sending glasses of milk flying.

"They didn't say a word. They just silently mopped up the mess with dishcloths.

"Outside there were still families working away, smiles on their faces. Boiling with anger, I strode through the insanely clean town to the station. I felt like my body was full of unclean waste, dribbling out with my sweat. It made me even angrier."

The man gulped down the whiskey. A sheen of oily sweat covered him as though the alcohol circulating through his body really was welling back out his pores.

"I was still angry when I reached the office. There didn't seem to

78

be any point telling my buddies about it; who'd have believed me? If there'd been someone from my own town, I would have said something.

"But when I was getting ready to leave that night a guy who lived in the next town over stopped me.

"'I'm just guessing,' he said, 'but has that... *unusual* family showed up in your town?'

"'Your place, too!'

"'That's right.'

"'And everyone in your town. They started acting crazy?'

"'Yeah.' He sighed deeply, and then this is what he said:

"'That family isn't human. I can't believe they're human.'

"He looked around like he was scared. 'I don't even think they're alive.

"'I know I'm alive,' he continued. 'My life may be a mess, but at least I'm alive, no doubt about that. But they, they and the people they've influenced, the neighbors, my family, all of them. I can't believe they're alive.'

"'I wouldn't go that far.'

"'Just you wait. You'll see.' He stared at me with tortured eyes. 'They don't sleep, you know? They don't eat, either. So of course they don't piss. They don't even sweat. They don't get angry. They don't argue. All they do is smile.'

"'Naw, that can't be true.'

"'It is.'

"We continued our conversation at an outside stand selling *yakitori* chicken, talking while we stuffed the meat into our mouths. My friend's town had been hit a few days before mine, but it seemed our experiences were the same.

"'You said something a while back.'

"'They're not human?'

"'Yeah, that. They don't sleep, they don't eat. You made sure of that?'

He nodded.

" 'That's the only way I could figure it. Didn't you just say so your-self? That little kid still looked fresh the next morning, didn't he? When they began to get to my family I scolded my wife, same as you. Who are they, I asked. How can you say they're so good? Their kids don't go to school; they don't go to work. And first my wife said it was because they'd just moved in. She didn't even know where they lived, but still she was taking their side.'

"Before long his wife, just like mine, stopped answering. No mat-ter what he said, she'd just watch him with that pitying expression. Finally he decided to trail the strange family, and did it one Saturday night until morning.

"They didn't sleep even once. They walked around town, picking up garbage. They stood mutely in front of guys trying to piss in the street. Sometimes they even stood outside the shutters of other folks' houses. They had to be eavesdropping on what was going on inside.

"Of course, when my friend saw that he got as angry as you'd ex-pect. He started chewing them out on the spot. But they just stared back at him with those translucent eyes, eyes like there's light in the depths behind them, and he couldn't go on. He felt overcome by a nauseating feeling that his body was packed with stinking waste. After that he just lived day by day, staring, not quite believing, with fatigue-swollen eyes as the family began their rounds again the next morning, their eyes still clear, helping in the big clean up, never slip-ping away to sleep, never taking a bite to eat. Just watched them, all the while churning with rage at the unclean feelings inside him.

"That night, my friend and I really went to town."

The man laughed uncomfortably and fixed his gaze on the dark-ness beyond the train window. Far, far away, another faintly glowing town floated in the black.

"If anyone's still living there, they're probably on a rampage same as we were. We swilled down the *sake*, threw it up, lurched from bar to bar in search of the cheapest women. We shouted for them to do it there, on the spot. We stuck our hands up their crotches, we were too much even for those fine ladies, and we got tossed out into the street and staggered up covered with mud."

He laughed dryly.

"Probably you think it was an asshole thing to do. A pair of over-grown punks. Now, I wouldn't exactly call my colleague and me gentlemen. But let me tell you, even we'd never gotten so royally pissed before in our lives. But the way we felt that night, we didn't have a choice. And after a while, we started enjoying making people watch us like that.

"I don't know what time it was when I got home. After pounding on the shutters and banging the door, I finally got in, and the first thing I did was I knocked my wife flat. She just lay there on the floor, like a doll. But she kept glancing toward the shutters. It was then I noticed her eyes were shining faintly in the dark. And at the same time I noticed that – maybe I should say I felt – somebody outside. I flung open the shutters. And saw *Them*. The whole family, even the kids, standing there. The whole pack of them were staring at my livid face with their shining eyes.

"The father, cool as a cucumber, signals the kids with his eyes. 'Well, shall we go?' And they made their way out of our little patch of yard with silent steps. I was speechless. I watched them enter the garden of another house and line up again in front of the sliding garden doors. Seconds later the doors burst open, and a shadow came dancing out. Flash, something glittered in the dark, and I finally realized it was light reflecting off a knife the guy was waving. All I could do was watch.

"Now the owner of that particular house was a bit of a gangster, and we neighbors always steered clear of him. He was drunk, angry drunk, and he snarled like an animal as he wielded a dagger and its plain wooden sheath. The blade plunged into the father's chest, then the mother's arm, a second slash at her husband's neck, her neck, and finally the three children. He hacked at them and slashed at them. And finally, standing there in a daze, he began to cry, or maybe it was a moan.

"They were not, after all, human.

"It wasn't blood that poured from the gaping wounds in their cheeks, their arms, their chests and legs. It was a dazzling light. No pulsing organs anywhere. Only openings on an empty cavity.

"The man sobbed to himself, letting the bloodless, *clean* knife dangle at his side.

"The children, with their shining wounds and clear eyes, watched the man. They watched the tears and snot pouring from his eyes and nose. They watched his naked body and the shriveled member limp between his thighs. They watched the sweat covering his body, his muddy legs. They watched. And their parents, their wounds radiating light, watched, equally serene, with an expression on their faces as if to say, 'Please bring happiness to this poor man.'

"A crowd was gathering in the street, larger and larger. Before I knew it, I had stepped out into the middle of it, still in my bare feet.

"Just then, a women slid quietly up beside the crying man. 'Dear,' she said. 'Dear, that's why I told you. Why do you try to fight them?'

"It was the gangster's wife. She was a serious girl, much younger than he was, and he was always beating her. She'd walk close to the walls when she went shopping, keeping her face down to hide the bruises under her eyes.

"But now this woman raised her head, and with everyone's eyes upon her, laid a hand on the man's shoulder.

"'Shut up,' he snarled, and knocked her hand away.

"'Please. Let's go back inside.'

"'Shut up! Who do you think you are!'

"Still waving his knife, the man began to sob, a low moaning.

"'It's all right,' his wife said softly. 'Go on. It's all right to stab me. Please, it's all right. Stab me, if it makes you feel better.'

"The man's knife quivered, trembled, a fraction of an inch from her breast.

"Finally the woman laid her hand gently on the knife and looked over at the shining family.

"The father gave a slight nod.

"The woman pulled the knife away, but the man didn't resist. He just gaped at her. The man's wife took the white blade and smoothly drew it across her wrists. The cuts opened their mouths like lenses, and from deep inside sprang a brilliant white light..."

The man sighed deeply.

The train rolled on.

The shining town was far behind us, and utter darkness spread out on every side.

"What happened next?" I prompted.

"A quiet murmur spread through the crowd," he said. "From the knot of people another woman stepped out to take the knife, and cut. This time her own neck... And again she radiated light. The knife passed from hand to hand, and old people, children, their mothers, one after another began to slice open their skin.

"On and on it went, solemnly, a ceremony. And at the end, nearly two-thirds of the town had become a family of light, gathered together on the opposite side of the road. Like a scene from some old Western, they faced our cluster of black shadows.

"Of course, my wife and children were with the light.

"In the very front row of Their group stood the shining family. More dazzling than all the rest. Finally the father, in a voice that was – maybe you could say awe-inspiring, or somehow theatrical – he called out to us.

"'There is nothing to fear,' he said. 'There is no reason to despair because you cannot be like us. Nay, come together with your families, and live as you always have. The unclean lingers within your bodies, and prevents you from joining us. But the love of your wives and children will make you clean.'

"The man spread his arms wide.

"'Come, my friends, let us call out. To our beloved husbands, our beloved fathers, our beloved children and those poor, unfortunate women...'

"But we turned our backs on the cries that welled from their mouths. Perhaps there were a few of us who did listen. But most of the men, and the small handful of 'unfortunate' women, earthy women reeking of the flesh, turned their backs and abandoned the town.

"NOW DO you understand?" he demanded. "Now do you know what those shining towns are?"

"The towns of the family of light?" I ventured.

"Yes. Whole towns shining with the light from their bodies."

"But what on earth are they doing!" I said. "Not working, not eating, not sleeping, not playing together, what on earth are they living for..."

"So that bothers you, too?" The man laughed. Smiled, squeezing the sweat out his pores, exposing his meat-colored gums. "Then you aren't one of them after all. This train's for meat people. The family of light and the family of flesh have built their own towns out here, and this train connects the towns of the flesh. We're in the minority, so we've got to pull together, solidarity forever. It's not easy for folk like us, for folk stuffed with organs, packed and coiled inside like snakes."

He laughed again.

"We'll be arriving any minute now. Why don't you get off, too? We can issue you a passport at the station."

The man reached for his inside coat pocket, and pulled out his passport. He flipped it open in front of me.

The picture was not of his face, but of what looked like a stomach, seeming to wriggle and squirm on the page. It was a picture of living organs.

"How about it?" he said. "This is the scar."

The man rolled up his shirt, and showed me a line of stitches across his abdomen.

"It hurts when you cut through the skin," he said. "But pain is a meat person's pride."

– First published in Shūkan Shōsetsu, *May 3, 1976*

MAYUMURA TAKU

I'll Get Rid of Your Discontent
Translated by M. Hattori and Grania Davis

I DON'T know where you can buy one, but I found mine at a shabby old store. The curious object looked like a blueish Chinese won-ton placed in a small plastic box.

"Excuse me, what's this?" I asked the elderly shop lady.

"Well, I don't really know, but it comes with instructions."

"You mean this sheet of paper? But it's folded and pasted so I can't read it."

"I know. I can't read it either. You d have to open it up first. Can't do it, though. It *is* for sale after all," she answered.

I'd never seen such an object, so I bought it out of curiosity. It was very cheap.

As soon as I got home, I took the strange object out of the box and broke the seal on the instructions, which said, *"This is a present for you. Hold onto it when you feel anxious or very angry, or when you are terribly embarrassed. Then you'll feel much better. You can carry it in your pocket to work..."* I almost cried out with surprise. It would be a good story, if it were true. I continued with the rest of it, *"You should use this only when circumstances are especially bad, because it is effective only three times. Do not use it a fourth time. If you forget this warning, something fatal will happen to you. After using it three times, please throw it away."*

It sounded like a fairy tale. I like this kind of story, even if it's just a fantasy. I would carry it with me, true or not – although I'm not one of those unfortunate people who destroy their lives over temporary upsets.

However, the chance to try it came earlier than I expected. At my office, my superior blamed me for something, but I was completely innocent. I was upset and blurted out a loud explanation, but I felt angry even after he accepted what I said.

Rashly I continued, "You had no reason to think it was me. You must have it in for me."

When I spoke, the boss became very irritated. He thought for a moment about what had been said, and grew even more annoyed. I didn't care a bit if he was angry. I was about to tell him what I thought – then I remembered the strange object in my pocket.

I found it with my fingers and grasped it tightly. I felt a momentary shock. I closed my eyes and exhaled deeply. Then my surroundings looked slightly different.

A middle-aged gentleman sat in front of me. He was a father and the husband of a family. The fine furniture of the office was all around me. I was merely an employee, just like many who work to earn their living. It was natural for him to be annoyed at my harsh words. What was the point of quarreling with each other? I apologized to him and bowed deeply.

"All right, never mind. It was only natural for you to get angry. It was me who was to blame," he said with a smile.

I left the room in the best of spirits. I realized that I had never felt so fine. The strange object in my pocket seemed to solve my problem. For several months afterward things went smoothly. I'd never had such a comfortable and fruitful life. But my youthful mood turned defiant again.

One morning I left home slightly late – I'd have been late to the office unless I hurried up. As I rushed to the station I hoped the train wouldn't be delayed. I was often annoyed with this train line because the trains were late. Just as I suspected, the train wasn't on time. I was impatient, worried about being late and receiving a poor evaluation at the office. As the train slid into the platform, I rushed to the conductor full of quarrelsome complaints. Then I grasped the strange object in my pocket – with the same curious result. I felt very calm and satisfied as he gave me a certificate that the train had been late. I left the station for my office with a feeling that I could coexist contentedly with everyone around me.

The third time I used the object was when I went to see an art exhibition with my friend. I couldn't help laughing at him as he fatuously discussed a row of obscure paintings. "The painters themselves don't understand these things – it's pretty rich that you're trying to explain them!"

He stared at me with a surprised look. "I thought you had a greater sense of aesthetics, but..." he muttered.

This made me angry, so I replied, "I have plenty of aesthetic sense, but I don't pretend to appreciate what I can't understand."

"That's not like you," he said, "Don't talk like a loudmouthed lout."

Instead of responding, I clutched that strange object. I didn't want a falling out with my friend. I was aware of the same sudden shock, then I vacantly opened my eyes.

The useless squares of gaudy colored paint hung in a row – they had nothing to do with real life. The people loitered, feeding their vanity. My friend was one of them. I shouldn't be in such a phony place. I told him I wanted to leave, but he didn't answer. I was sorry that he felt bad, but I thought he would recover his temper after enjoying a drink. He wasn't really that angry. I left and went home without stopping anywhere.

When I got home, I took that strange object out of my pocket and examined it. I had already used it three times, and now it had to be thrown away. The curious thing on the palm of my hand looked just the same as it had when I first saw it. I decided to keep it with me instead of discarding it. I relied on it to help me cope with daily life. I held it up.

Do not use it a fourth time. If you forget this warning something fatal will happen to you.

The warning began to influence me in subtle ways. I didn't know why I was carrying it with me, though I had no intention of using it again. I wasn't angry or irritated at anything, but sometimes I involuntarily thrust my hand into my pocket and tried to grasp it.

No. No!

I mustn't grab it! Something terrible would happen to me – something fatal. Who knows what? Yet the strange object is so powerful that it can help me, whatever may happen.

The ambivalence began to affect my behavior. I was sure that someone would notice. I knew I must throw it away, but each time a strong attachment kept me from acting on my resolve, as I excused myself for my indecision.

But at last the crucial moment came. My great efforts on behalf of the company were ignored, and I was passed over for a promotion.

Staring at the promotion announcements on the bulletin board, I suddenly found myself grasping the object tightly in my hand.

I felt as though something was draining from my body... It flowed out calmly and slowly... I stood there, motionless...

I don't know who made this thing, and why it was for sale at all. I don't need to know the reason – and I don't need to use it any longer. Nothing fatal happened to me. That day, after I grasped it for the fourth time, everything has been going very well. It brought me genuine happiness. I am never discontented or angry about anything. I've learned that life requires lots of patience. Now I'm regarded as a model employee. I'm never absent or late to the office, even if there's some problem at home. I'm pleased to carry out any orders given by my superior, no matter how difficult. I am never disobedient. I can accept whatever comes along. I'm more concerned about the well-being of the company than about promotions. An individual mustn't be respected above the company.

So what happened when I held it the fourth time? Where was the fatality? I've never felt as happy as this. If you find one in a shop, you'd better keep it in your pocket – I recommend it!

– *First publication:* Uchūjin *(Cosmic Dust) 57 (July, 1962)*

ISHIKAWA TAKASHI

The Road to the Sea
Translated by Judith Merril and Yano Tetsu

I MUST *go forth to see the sea!*

So the boy resolved. And, being the kind of boy he was, no slings or arrows would stop him once his mind was set. Without a word to father or to mother he set out from home.

Which way to the sea? The boy didn't know. But any which way he went, if he just kept tramping along in one direction, he was bound to come to the sea sooner or later. This was the wisdom of a boy just turned six.

The boy had never seen any sea except inside his picture-books.

...full of blue water everywhere, the open ocean stretches without end. And in it – there's a whale! – and a shark – seagulls! *– a mermaid and an octopus – kelp, coral, and a* mole! *And over there, and here and here and there again, great floating vans named "ships" – and* that *one is even a* skull-ship *with* tattooed pirates *riding in it! And the horizon out at sea – water, water, nothing, as far as you could see but* water *– what in the world would such a sight look like...?*

His mind could not hold on to such a watermuch.

Adrift in dreams of sky-sea-blue, the boy trudged purposefully on.

At the end of the town, he met the old man. This old man was always sitting there by the side of the road, staring at the sky: he was kind of funny in the head.

"Hey, boy!" The old man hailed him, "Where you going?"

"The sea," said the boy, and kept on walking.

"The sea?" The old man opened his toothless mouth and laughed. "That's a good one!"

He grabbed the boy by the arm and pulled him to a stop.

"Going to the sea? Okay. You'll just have to go to heaven first." He pointed a withered old finger, trembling uncontrollably, at the sky. "The sea is right up there over your head!"

In the clear blue sky there was nothing but the sun, shining bright. The boy didn't say a word. He just pulled loose from the old man and trotted off, pursing his lips a bit and clucking his tongue: *That old man has got too old – his whole head is mixed up now.*

PRETTY soon the boy got to a small hill. Standing on the top of the hill, he looked all around him everywhere, but the presence of the sea was nowhere to be sensed. The boy dropped on his haunches and had something to eat while he watched the gradual shifting of ground-shadows cast by the slow passage of the sun.

Beyond the plain was a range of mountains and the sun was just beginning to slant down in that direction. *The sun sinks in the sea:* that's what he had heard, so – *Let's see what's on the other side!*

The boy straightened his back, set his lips firmly, fastened his eyes on the distant hills, and started walking —

Beyond the mountains were still further mountains. Beyond those mountains stretched a plain. At the far end of the plain, another range of hills confronted him.

The boy kept marching along, all alone. Not one town, not one village, not one person, not one living creature did he meet.

His supplies of food and water were getting sadly low.

He did not understand how the sea should be so far away.

The boy kept going. How many times did he sleep on the ground? It didn't matter. When he was sleeping, when he was walking, he was always seeing his visions of the sea.

He took every shape of the sea. Sometimes he was a fish, sometimes a pirate, another time a harbor, then a sail swelling in the wind – he was always changing from one shape to another; and now – *a storm-toss'd ship, bathed in spray-spume, shot through with lightning bolts, pounded on by thunder-claps, just about to sink at last—*

The boy's legs had stopped walking a while back. Now two moons shed their light on a still, small figure stretched out on the red-brown desert sand.

THE SPACESUIT had a two-hundred-hour range before it stopped functioning completely.

The boy was smiling a bit even as his breath stopped. Under the night sky of Mars he lay facing a green star – the sky-floating Earth. The sea was there, but he could never reach it.

Nobody goes back there any more.

– First publication: Mahotsukai no Natsu
(Summer of the Wizard: Collected Stories),
1970, Hayakawa Shobō

YAMANO KŌICHI

Where do the Birds Fly Now?
Translated by Dana Lewis

NOTE: THE READER *is encouraged to rearrange*
sections A *through* L *as he or she sees fit.*
– The Author

1. *Concerning the birds*

For a long time I wasn't interested in birds. If birds occasionally flew in front of me, I didn't trouble myself much about it. I have a feeling that even before I noticed it, birds flew in front of me any number of times. On such occasions I simply thought, "A bird flew by." No doubt there were times I neglected to even perceive them as birds. I only noted that some irrelevant object had passed before me.

There was just one time that I showed a little interest in the birds. I was walking the streets with a friend. A bird flew by when we were stuck for conversation, so I said, "Hey, it's a bird!"

My friend only responded, "Where?"

Probably he paid less attention to birds than I.

2. *The events of a certain evening*

I was strolling with Noriko, going no place in particular. It was a cool, bracing evening, and we didn't feel the least bit tired even though we'd been walking for two hours. Long-distance trucks ran down the highway, their lights illuminating the trees along the sidewalk. We turned to climb an open-cut road and came out on a height in the middle of a quiet residential district from which we could take in a sweeping view of the town.

There seemed to be a small river flowing beneath the bluff, but there were no lights nearby and we couldn't be sure. The city lights were unexpectedly sparse, only the downtown glittering in rich colors. The perimeter was surrounded by a vast darkness.

While Noriko and I stood there, enjoying the panorama, a bird flew by.

"There goes a bird," I said.

"Where?"

I pointed into the nearby shadows.

"It's too dark to see," said Noriko.

True, as soon as she pointed it out, I realized that there wasn't any light that could have shone on a passing bird. I shouldn't have noticed one even if it had cut right in front of me.

At that moment I first became aware of the singular existence of the birds.

"Do birds fly in front of people all that often?"

Noriko cocked her head as if she didn't understand the question.

"Cats, for instance. Cats cross in front of people all the time."

"I guess they do."

"Dogs, too. Dogs and cats react when people approach."

Noriko nodded.

"Then what about birds?"

"I've never really noticed."

"Take swallows – swallows sometimes fly in front of people. Swallows build their nests under eaves, and they fly around buildings. They don't care. But sparrows fly off when people come. They escape to roofs or telephone lines. Pigeons aren't afraid of people, but they don't fly down low."

"So?"

"So?"

"So what about it?"

"What about it! In other words, swallows are the only birds that fly in front of people! You don't see many other birds in the street, do you?"

"If you insist," said Noriko.

"But probably even swallows don't fly under people's noses all that often," I persisted.

"I imagine not."

We started walking again. Noriko wasn't interested in the conversation. A road sloped gently down from the height, fields and houses alternating along it. Noriko observed each house one by one, and took it upon herself to critique their mediocre architecture.

"What's that?"

She led me to an aging bungalow surrounded by a wooden fence with small gateposts. A bill had been posted on one of them.

OWNERSHIP SUBJECT TO LITIGATION
BETWEEN SATA GONZAEMON, INVESTOR,
AND ISHIGURO SANPEI, ARCHITECT.
VANDALISM, FURTHER CONSTRUCTION, OR TRESPASSING
STRICTLY PROHIBITED.

"What a waste," Noriko said. "People could live here."

She went through the gate.

"It says no trespassing!"

"Nobody's looking."

Noriko opened the front door. Apparently it was unlocked; we could trespass very easily. Inside there was no floor matting, no furniture. Only a window sash silhouetted against the scanty light gave the house a curious air of habitation.

"It's creepy."

"Then you can come back out."

"But interesting," she added, stepping up from the entrance into the front room. The floor creaked, and the house posts trembled in response. It was then that Noriko must have seen something, for suddenly she screamed. And in return:

"Uoh!"

A voice!

"Eeek!"

"Uoh!"

"Someone's in here!"

"Uoh!"

Noriko flung herself on me, and I inched back as well.

"Who's there!"

"Uoh! Even if I tell you, what can you learn from a name? To you I'm just a stranger."

A man reared up in a corner of the room.

"Why'd you frighten us?"

"It was you who frightened me, when she started shrieking like that."

"Didn't you say, 'Uoh'?"

"I was surprised."

"You stayed surprised a long time."

"The last 'Uoh' just slipped out."

Noriko was regaining her composure.

"This guy talks funny, just like you," she said.

"I'm like him, you say?"

The man came close and peered into Noriko's face.

"Eeeek!"

"Uoh!" he replied. Then he shook his head and cocked an ear. The sound of a siren, previously lost in the commotion, was now clear to hear. The man ran to the window, rushed back, and searched the floor for his gear.

"We're in for some strange company, thanks to your young lady and all her yelping. This should get interesting."

He had a gun in his hands as he spoke. The patrol car siren drew close and stopped. Lights shone on the windowpanes. The man broke out the glass with the gun and promptly shot out the head-lights. Amid the shouts of officers, the engine turned over again and the patrol car retreated.

"I've got another pistol," the man said, still peering out the window, gun at the ready. "Wanna give it a shot?"

I tugged Noriko's hand without answering and we felt our way to the front door. We got there just as gunfire opened up outside. We'd be shot dead if we rushed out now. I decided to watch how things developed, and we huddled together by the door. After a long exchange of fire, a second patrol car pulled up. More and more reinforcements arrived, raising sirens one after another.

The police switched tactics. The shooting stopped and a voice shouted over a loudspeaker.

"You're surrounded! Throw down your gun and come out peacefully."

Noriko and I opened the door and stepped into the lights.

"We're innocent! Don't shoot!"

Still shouting, we ran in the opposite direction of the armored minibus the man had been aiming at and escaped unharmed beyond the line of patrol cars.

Time after time the police shouted over the loudspeaker, and time after time the man fired back at the sound. A group of officers circled around to the back, and those in front resumed fire.

But at that instant there was a flash, and the whole roof of the house exploded in flame. I urged Noriko on, and we lost ourselves among the bystanders while the officers were still distracted by the blast. We quickly fled the scene. Looking back over my shoulder as we ran, I saw red flames swirling toward the pitch-black sky from throughout the empty house.

At that moment, a bird passed before my eyes again.

A. *The flight of the birds*

The day after the affair at the empty house, I noticed it wasn't reported in the papers. Nor did Noriko remember anything about it.

"Then what did you do last night?" I asked her.

"I took a walk with you, didn't I?"

"That's right. And we went to an empty house."

"No, we didn't go to an empty house."

"You don't remember meeting a strange man in an empty house?"

"I remember perfectly well what we did last night, and we didn't go to any empty houses and we didn't meet any strange men!"

"Then where did we walk?"

"We went up a road from the national highway."

"We came out on a height with a fine view."

"Yes."

"And we talked about birds."

"No."

"I see," I said.

I retraced the same route with Noriko. The roads were just as she said, but she didn't remember anything about the empty house where the gentle road descended from the height.

And moreover, the house had not burned down.

There was more to the flight of the birds than I had thought.

B. *The ecology of the birds*

I observed those birds.

Their beaks were very sharp: practically cones. Their necks were thick and short. Their wings seemed to flow from the base of the neck, and their tails spread wide at the end, exactly like a fan. I couldn't be sure of their size, but since they seemed to fly about a meter in front of me, they should have been some twenty centimeters long. Nor could I speak with certainty of their color. The general impression was ash gray, but it seemed to be a meld of many different colors. Perhaps their legs were hidden – I have yet to see them – and I could not make out their eyes.

The birds flew in slanting straight lines as though striking a canvas boldly with a brush. They seemed to go off in a direction slightly away from me. Their sharp beaks split space. I should probably say that what ran across the white canvas was not a brush, but a sharp palette knife. And the line born there was not like a Mondrian, but a Fontana. The sliced-open canvas revealed another picture beyond it, but because that second picture closely resembled the first, it was afterwards all but impossible to find the tear.

When the birds flew, they always appeared from somewhere and vanished somewhere.

I never had a distant view of the birds.

C. *The events of a certain midnight*

Birds were flying in front of me every few seconds. Time and time again I lunged to catch one, and time and again I failed. Perhaps because the birds flew so often there was no dawn, no matter how much time passed. It felt like it had been twenty hours since the sun went down, but the night was still sunk as deep as though it had reached the bottom of the subconscious. There was no sign of sunlight spilling over the surrounding hills and horizon line; the shadows of the trees had melted in the dark. Perhaps, I thought, morning would never come again.

Only at the instant the birds flew, something like a thin mist scattered momentarily in the darkness. This was the dimensional spray of split-open space.

I pondered what would happen if I couldn't catch the birds. What could I do for myself under such conditions? Other than catching the birds, was I only able to flee them?

But I didn't want to flee.

At last the intervals between flights began to lengthen. I moved through the darkness. Over and over I ran into trees or lost my footing on the soft earth. Once I tumbled nearly five meters before getting snagged on a tree. Yet the flights of the birds continued to decrease.

"You're a bird caller, too?"

Unexpectedly, I heard a voice nearby. I looked around, but could see nothing in the dark. Finally, by the sound of dry leaves trampled underfoot, I was able to ascertain only the existence of my companion.

"A bird caller?" I asked back.

"Isn't that so?" said the voice. "But it seems the flock has passed."

Certainly the birds were gone.

"You've done very well to come this far," said the voice. "This place is probably quite close to the nests. But until you next meet a flock of birds, you won't be able to get any farther into the interior."

D. *An evolutionary theory of the birds*

The man and I lay on the grass and talked without knowing each other's faces. The dew-laden grass was cold – there were thorns mixed in – and insects crawled about in it, stinging our skin. The stars spreading across the night sky still clung to their old constellations, so I didn't think I'd come to some preposterous other world. Yet even so, I felt somewhere something different from my familiar environment.

The man called himself Ōtsuka. He had all kinds of theories about birds.

"Have you ever had a chance to observe a bird's body? Aside from bones and organs there's almost nothing else crammed in. The bulk of a bird's volume is wing; there's almost no fat and no excess viscera. Yet when a bird takes to the air it should need considerable energy. Where does all that energy spring up, in a creature that has no reserves? This thing we so easily call a 'bird' has sacrificed all its other faculties for the sole purpose of flight. The bird is a truly awesome organism, don't you think?"

"That's how they've survived so long."

"Certainly so. And yet, thanks to this great sacrifice, birds have evolved relatively little compared to mammals. Mammals and birds appeared at about the same time, but while mammals can boast man's intellect, the carnivore's fighting prowess, the ungulate's aptitude for escape, birds – other than some special cases like the ostrich, of course – have not undergone any striking evolution at all. Most birds are little different from the archaeopteryx."

"That's because they over-specialized," I said. "Like dinosaurs and mammoths. Irish elk and saber-toothed tigers."

"No, it is a little different. Those all died out, but birds survive. Birds haven't gone extinct; they just haven't evolved."

"Other animals haven't evolved that much. The reptiles are still around. It's the same with birds and insects."

"Ah, yes. But those are just archaic holdouts. Birds should have reached the very pinnacle of evolution. Just like the mammals, don't you see? Is it plausible that the bird family should prove to have been an evolutionary dead end, when the mammals gave birth to Man? We can think that, yes. Just as, among the mammals, the perissodactyl species, at their furthest point of evolution, are going extinct. Yet there is also a possibility that this is not the case."

"The birds we've seen?"

"Exactly so. Birds learned to fly to escape from other animals. They made their escape through the epoch-making solution of flight. Would it be so strange if the birds again assayed an epochal escape?"

"You're saying they fled from two dimensions to three, and now they've gone on to four."

"It's not unthinkable, is it?"

"I didn't say it's unthinkable! Just that you can't prove it."

"*We* can prove it."

"But how do they fly across dimensions?"

"That I do not understand."

"Then why can we cross over with them?"

"That probably has to do with human consciousness. In our minds there are worlds transcending reality. Or perhaps I should say, worlds *trying* to transcend reality. For the birds, they present a splendid passageway. If you were faced with a wall, and a door through the wall, you would probably use the door, even if you had the strength to hurdle the wall."

"So the birds that I thought were flying in front of me were really flying *through* my mind?"

"Probably so."

"So it's impossible to catch them."

"No doubt you wished to transcend reality."

"I guess you could say that. I was trying to escape."

"That impulse intersected perfectly with a flock of birds. On the evolutionary grounds I was mentioning, you see."

"And that's what you call bird calling."

"Yes," said Ōtsuka. "When you try to transcend reality, the birds pass through. If they pass through once, it becomes their flyway. I just came here because I like birds, but to encourage them to fly through me I tried reading *Nadja* and *Au Chateau d'Argol*, and studied Max Ernst's paintings every day. That was my bird calling."

The sky was finally beginning to pale, and the thinly floating shadows of trees cast a radial pattern around us. As the gray slid to blue, the flat shadows of the trees also changed, into three-dimensional layers of leaves.

E. *The events of the previous day*

Even after the birds erased the incident at the empty house, I remained blithely optimistic. The world around me was changing with each flight, but it was only a little at a time, and there were no sudden shifts that affected me directly. If anything, I found myself enjoying the transfigurations wrought by the birds.

I went to the library and reread old newspapers, comparing them against the memories filed inside my head. As when the girl behind the curtain is made to vanish by slight of hand, I was able to spot many an adroit change in reality. I can't say these were all "small" changes for those involved. But since they came about through my own dimensional movement, they were minor as far as I was concerned. Perhaps it isn't strictly true to say they were none of my business, yet none affected me greatly.

Palestine Liberation Front seizes control of Jordan →
PLO and Jordanian government agree to ceasefire

Speed Shinbori wins the Mainichi Crown →
Kurishiba wins the Mainichi Crown; Speed Shibori runs second

Osaka World Fair extended one month →
Osaka World Fair ends on schedule

Janis Joplin releases third album →
Janis Joplin dies suddenly

If one bird flew before me, only a small change occurred, like when – to use spatial logic – one's field of vision shifts ever so slightly when one takes a single step. If I flew halfway around the world in a jet I would no doubt experience considerable unease, but there should be nothing much to worry about if I walked there a step at a time.

There was a chance, however, that this accumulation of small changes might eventually transform the environment around me. One's field of vision may not change greatly with a single step, yet a hundred can reveal a very different landscape. For me, the changes that had occurred since I came to this place were not just chronological; they were part of my dimensional relocation from one world to another.

I left the library, and laughed aloud as I circled the fountain in the park. I had been completely deceived. This beautiful, mountain-ringed town illuminated by the bright sun, the clear air from the mountains, the white buildings glowing in that crystal air, the vivid pattern of these scenes was nothing more than a photographic slide. With the flight of a single bird, it would be switched to another succeeding picture.

We call this existence.

I went to meet Noriko at the coffee shop where she worked. After opening the colored glass door, I paused for a moment to adjust to the dark.

It was a small shop with just three employees, and there were certainly three girls there.

But none of them were Noriko.

F. *Concerning Noriko*

When I fled here from Tokyo, the first thing I did was to call up my only friend in town. But he'd already been questioned by the police, and said he couldn't give me shelter.

I regretted coming here then, driven simply by a yearning for the clear air between the mountains. If I'd gone to another city I would have known lots of people, and had a place where I could go to ground.

Aimlessly I wandered the streets. I no longer had a place to go, and the whole town seemed somehow empty. It was like walking through one of those *nihonga* Japanese paintings, where there's always a mountain looming behind the buildings. But with night the peaks were lost in the darkness, and a cold wind out of nowhere attacked me like it was crazed. Stores closed early, and even the lights of the entertainment district winked out one by one. Pedestrian traffic disappeared in an instant. Only buses ran down the thoroughfares, transporting dim, boxed-in light.

I went into a small coffee shop. I was completely exhausted, half asleep, my head full of random thoughts. Fragments of consciousness popped up and vanished in my mind.

Suddenly I noticed someone had thrust a sheet of paper at me. Before looking at it I followed the hand that held it, and found a girl's face.

The girl gazed at me with a gentle smile.

The paper was a simple handbill.

"Please read this," she said.

I nodded, and finally took the handbill. The girl left immediately. I skimmed the sheet. It denounced the unfair dismissal of some pacifist workers at one of the region's major manufacturers.

I was fed up with this stuff. I'd left Tokyo to get away from it. But somehow I felt something fresh in this anti-war movement in a little town between the mountains. I'd only left Tokyo the day before, but already I felt something akin to nostalgia as I read the handbill.

And one more thing: in the gentle, smiling face of the girl distributing pamphlets without distinction to all the coffee house customers I felt a serenity missing from the brutalized Tokyo movement.

When she approached again I said, "I'm a student from Tokyo, but the police are after me. If there's anything I can do, I'll help. But can you give me shelter?"

Still smiling lightly, the girl nodded.

"Probably," she said. "It's all right, I think."

Of course the girl was Noriko. She'd been working for that manufacturer, but she'd quit to protest the firings.

"I'd really meant to quit all along," Noriko told me. "An office girl doesn't make much of a salary: it isn't like you've got prospects for the future, or that the work's interesting.

"What I'm doing now is much, much more fulfilling," said Noriko.

For more than a month I faithfully helped the local movement. The work was nothing more than pamphlet writing and stencil cutting, but everyone called me "the activist from the front lines in Tokyo," and treated me like I was special. My pronouncements were always heeded, and I was able to indulge in a quiet sense of good fortune. I loved Noriko. I thought I would stay and live this way, modestly, in this town. Our comrades raised money for our wedding.

Yet even then, I sometimes found myself wanting to return to Tokyo. Or rather, I should say the feeling was always there in a corner of my mind. Even as I enjoyed my small piece of happiness, I was fanning my dissatisfaction with it.

G. *Pursuing the flock*

When Noriko vanished, so did my desire to return to Tokyo. The two thoughts – of Noriko and Tokyo – had existed by being opposites, and when one was erased the other lost all meaning.

But Noriko's disappearance also revealed a fatal flaw in my reasoning. As far as I was concerned, the flights of the birds weren't limited to small changes after all.

True, when a bird flew before me it was the bird that flew, not I. But nowhere was there any guarantee that once it flew away again, I would be in a place I desired. Granted, a bird's single flight was like a single step; it could only fly to worlds close to mine. Yet there were instances when that could affect me greatly. Cannot your entire field of vision change with a single step! It had been simple chance that I'd escaped serious harm until now.

Losing all direction, I was bewildered. The bewilderment called more birds. The birds flew one after another. In no time at all the town's anti-war movement was transformed. In the course of a day I lost every friend I had.

I gave myself up to the birds. At some point I began chasing the birds. Desiring the birds to fly before me, I emptied my mind and kept on walking. The birds flying through my consciousness walked me in the direction of the flock.

I saw now that the flights of the birds were not identical after all. If some spread their wings and arrowed off like downhill racers, there were others that lifted their heads and peered at the sky. Others bowed their bodies as they ascended.

I left the city. Passing through a scanty belt of rice paddies, I entered a stand of trees like a jungle gym. I didn't know what kind they were, but it was clearly some kind of orchard.

The orchard road leisurely climbed a hill. The trees were about three meters tall. At that height the branches spread out to form a canopy. All I could see was a ceiling of branches and leaves and the countless pillars of trunks supporting it. Still inside the labyrinth, I met the end of day.

I kept walking even after the sun went down. By now I seemed to have left the orchard and gone even deeper into the mountains, but I entrusted myself completely to the birds and entered a second, deeper labyrinth. Still the flights increased. The grade steepened to an acute angle, and I suffered an illusion that the surface of the earth itself had tilted. In the almost impenetrable darkness, I continued to gaze only on the spray of dimensions split open by the birds.

H. *The events of that morning*

The night ended quickly. The stars went out one by one in the pale light, and the black trees turned to green. I got up slowly and looked at the man beside me, who had called himself Ōtsuka. He was sleeping. His hair was gray. He could already be called old. His appearance was respectable, but somewhere in his face was a starved loneliness.

"Night seems to be over," I called out. He slowly opened his eyes and looked up at me.

"Ah," said Ōtsuka. "You are young."

I inspected our surroundings. The trees were small, but sturdy. There were patches of wild grass with something like hard fruit-like seeds. The damp earth was red.

Ōtsuka stood, and we began to walk.

"Shall we try going down to the town?"

Ōtsuka suggested it. I nodded.

Ōtsuka seemed to know the local topography well, and he quickly picked a direction. There was nothing at all resembling a road; we descended searching for footholds among the trees. After advancing for a while, Ōtsuka stopped in his tracks and looked up at the top of a tree. A small white bird perched in the branches.

"That's an unfamiliar bird," Ōtsuka said.

I nodded and continued on, but Ōtsuka, not making a move, just stared at the bird. Not having any choice in the matter, I sat at the foot of a tree and waited for him to move on.

Ōtsuka took out a notebook and began to sketch. At last he came over to me.

"That is a completely new bird," he said. "Please think of a name for it."

"Uhmm, since it's white, how about 'whitebird?'"

I spoke without thinking, but Ōtsuka licked his pencil and wrote "whitebird" in the notebook.

After that we often saw birds, and every time the routine was repeated.

As we descended the mountain the trees got larger, and the number of birds increased. Ōtsuka collected sketch after sketch in his notebook, and I made up name after name. A bird that pounded wood like a woodpecker but looked like a sparrow became a "sparrowpecker"; to avoid being obvious, a bird like a Buddhist monk was a "Christbird." The fruit orchard itself had become a mixed copse of trees. There was no road, and no sign of human civilization. But the birds increased even more, until we couldn't go a hundred yards without sighting a new species.

Ōtsuka continued to observe them as though possessed. When I asked him if he thought all the people had disappeared, he replied with only a distracted grunt.

At last we emerged into what had previously been the belt of rice paddies. Here, too, there was only a primitive expanse of grassy fields and marshes. But something like a town could be seen in the distance.

"It's the city!" I cried, shouting despite myself.

Ōtsuka put a finger to his lips and silenced me. His interest lay in a brilliant red bird like a phoenix that came flying from the grove.

I. *The taxonomy of the birds*

There were twenty kinds of birds in Ōtsuka's notebook. For the time being he had classified them using a standard schema.

SPARROWS (OR CLOSE RELATIVES)

Parallel swallow – the bird that brought us here. The migratory bird of the parallel worlds.

Great lark – closely resembles the lark, flies high in the air.

Sparrowpecker – resembles a sparrow, pounds wood like a woodpecker.

Grillbird – coal black, meager body.

Whitebird – small, white bird. Even the bill is white.

Ratbird – mouse gray, with a thin, long tail.

SWIFTS (OR CLOSE RELATIVES)

Dustbird – smaller than a hummingbird, almost like an insect.

BROAD-BILLED ROLLERS (OR CLOSE RELATIVES)

Christbird – the orange beak is beautiful against its blue body.

GRESSORES (OR CLOSE RELATIVES)

Scarlet heron – exactly like the Japanese crested ibis.

Bigamous heron – long beak and lecherous eyes.

LYREBIRDS (OR CLOSE RELATIVES)

Phoenix – large, splendid red bird.

CRANES (OR CLOSE RELATIVES)

Baldcrane – white head, resembles a Japanese crane.

UNCLASSIFIABLE

Birdbird – long legs, petite body.

Broombird – found with the dust bird; wide, spreading tail.
Perhaps the male dustbird?

007 bird – nimble, runs around trees.

Bourbon bird – red eyes, zigzags in flight.

Broadbird – large body, barely moves.

Hoshi crane – round body, with large beak and eyes; probably
no relation to cranes. Resembles a certain science fiction
writer.

Glider – long wings, soars like a sailplane.

Rumpbirds – small, line up when they fly.

I came up with most of these names. Ōtsuka, neither angered nor
impressed by my horseplay – indeed, totally indifferent to it – recorded them just as I gave them.

J. *The events of two months before*

For a long time Funabashi and I faced off across the table. I talked
on and on, and then there was nothing more to say. Funabashi was
silent from beginning to end.

There were several other men and women in the room. Inoue
had gotten his guitar out and plucked softly at the strings, both
his feet propped up on the desk. Omiya idly skimmed the handbills
and pamphlets stacked beside him. The big desk seemed to fill the
room, and was jumbled high with stacks of books, magazines, and
pamphlets. Where the surface was exposed, the grain was lost in the
grime, and x-acto knife gashes had destroyed its smoothness.

"Wonder if it's raining?"

Ishida looked out the window, hoping for some change.

It wasn't raining.

"Then you really won't go along," I said finally.

Funabashi didn't reply, didn't shake his head. Just lowered his eyes.

Inoue plucked at the guitar again, but the formless noise just put us more on edge.

"Why do I have to join in?" Funabashi muttered.

"That's your problem. If you've got your own rationale for dropping out, that's fine by me."

Funabashi and I had been close friends since high school. He'd always followed my lead. But now this familiar Funabashi had come out against violence. Since he wouldn't talk, I don't know why. Family reasons? He'd arrived at some different ideas? Or maybe he was scared? I couldn't care less. What mattered to me was that if he didn't join in, the others wouldn't either. And that meant I was in trouble.

Omiya restacked the pamphlets on the desk. Inoue set down his guitar and stood up. Without reaching any conclusion, everyone was getting ready to leave.

"Logic-rejecting opportunists like you empower the old system," I rebuked Funabashi resignedly. He got to his feet, taking advantage of the others' preparations to try to make his own escape, but I lurched up and blocked him.

"Hold on! You haven't answered a thing I've said!"

"I'm leaving."

He shoved me aside.

"You're saying it doesn't matter?"

"Yeah."

"*Why* do you say it doesn't matter?!"

"The opportunity's no good," Funabashi retorted. I clenched my fists, but he edged warily around me and slipped out of the room.

I was left behind, alone. Far off I heard laughter, but I couldn't tell if it was Funabashi's group or not. I faced the mimeograph and lined up combative words one by one on the stencil. I felt miserable and forlorn, as though I was the only person left struggling to do his best.

Two weeks later we staged a small street battle. Funabashi didn't show, and his friends didn't either. More lower-classmen would stay away the next time. But for me there would be no next time. Funabashi was arrested just for being on the student council. He spilled everything about our "criminal conspiracy." And we became fugitives.

K. *The events of that afternoon*

What with Ōtsuka's bird watching, it was noon before we reached the town. We realized as we approached that it was in ruins. But Ōtsuka seemed uninterested and barely mentioned it.

"It's almost as if you expected it to be like this," I said.

"It's nothing of the sort," retorted Ōtsuka. "It's just been a tremendous stroke of luck to see so many birds."

"Do you think other birds can dimension-travel like the parallel swallow?"

"I imagine most of them can. But birds normally fix on a territory and a flyway, so it's quite possible the swallows are the only ones that come to our world, while others fly to different dimensions. The parallel swallows probably visit our world from another one quite near here."

Skirting a collapsed house, its roof tiles covering the ground, we came upon a road. It continued on into town, with rusted hulks of automobiles abandoned along the way. The car interiors had become rookeries for dustbirds, and countless numbers of the tiny creatures flew busily in and out of the windows.

Most of the wooden houses had collapsed, and only the concrete buildings preserved an afterimage of the city. Judging from the state of things, it must have perished at least ten years before.

The destruction of all the wooden structures was probably the work of the birds. Scenes of utter desolation and others little changed from our own world existed side by side. Thin grasses stretched roots across the asphalt. Yet medicine advertisements still hung from buildings completely unscathed. Trees lined the central thoroughfare just as before, still spreading neat green leaves beneath the clear blue sky.

We entered a building. The birds had shattered the glass door, and a bird like an owl flashed its eyes in the dark corridor.

"He looks like an owl. Let's call him 'Daddybird.'"

The bird beat its wings when I spoke, and suddenly barreled straight at us. It retreated when we shouted, but the moment we relaxed it charged again. I grappled with it with both hands and, somehow grabbing a leg, swung it against the floor. Blood dribbled from my hands.

"We might find some medicine if we search," said Ōtsuka. He opened a nearby door. Inside were neat rows of office desks. There were no cabinets, and the desk drawers were empty. The next room was completely bare, and in the third, where a barber's sign had been hung out, there were only chairs and mirrors.

"It's all right," I said. "It's nothing serious."

The bleeding had already slackened, and my hands, despite being stained beet red, didn't hurt that much. But we kept on looking anyway.

There were closed curtains in just one room on the third floor. Some furniture could be seen in the thin light. We went in and opened the window.

A body lay on the sofa, reduced to bones.

The skeleton held a rifle in one hand. Cigarette butts, empty cups and a whiskey glass were strewn nearby.

"One who survived to the last," I said.

The rifle was still usable, and there were more bullets in a cabinet nearby. Other than that, we found several dozen packs of cigarettes, a few boxes of chocolate bars and canned food, matches, fuel oil and medicine.

We carried out the bones and ate in the room.

"The birds may have killed all the people," I said.

"Nature's way, no doubt," replied Ōtsuka.

"And the rifle he was holding... There may be stronger ones out there. Predators."

Ōtsuka nodded.

We stuffed our pockets with cigarettes and chocolate and set out again, taking the rifle with us.

A wind came up in the afternoon, sending the paper and plastic remnants of human civilization swirling into the sky. Suddenly a huge yellow bird with a beak like an eagle's burst from a collapsed wooden house. I shouldered the rifle and fired. The bird fell on the roof tiles. But at the same moment more erupted from the debris.

"Run for it!" I shouted.

Still shouting, I dashed for a building. But Ōtsuka just stood there without moving, frozen to the spot. The birds attacked Ōtsuka. I aimed the rifle.

In that instant, he and the birds flocking around him vanished.

I stood paralyzed, the rifle trained on empty space.

It was just as Ōtsuka had said: other birds could cross dimensions. I didn't know if he had tried to cross over with the birds, or if they'd carried him off against his will. Whichever it was, there wasn't much you could do if you were attacked by the giant birds.

L. *The events of a month and a half before*

The tears had nothing to do with my emotions. Just when I thought I'd gotten away, teargas soaked my eyes and brought the pain. But the pain and the tears were cathartic. Or maybe if there hadn't been any teargas, I would have had to work up that much more emotion, just to shed the same tears. The tears outracing my feelings produced a strange composure. I felt an almost pleasant sense of relief.

While I was fighting I'd been content to have comrades fighting beside me. I was able to feel magnanimously that even if Funabashi and his friends skipped this action, they'd surely turn out for the next. There was fulfillment in the weight of a Coke bottle turned

Molotov cocktail, and the sparks shooting from its mouth sped from my hand like flames of anger against State and Civilization.

It was the same while I was escaping. The solidity of the concrete beneath my feet supported me. My field of vision was filled with a static city. These streets that had lured people with poisonous colors, burying the inner world with noise, were now blurred by the smoke from Molotov cocktails and teargas canisters. Show windows closed, neon extinguished, the city seemed completely cut off from the temporal world. Here, my running self was the only dynamic existence. Through the cessation of time around me, I felt the rebirth of that time that slumbered within me.

I could see the moon above the black shadows of the buildings. The moon was running with me. I was being called to the moon like John Carter was called to Mars. As I ran I tried to fly to the moon. Inside my personal time, that seemed an easy thing to do. But the tears wiped the moon from my sight.

When the tears stopped, my pain turned to agony. As though gravity had suddenly increased, the mass of road and building pressed my body to the earth. I was utterly exhausted. My eyes, my shoulders, my back hurt. I woke from fantasy and, fearing the gaze of others, shrank all the cells of my body. I must sleep behind the tightly closed doors of my consciousness. The street again attacked me, and in my violent hatred for Funabashi I knew my own victimization. For me, far from again facing the challenge of battle, only flight remained.

3. *The events of that evening*

I discovered a steam engine at the train station. It was rusty, but I didn't see any broken parts, and the rusty rails were undamaged as well. The tender was full of coal, but the water had all evaporated.

I carried bucket after bucket of water from barrels where the rain had collected, and after some hours of trying finally got a fire lit under the boiler. Black smoke rose from the stack and vanished in the thin mountain air. But perhaps the operating method I'd come up with was wrong, or maybe the locomotive was damaged after all. It refused to budge, almost as though it had sunk roots into the rails.

Only the whistle still wailed. I yanked the valve again and again, blowing off all the steam there was. The whistle echoed back from the mountains and felt good. When I at last started resignedly back to town, I saw a figure running toward me along the rails.

"Uoh! There're people here!"

The man shouted as he ran. Jumping down from the engineer's seat, I walked toward him with the rifle on my shoulder.

"A survivor?" the man asked, gasping for breath.

"Just now you said, 'Uoh.' You're not the guy from that empty house, are you?"

"Empty house? Uoh! Not the loving couple?"

"So it is you. You weren't killed?"

"Me, die? Don't be stupid. I threw a hand grenade when the birds flew. Nice stunt, huh? And so, uhm, what happened to her?"

"She doesn't know the birds."

The man laughed at my answer.

"Is that so? Now *that's* interesting."

Probably he was thinking about the connection between an individual's consciousness and the dimensional worlds. He laughed on and on and wouldn't stop, no matter how angry I got.

We left the station and returned to the center of town. As the evening sun began to set, birds darted frantically about and flocks sped off at different altitudes and in all directions, burying the entire sky.

"Have you been traveling with the birds for long?" I asked him.

"Yeah. From way back."

"You and I seem to have wound up in a lot of the same worlds."

"Purely coincidental. But seeing how this one's close to where you used to live, maybe not so surprising."

"Then why'd you come here?"

"This is home. I came from here. I met up with migrating birds when I was thirteen, and eventually I started to travel."

"So did all the people here go somewhere, too?"

"Naw, the birds got most of them. The birds flying through us are just one species, right? Only folk who met up with them got away. Just a few people here could see the birds, same as in your world."

"My companion was attacked by a yellow, eagle-like bird and disappeared."

"That's the one. It's a kind of raptor. Attacks people, see? Most folk here got carried off. They say there are mountains of human bones in the world where those guys nest."

"Then they'll kill us, too, in the end."

"Naw, they almost never show up here anymore. They've already eaten all the people in this world, so they've gone on to the next. Someplace where human civilization still flourishes, heh?"

"The world I used to be in?!" I demanded. "You're saying it'll turn out like this?!"

"You betcha," he said. "The migratory birds have already shown up there, so the predators can't be far behind."

"Can't we go back and do something, take measures?"

"No can do. How do you get away from birds that pop out of another dimension? Kill a hundred, kill a thousand, they just keep on coming. Gotta destroy the nests to wipe 'em out. But you can't get to them unless they take you there. Escape with the migratory birds; that's the way to survive."

From the way he talked, I gathered he thought nothing of mankind's extinction. And perhaps he was right. Maybe, like Ōtsuka said, it was nature's way.

"The migratory birds," I asked him. "They'll pass through here again?"

"Sure. They're migratory, right? In half a year they'll come back on the same flyway. You can go back to your original world along with them. If you want to, heh?"

I nodded. The surroundings dimmed; the birds were almost invisible. Only the buildings of the town still cast purple shadows against the sky, erecting gravestones to civilization. The scene was cut off from the temporal world, exactly like the one I had seen during the street fighting a month and a half before.

In the end, the world I had known would come to this. The show windows closed, the vivid colors of neon signs extinguished, it would enter eternity's static plane. The wooden buildings would crumble under the birds, the birds would build their nests there, plants would spread their roots on the roads, and the birds would fly off across the entire sky. I thought I would return there with the parallel swallows in half a year's time. I would wait with Noriko for the coming of the yellow eagles, and we'd pass the last days of human civilization together.

4. *Where do the birds fly now?*

Early in the morning, the cries of the Christbird are heard. Next the scarlet heron and gliders appear over the town, and in the afternoon the phoenix comes as far as the city center. In the evening the Hoshi cranes walk about, and rumpbirds form long lines and fly away. Yet the parallel swallows are not to be seen.

"In two months." So thinking, I walk the streets, rifle on my shoulder. I've seen the yellow eagles again only once. I'm not troubled for food or daily necessities. That man went off somewhere, and I have long been alone in this town.

I have come to like birds very much. I am satisfied every day just watching the birds. The birds have nothing to do with me. I do nothing for the birds, and the birds do nothing for me. Yet the birds and I both live in the world. The Hoshi crane walks slowly in front of me, the great lark ascends overhead. The gliders wheel lazily nearby and the baldcrane is off in the distance, flying in flocks.

The same as the birds, I am just walking in the world. I have lost all sense of time.

Two more months? I have forgotten what that means. In two more months the parallel swallows will come. Why is it I am waiting for the parallel swallows?

Why is it, that of all the birds, I think only of the parallel swallows?

– *First publication:* Hayakawa SF Magazine, *February 1971*

TOYOTA ARITSUNÉ

Another *Prince of Wales*
Translated by David Aylward

I'M ON the U.N. War Supervision Commission. It's like being a baseball umpire, a boxing judge, or the referee in a sumo match. That kind of job demands single-minded concentration, but it never works out that way. I have to wade through all kinds of shit. My office is in the new U.N. Headquarters in Washington, capital of the United States of North and South America. Of all the departments there, mine gets the most public interest. That can be a good sign of how well you're doing your job.

The videophone on my desk rings all day long. Avid young war fans call in to say things like, "Hey mister, tell me when the next war is on, will ya? I really wanna see it so c'mon, tell me, huh?"

That kind of thing is OK, but just let one month go by without a war, and listen to them scream! Some frustrated old bag will ring up and throw a fit of hysterics, blaming me for everything: "You men aren't doing your job! You get money from every country in the U.N. and what do you do? Just sit on it. It's gross negligence!"

But it's not my fault if there's no war. My job is supervising them, not starting them. In peacetime, I'm in my office all day long; then there'll be a sudden outbreak of hostilities, and I'll have to fly to the spot right away.

One day, I had just had about five calls like that, when the door opened and one of my co-workers came in. Isabelle is a good-looking girl of mixed Spanish, Bantu, and Indian blood. She has the rather strange hobby of collecting gods, and has miniature idols of each one lined up on her desk. She's always praying to them for a war to start.

This time, she turned first to a crucifix and prayed in Latin, "Oh Lord, grant us destruction and massacre every day of our lives, Amen."

Then she prayed, in various languages, to the goddess Ishtar and the war gods Ares and Huitzilopochtli. Finally, facing a miniature Shintō shrine I had given her, she said in strangely accented Japanese, "Hail Hachiman, great Boddhisatva, let disturbances arise in every nation, until all under heaven is torn with strife!"

She turned to me and winked. "Even your god doesn't seem to be very effective, Keith."

"No," I agreed, "But he's one of my Guv'nor's gods. Maybe I'll introduce you to one on mum's side. You probably don't have any Druidic idols in your collection yet."

The full name's Keith Kimura. My father is Japanese, my mother English. These days, a racially mixed child like me is quite common, and even a mixture of three or four races like Isabelle, is not rare.

"I wonder why there haven't been any wars?" she complained. "I've mobilized practically every god in the world!" She sounded like the callers I'd been getting lately, hoping the War Supervision Commission would start living up to its name, and find some wars to supervise.

"Watch what you say, or we'll get the sack. Starting wars is none of our business. It's our job to put limits on them. Anybody throwing nuclear bombs around now could destroy the world. You should ask how we can limit wars even more."

We should have realized that earlier, of course, but it was only in the twentieth century that people were forced to reject war. The League of Nations had no military deterrent, and it finally ended in empty phrases. Then came the U.N., but again the deterrent was only lukewarm. Even America, which had set up a U.N. army to be used with fairness and justice in the Korean War, failed to show either in Vietnam. Admittedly, war in itself had no fairness or justice about it. At that time, if you wanted to make war, you just went ahead. Now, even the U.N. alone can make two countries at war play by the rules, and if they violate them, it can punish them severely.

"I know all that, Keith. But people enjoy wars! If a long time goes by without one, they get withdrawal symptoms. The televisions of the world are waiting; the war correspondents are all ready. If you don't dole out something to satisfy their passion for war, they're sure to do something dangerous. There'll be a general war like in the old days!"

While she was speaking, Isabelle stroked the heads of the gods in her collection. I noticed a twentieth century G.I. Joe doll mixed in with the rest. Isabelle seemed to think it was another war god.

"Speaking of that," I said, "there was an interesting war between Spain and Mexico a little while ago. Mexico had declared war in retaliation for the Spanish invasion of the sixteenth century, so the U.N. limited their equipment to the same period."

"I know; and the one between the Arabs and Israelis was good, too. The causes of that war went back two thousand years, before the Jews were exiled from Palestine. Each side was restricted to five thousand men, and there wasn't even one death. There were plenty of lumps though, on both sides..." When she got that far, Isabelle rocked with laughter. She swung her right hand in a gesture as if throwing a stone. That had been just about the ultimate weapon at the time of David and Goliath.

When you think about it, war in those days was a perfectly reasonable way of reaching a settlement. If you won a battle, you gained territory, gold, and women. And if you lost, well, you didn't get hurt all that much. There were even rules, too, so it was all quite rational. For instance, the tournaments of the medieval knights, where both parties were allowed to choose their weapons beforehand. Their attendants would then bring their choice out to the field on a pillow. In an affair of honor, the parties would carry weapons of similar destructive power, like an axe against a morningstar, or a sword against a billhook, so there would be no unfair advantage. And after the cannon was converted to practical field use, it was battlefield etiquette to hoist a red flag before using it, to give the enemy time to take cover. This was because the destructive power of the cannon was so much greater than any other weapon of that time. It was after the beginning of the twentieth century that war became a cruel tragedy. Win or lose, you gained nothing in return for a vast number of dead. To be on either side was equally futile.

While Isabelle and I were discussing these points, my videophone suddenly blared the call sign for a direct line from the Secretary-General's office. We both leaped up to stand at attention in front of the screen, where the Secretary himself came on to make an announcement.

"Keith! Isabelle! England and Japan have both made applications for a war. After investigating their reasons, the U.N. computer gave them the go-ahead. Equipment is limited to that in use up to 1941. I'm assigning you to Japan as observers for the War Supervision Commission, to see that the rules aren't violated. Another team will be sent to England. You should start immediately!"

This was the first new war in four months. After the Secretary-General's announcement, Isabelle was in high spirits. She made the sign of the cross, clasped her hands, and prostrated herself in the Islamic style, giving thanks to the eight million gods of all times and places, East and West, for granting her prayers.

2.

ISABELLE and I got into an aircar with U.N. markings on it and flew to my father's native country. We found the whole Tōkaidō megalopolis in a warlike mood. There were posters of the demi-god Susano-o-no-Mikoto beheading the Loch Ness monster against a "rising-sun" background, and the Beatles had been hung in effigy from the gates of shrines.

When we got to our hotel in the Tokyo district, Isabelle said to me anxiously, "We've got a problem now, haven't we, Keith?"

"Why? What you were praying for happened, didn't it?"

"But... England and Japan are both your parents' countries, aren't they?"

"Maybe so," I answered, "But what's that to me? It'll be a limited war, so there can't be any massacres, or bombing of non-combatants. Not to worry."

Our duties as U.N. War Supervisors came first; if we happened to be connected with the countries involved, it was a mere detail.

Isabelle looked down from the hotel window to the street below.

"There's a lantern procession passing," she said.

The lamps had been put out on all the streets, and a parade of several thousand people was marching along with lighted lanterns, to celebrate the declaration of war.

"Yes, it's on the schedule here," I said, "When the U.N. grants an application for war, the tourists come in droves. The Japanese always like to put on a good show for them."

The lantern parade was followed by an illuminated float and a traditional warriors' procession from Nikkō. It was an impressive sight. Since it was my own country, I thought I should explain a few things to Isabelle.

"Japanese are funny people. To them, war is a rite to be carried out with strict formality. It's not a sport, like it is in Europe."

My explanation went like this.

When European countries fight among themselves, and one is no match for the other, it can easily surrender. For instance, during the Second Great War of the twentieth century, Englishmen in Nazi prison camps were given a lot of freedom. They could even get parcels from home with things like lenses for glasses and medicine for chronic ailments. Even the distinction between officers and men was kept.

On the Nazi side, soldiers went on leave right up until just before the collapse of the Third Reich. If they had believed their country might be completely ruined, they would have stayed on duty. But they knew if they were defeated in the "game," their European enemies would stop short of total destruction. Even when the other side's score begins to mount way up, they'll take "time out" from the game if they can.

But the Japanese look on war as a great catastrophe. From the time they leave for the front, it is a matter of life and death. Naturally, if the tide turns against them, no more leave is granted.

There are always tragedies when two different cultures collide with each other. Take the case of the B-29 pilots who bombed Tokyo during the Second World War. If they were shot down, they would always parachute from their planes, thinking they'd be rescued and made prisoner. But to the Japanese, this made no sense. They could understand if the pilots had made a forced landing on water and waited for rescue by a submarine. But they had jumped over enemy territory, where there wasn't a single American.

It's the same kind of thing as the old Tom and Jerry movie cartoons. There are a lot of gags where Jerry the mouse will suddenly stand still in the middle of being chased and shout, *"Stop!"* Without thinking, Tom the cat *will* stop. Then Jerry will start running again.

In Japanese eyes, American pilots downed over the Japanese mainland should have resigned themselves to certain death. There were only enemies around them, so there was no chance of rescue. In fact, Japanese officers executed all those who had been on more than three missions. To them, men who had massacred several thousand non-combatants indiscriminately should have expected such punishment. Why should their war crimes be overlooked just because they were prisoners?

"But at the War Crimes Tribunal in Tokyo after the war," I told Isabelle, "The officers were sentenced to be hanged for committing atrocities. By the European rules of the 'game,' the crimes of prisoners of war should be written off. But to the Japanese, war is no game."

"They seem to be enjoying it now!" said Isabelle.

"Well, this is only a festival, but they're still in earnest. Their minds are an odd mixture of sincerity and superficiality, and their moods change very quickly. If they knew it looked like they were just having fun, they would adopt a serious manner right away. This is the face of the people of Japan. In a war, everybody does their damnedest, with plenty of noise and cheering. But once they're defeated, they go on as if it had all been just a bad dream.

"In the Momoyama Period, the Christian missionaries thought they were making converts hand over fist, because so many Japanese used to wear crucifixes around their necks and march along the highway chanting the Ave Maria. But they had only taken it into their heads to imitate European culture for the novelty of it. Of course, they did it in all seriousness, without realizing they were just being superficial."

"Maybe so. I suppose these people look so happy because they expect to win the war?"

"No, they're just having a good time, but this way, they can pretend they're doing it to get themselves into a fighting mood. It looks like devotion to their country, instead of selfish pleasure-seeking."

After the parade had gone by, Isabelle and I went back to sit on the sofa. I calmly put my arm around her shoulders. Her skin had a bronze luster to it that excited me to look at. It was just my luck the door chime sounded right then.

When I opened the door, there was a boy in his late teens standing there. He looked like he had stepped out of a fancy dress shop. He was wearing a Japanese army uniform of a hundred years before, and carried an old Type 38 infantry rifle on his shoulder.

"Hello, I've come to volunteer! We're at war with England, and I don't want to miss the fun. You're on the War Supervision Committee, aren't you? You can send me to the war right now!"

The boy chattered on animatedly. I didn't know how he had managed to locate the hotel we were staying at, but he'd obviously made his preparations too far ahead.

"You're in the wrong place, son. The Japanese government is doing the recruiting. Why don't you go to your local office and try there?"

"But they've got over a hundred times the people they need. I thought I'd be better off to track down a War Supervisor and tackle him instead. Please, can't you do something for me?"

The boy wouldn't let me go. He had a real war mania; I could see it wasn't half-hearted when I got a close look at his gear. All the same, he'd got the wrong man to help him. I had no authority to interfere in the preparations for war.

I explained all this and finally managed to get rid of him, but that was only the beginning of the rumpus. The doorbell and videophone went on ringing and the stampede of volunteer soldiers rapidly turned my room into a barracks. We didn't get a minute's sleep all night.

3.

ISABELLE and I took off from Tokyo the next morning in our aircar, rubbing our eyes. We were going to inspect the country's war preparations.

The restrictions were that only weapons from before 1941 could be used, to correspond to the last declaration of war between Japan and England, and that the personnel could be no more than twenty thousand men. The equipment appropriate to the period had been researched, using data from the U.N. data banks and consultations with various world authorities on the subject. From this, an outline of instructions was made and distributed to all quarters.

The events of the war would be broadcast all over the world by satellite relay. Any heroes to appear in it were certain to become globally-known stars. Youngsters from all over Japan were jostling each other for this narrow opening.

Since no one was allowed to make any preparations before the U.N.'s public announcement, everything got going at the same time from that moment. The rules and instructions had to be thoroughly enforced. Any nation violating them would be punished, and if the violation was heinous enough, they risked the ultimate fate of being wiped off the face of the earth. Not surprisingly, there had been no precedent for measures as drastic as this; it was only to be used in a case where a general all-out war was planned. At any rate, the ICBMs at U.N. Headquarters were not simply there for the sake of coercion; they were on the alert, ready to be fired at any point on the earth's surface.

For the most part, the Japanese government adhered to the instructions. I say "for the most part" because some members of the radical fringe were actively inciting people to disregard them, but the government did nothing about it. As I said before, the Japanese were not used to the idea of war as a game. Sometimes people fumed up who took things too seriously. They should have been content to enjoy the excitement of war for its own sake, but some of them were suggesting that nuclear bombs be used. They claimed that by 1941, Japan had been capable of manufacturing atomic weapons – an obvious distortion of the facts. But Isabelle and I moved quickly to deliver a warning, and their aggressive plan flickered out.

The reason the Japanese had given for declaring war was the vicious propaganda campaign that was being conducted against them in England. Enraged by the Japanese economic invasion of their country, the English could find nothing good to say about them. They were cruel, avaricious people. They mistreated dogs. Their whisky was a steal from Scotch. They would not stop until they dominated the world commercially. All these allegations had the effect of slowly bringing world opinion around to sympathy for Japan.

Then some madman started a movement to drop a nuclear bomb

on Japan. It might have been another example of the peculiar English brand of black humor, something to laugh and forget about, but there seemed to be a serious note appearing in it somewhere. There had even been some funds raised in support of the plan.

All this culminated in England's declaration of war. Isabelle and I went to visit an automatic munitions factory programmed to manufacture parts for Type 97 "Kate" carrier-based attack planes and Zero fighters. In the twenty-first century, practical thermonuclear energy was very cheap, and since the widespread use of computers had increased the rate of production, anything at all could be made in a very short time. In one part of the factory assembly line, the completed Zeros were all ready for flight.

The officer who was showing us around had some questions.

"Since it takes so long to train pilots, we're going to have to use hypno-education. It won't be a violation, will it?"

The man had fought in other wars, but since he didn't know how to fly a prop plane, he had to depend on hypno-education for his own instruction, too.

"No, it's not a violation. You can use a simulator for flight practice, too. As long as you don't use the equipment in direct warfare, it doesn't have to be from the 1941 period.

"When Persia and Greece fought recently," I explained to him, "They re-enacted the sea battle of Salamis. The tactic of that time was to sink an enemy ship by ramming it with your bow, and the outcome often depended on skill in seamanship. Learning how to handle ancient sailing ships required hypno-education, so it was permitted by the U.N. Following that precedent, it'll probably be allowed for pilots, too. But three-dimensional radar, for instance, was unknown in 1941. And since searching for the enemy is considered direct warfare, you can't use it."

He asked a lot of other questions, mostly about air warfare. He seemed to be thinking that the Japanese forces would have to fight a decisive air battle.

Then Isabelle took a micro-fax out of her pocket. She called me aside and whispered in my ear. She didn't want our escort to hear, for fear of showing partiality to one side. "Keith, I've got a report on the situation for the English side. Ten capital ships of the *Prince of Wales*, *Repulse* and *King George V* class are being built."

I whispered, back into her own small ear, "It's starting to get interesting, isn't it? For the honor of the British Empire, they're going to stand or fall by their navy."

Then, together with the officer, we went off to inspect the completed Zeros. By "inspect" I mean just from the outside. The assembly line had been fitted with U.N. designated automatic selection machinery, to catch any unauthorized special parts and remove them. Only after passing this inspection did the completed planes come off the line. All I did was walk around the Zeros once; then I winked at Isabelle and we flew off in our aircar.

Our next destination was the induction center. Landing the car, we found a huge crowd of people in a terrific uproar. Adding up a hundred times the volunteers that were needed came to a million men, so they had to be handled on a nationwide scale. Such a high rate of competition was understandable, because, for those who had grown up during this dull peacetime period, the fastest way to success was to become a war show star. At mobilization points across the country, computers gave each volunteer an oral test and only those who passed it were allowed to take the practical test.

Even here, since there was a checking system to see that the number of military personnel was not over the limit, we had nothing to do for the present. For a while we just loitered around, discussing some of the volunteers.

"There's a handsome fellow," Isabelle remarked, "He has a sad expression, as if there was a shadow in front of his eyes. If he puts on a good performance, he'll be very popular."

"That's only cosmetic surgery. I like that girl over there better. If you were doing a script on an army nurse, she'd be just right."

We talked for a while, getting more and more bored. We didn't seem to be doing much in the way of supervising.

4.

ON DECEMBER 10, 1941, the battleship *Prince of Wales,* with an escort of nine other ships, sailed from the Liverpool navy yard to Singapore and then north through the Strait of Malacca. Approaching Japan by this route, their strategy was to bombard the mainland, and hopefully to bring the war to a conclusion.

Isabelle and I took a helicar up thirty thousand feet to get a good view of the battle from overhead. It was over the area that computers had calculated to be decisive, and the air was crowded with other cars. Here and there were sightseeing parties carrying telescopic equipment; news commentators' helicars, with markings on them, threaded their way through the mass. To avoid accidents, a temporary satellite had been stationed high above us to control the traffic remotely by computer.

I turned my telescopic sight to the north. "Here comes the Japanese fleet. They're all aircraft carriers. I can see the *Akagi, Kaga, Hiryū* and *Sōryū.* The plot thickens."

"Rice crackers! Candy!" A strangely shaped helicar passed by us. It was decorated like a portable shrine, and a cheerful-looking vendor was using a manipulator to pass his orders through the hatches of his customers' cars. It was a traditional Japanese service for sightseers.

"Sweets! Ices!" The next car that passed us was completely decked out with Union Jack and all. There was even a bronze relief of the lion of England on the side, looking much like a Chinese one; this one's idea of a snack was sandwiches washed down with beer.

The two helicars stopped in front of us and the drivers glared at each other threateningly.

"Out of the way, you foreign dog!" the cracker-seller shouted. "I wanna watch your pirate fleet get massacred!"

He had probably learned this belligerent way of cursing from the hypno-educator. It was in just the right style of the good old days.

"Shut up, you filthy Jap swine!" the "foreign dog" screamed back.

A fight breaking out at that point might have been serious, so I declared myself as a U.N. War Supervisor and the two helicars scattered.

While this was going on, far away on the surface of the sea the fleets of both sides were closing with each other. The Japanese were the first to spot their enemy. A submarine scout and a reconnaissance plane found the *Prince of Wales* and the *Repulse* and radioed a message back to the fleet.

More than a hundred shipboard attack planes, Kates and Vals equipped with bombs and torpedoes, took off from the carriers one by one. The first ship to be sighted was the *Repulse*, in the vanguard of the British fleet. The eight leading planes dropped 500-pound bombs, blowing off one of her gun turrets; then the eight planes in the second wave attacked with torpedoes. Two of the torpedoes made a direct hit on the rear of the *Prince of Wales*, damaging her steering.

The British fleet wasn't just sitting tight through all this. Their pom-pom guns were pounding away, covering the whole sky with their barrage. One of the Japanese planes, with its wings shot off, fluttered down in a spiral and disappeared under the sea. A cry of dismay rose from the communicator. The spectators in the helicars around us had linked up their circuits to get more direct news.

"It sounds like they're all cheering for Japan!" said Isabelle.

"The one that just fell was a dummy," I whispered back, "The U.N. is sponsoring this world-wide 'big war show' so it has to liven things up as much as possible."

"Do you think we should do that kind of thing?"

"Why not? There's no pilot and it doesn't attack. It only falls when it's hit, so it doesn't discriminate against Japan."

In confidence, I told Isabelle what I had been instructed by the Secretary-General. It wasn't only Japanese planes that were U.N. dummies; there were some planted in the British fleet. The tenth battleship was only firing blank shells, and it was rigged to blow up and sink, gushing out convincing smoke and flames.

The Japanese planes attacked at the lowest altitude, one after another, pouring on bombs and torpedoes. The *Prince of Wales* was listing badly, but was still making plenty of hits with its anti-aircraft fire. Far behind her, two other ships were spouting pillars of fire. Soon their bows rose into the air, and, still fighting bravely, they exploded and sank. One of them was the dummy, which had been synchronized to blow up when another ship did, to make things more exciting.

The decks of the *Repulse*, in the lead, were ablaze after she had been hit by five or six torpedoes, and she began to sink too. After that, there was so much smoke I couldn't see anything in my telescopic sight. I switched to a television relay concealed in one of the dummy planes. With this, I could see everything clearly.

At the end of a brave but vain expedition, most of the British fleet floated in a terrible condition, covered with wounds. The anti-aircraft fire was furious but their aim was getting so bad that they couldn't hit the Japanese planes flying defiantly around them. The whole fleet was at the mercy of its enemy. There could be only one outcome to the battle.

"It's revenge for the Bismarck!" I heard a voice say from somewhere, in a German accent. The war show seemed to be reviving some old grudges.

Before long, all of the British fleet had disappeared beneath the waves. Then a great wreath was dropped from a diving Japanese plane. It was a dignified repetition of an incident in the battle of the Malay Straits a hundred years before, vividly showing the essence of the Bushido spirit.

5.

WHEN everything was over, we got a call from U.N. Headquarters. Isabelle punched the switch and the beaming face of the Secretary-General appeared. He only had this expression when there was a war on. One of the early Secretaries used to get into a terrible state at such times. He would run all over the place trying to achieve a reconciliation. His helicopter crashed on one of those missions, leaving behind what was in those days a very serious situation. The present Secretary felt he could relax and maintain his popularity only if there were wars on the boil all the time. Now he looked positively ecstatic.

"Keith! Isabelle! Your next assignment has begun. Pakistan, India, Australia, China, Egypt and Russia have all declared war on England. You're to fly to China as quickly as possible!"

What was going on? This time, it was a group application. It was like bees stinging a crying face. Isabelle's expression was commiserating.

"What a shame, Keith! Your other home country... it's really too much. Everybody is swarming around, just to bully poor old England."

"No, it's all right. Let them. I don't care. You don't feel right if you attack someone weaker than yourself; but you can go for a tyrant whose strength has declined without any pangs of conscience. The more arrogant and overbearing he was in the past, the more enjoyable it is. You can let him have it without feeling the slightest guilt.

"That tuppenny island has had everything its own way too long!" I shouted, "But now that it's just a broken-down, second-rate power, it'll get some of its own medicine. We won't get a chance like this again!"

By this time, I was really carried away. Maybe my bad Japanese half had got the better of me. I was talking about my mother's country, but I didn't pull any punches. If my old lady had heard me, she would have cursed the day she'd had a child by a Japanese!

I wasn't exaggerating, either. It was true. No other country had had things her own way as much as England. She had always done whatever she wanted, ruthlessly. The unscrupulous things she did in India, for instance. After skillfully sowing discord in the Mughal Empire, she infiltrated it like a thief at a fire and craftily took it over before anybody noticed.

It was the same thing in China. During the most prosperous days of the Ch'ing dynasty, the British Ambassador didn't mind doing the "Three Obeisances and Nine Kowtows" before the Chinese Emperor, because he knew that if he groveled enough, the English would be allowed to buy tea and silk. But when China was defeated in the Opium War, there was a sudden change of attitude. Like a sneak thief, England stabbed her victim in the back. The British Army occupied Peking, and their commander himself gave his men permission to loot the Summer Palace. There are few other examples in history of a regular army given permission to loot. The soldiers ransacked it and then, like barbarians who valued nothing but gold, set fire to works of art that had been handed down for generations.

These cunning Englishmen had lived in luxury on the spoils amassed by their pirates' trade, but by the twenty-first century, it had all run out. *"The failure in life has no other pleasure but criticizing others."* It would be better if they had stayed in their little island and kept quiet, but the now senile empire could do nothing except bewail its fate and heap scorn on other countries.

By now I had completely reverted to my Japanese nature, and was getting angrier and angrier. Of course, no true Englishman would have lost control like that. They would never suddenly burst out and slaughter somebody like a Japanese would. It was a point of pride with them to keep their faces expressionless while they tortured people to death. The crusaders used to kill a man by giving him no water for days, then gloss over it by saying he'd died of disease. Another favorite trick of theirs was to tie their victims up at the water's edge and let them die agonizing deaths by being slowly drowned by the tide.

"How many millions of people on earth have been enslaved, tortured and beaten to death for the sake of this crazy little one-horse country?

"They always *gata-gata* about Japan's guilt; *korep'pochi mo nai!* The *yatsura* should pay for their own blood-guilt, the one they've had for four centuries!"

Isabelle's face registered shocked amazement as I went on shouting.

"Keith! Are you all right?"

I calmed down and apologized, embarrassed. "Don't worry. I go off like that sometimes; I get it from my father. Anyway, War Supervisors often go off half-cocked. But these things soon fade away."

Isabelle pointed to the facsimile output. Our next orders had arrived without our noticing them.

It was a report of declarations of war against England by Malaysia, Korea and Both Americas, as well as Scotland, Ireland and Wales. Although Wales was part of the island of Britain, the native people were not Anglo-Saxon, but part of the Celtic group. Wales had been kept distinct from England as a sort of supply area for servants and field hands. Scotland, of course, had been hostile to England from the time of Bannockburn and the execution of Mary, Queen of Scots. Ireland was never anything more than an English colony. All these things made their motives obvious.

"It's too bad, isn't it?"

I nodded my head sadly. "Yes, it's a bloody shame really." England was the world's scapegoat, just as the Jews, the blacks and, at one time, the Japanese, had been in the twentieth century. When there were people like this to heap all the blame on, everyone else was satisfied.

"This could be serious. We've got to do something to stop it," I said, with a black expression. I had become a completely different man from when I burst into my diatribe a while before.

But secretly, I was interested to see what would happen, and mocked my own pretensions. Behind my gentlemanly facade was peering out another quality inherited from my mother – a spirit of English cunning.

– First publication: Hayakawa SF Magazine, *April 1970*

FUKUSHIMA MASAMI

The Flower's Life is Short
Translated by Yano Tetsu and Judith Merril

FLAMINGO *lily... Oncidium... Cymbidium... Epidendrum... Dendrobium... Vanda suavis...*

THE ORCHID pattern is really good... but maybe it should start with the simple fluorescent spectrum after all...

In the cool, well-ordered room, Rina pauses to consider, delicate fingers playing idly over the keys of her personal ikebana-synthesizer. She makes up her mind: presses down with the ball of her middle finger slowly and steadily on a single key.

An unearthly flame of blue-and-yellow flares up in the innermost corner of the room, and fans quickly outward, widening and thinning into a curtain of blue light folded into dark pleats.

Rina's fingers begin a lithe and lively dance over the keyboard of the electronic instrument; the curtain of light starts to flutter as if blown by the wind, the color thinning and deepening as stripes of light shift through from top to bottom and bottom to top, from left to right, from right to left. It is, precisely, the movement of the aurora illuminating the heavens at the two poles.

The rhythmic play of light increases in rapid tempo until, suddenly, it freezes into place, transmuted into orchid-shape in deep exquisite violet – altogether different, of course, from any species of orchid that blooms in this world. High-energy high-speed electrons create an unearthly light unlike any natural light, any natural color, any natural flower; this is indeed the essence of the experience of 3-D luminescence.

Rina's shapely lips tighten; her eyes take on a feverish glow. Ten slender fingers, like small fantastic independent living creatures, race nimbly over scores of keys where the luster of 3-D luminescence is absorbed and reflected in an infinity of colors.

Too fast for the eye to follow, the orchid's petals stretch out long and thin; at the same instant, the stamen starts contracting and expanding with a movement like the pseudopod of an amoeba, evoking a mood of voluptuous sensuality.

Driftwood – decayed, earth-colored – appears behind the orchid; fern fronds – the brilliant green color of metallic crystals – grow out to hide the orchid's underside; from the pistil, a red mist spreads slowly in all eight directions. In time with the movement of the mist, the whole light-image begins to revolve... revolving... whirligig... and comes abruptly to full stop.

Done!

Rina held her breath, examining her creation, then pushed the set-key and fixed it in mid-air – a dazzling spray-shape like the materialization of a fantasy.

"Wonderful, Rina!"

The quiet voice came from behind her. Without turning to look, she recognized her closest friend, Yuri. Rina set the synthesizer down on the tabletop, and discovered that she was damp with perspiration, and that there was a feeling of satisfaction in that moisture on her skin.

Yuri's clear holographic image stood in front of the videophone console, shaking her head slowly as she studied Rina's arrangement.

"Absolutely fascinating! – as usual! There really is *something* about your 'living flowers'—"

Yuri habitually used the old-fashioned phrase for luminescent flower arranging. Actually, it was a holdover from olden days when ikebana, as it was called, still used genuine living flowers, flowering branches, and driftwood, as well as assorted plastic and metal materials, arranged in pottery bowls and vases. The only people who use such terms nowadays are professional electronic flower arrangers – usually only at formal exhibitions – but Yuri somehow managed to use the words without sounding at all ridiculous or pedantic. Of course, she was not simply a professional, but one of the top flower-arrangers, with a large number of students – but it wasn't just that. Probably it had more to do with her basic character, her unworried self-assurance.

Rina smiled. "Thank you."

"Nothing to thank me for – actually, I'm jealous."

That was typical of the way Yuri would say it.

"You're flattering me."

"On the contrary. If it were done by anyone but you I would have said it was the quality of the instrument rather than the skill of the arranger that made such magnificent flowers possible. If I had a fine machine like that, I might almost say my flowers were arranged for me."

Yuri spoke laughingly, but there was a sticky glint deep in her eye.

"Oh—? Actually, you'd be quite right—"

Still smiling, Rina glanced at the machine on the table. It looked new, but the style was an old-fashioned one, rarely seen nowadays, and the patina of long months and years of care and careful use shone on the smooth metal surface.

"You know, I'm not at all sure I'm good enough to use an instrument like this. It was handed down to me by my father, who got it from a friend of his, an electronics engineer who spent his whole life working on it as a hobby. I don't know the name of the artisan, but he was a genius, eh? So if the flower arrangements are good, the credit should all go to that man and certainly not to any skill of mine."

"That's just not true! You know I was joking – don't twist it around that way to make it serious!" It was out of character for Yuri to be so upset. "No matter how much of a work of art it may be, an ikebana-organ is still an ikebana-organ. The same kind of computer emits

145

the same kind of electromagnetic impulses; there's no difference in the way the emissions knock an electron out of orbit, in an atom of argon or nitrogen or oxygen in the atmosphere. So in the end, it's skill after all. Ideas and composition. Touch. In short, your skill!"

Rina gazed steadily back into Yuri's unwontedly intense face.

"That's not the problem. I – the sense of satisfaction I always used to have in flower-arranging – it's gone flat— "

Why? How could it happen? Rina was about to go on, but for some reason closed her mouth on the words – perhaps because she felt that whatever she said would enable Yuri immediately, intuitively, to see straight through to the bottom of her heart. And if that did happen, Rina was afraid that all the unconquerable loneliness and emptiness dammed up inside her would come bursting out in a flood.

"I'm sure it's just some sort of slump," she said with assumed casualness, "but actually I've been thinking I might even try getting into working with real flowers instead – like in the old times—"

"Stop. First of all, real flowers are short-lived, and on top of that, they're hopelessly inflexible and unadaptable. Really, that kind of thinking—" Yuri began, and leaned closer.

"Rina – there's something I want to say—"

"What?"

"How old are you now?"

Rina's cheek creased involuntarily. "What!? After all this time?"

"If I remember correctly – sixty-eight, eh?"

"That's right. An old lady now."

"What are you talking about? I'm seventy-two myself. It sounds incredible, but even a half-century ago, we would both have had one foot in the grave by now. But fortunately, we're living in the twenty-second century – so we can still pass for 'high miss'—"

"All right, so what does that mean?"

"Well, then – you're not planning on going into a long-term marriage any time soon?"

"No way."

"Right. Long-term marriage is simply—" Yuri broke off and her voice became wonderfully worldly-wise: "After all, it should be done before fifty. At our age, it's just too much trouble, somehow—"

"Exactly what are you trying to say, Yuri?"

Rina's tone was slightly edged. Yuri began speaking more briskly.

"In a nutshell: if you're not getting involved in a long-term marriage, I wondered if you might do me the favor of becoming an instructor at my flower-arranging school? No – let me finish!" Yuri checked Rina's response peremptorily. "I know you don't want to turn professional. But just try thinking about it one more time. When you have so much talent, it's a waste—

"I know, you're a perfectionist, and I understand very well the kind of purist feeling you have, of wanting to value your craft just for its own sake. But in the end, it's all hollow, isn't it? If you were teaching the flowers to students instead – well, that's something with its own very real sense of satisfaction. Your way of thinking just doesn't work in this leisure age! Anyway, please do think about it. Goodbye."

Rina started to reach out a hand to stop her, but the connection was already cut off, and the pallid after-image was fading. It was another trick of Yuri's, making the effective exit.

Rina stared blankly at the suddenly emptied space, aware of some deep inward uncertainty, apparently set off by Yuri's monologue: there was some thread of connection with the dissipation of illusion she always experienced after complete immersion in flower arranging.

In the end, Yuri had said, self-sufficiency led only to loneliness, and she realized it had actually been that way for at least two or three years now. Of course, she had refused to admit it at first. It was ridiculous: flower arranging was her whole life and there were inexhaustible depths to be plumbed in the world of her craft. To be bored, or to feel she had achieved everything that could be accomplished – such superficial feelings ought to be foreign to her.

But deny them or ignore them as she might, these unaccountable anxieties were certainly there, always deep in her heart, ready to take advantage of any unguarded moment of weariness of spirit to surface unexpectedly.

Why? she wondered. *Why just now, when there is nothing at all to worry about in my life?* With a gesture that had become second nature, her fingertips toyed with the keys of her instrument as she stood in thought. *In the old days, they say, there were people for whom ikebana was a livelihood, and critics are supposed to have been all the more severe for that reason – but the past is in the past – this is the twenty-second century! That shouldn't have anything to do with my problems now...*

How long had she been standing there, like that? Rina was suddenly aware that someone else was in the room.

She turned to look.

There, across the living-room, a man stood alone, wearing a dark and somber look, somehow familiar – a young man of about sixty-five, but dressed in a very old-fashioned Western style business suit. If she remembered correctly, it was a mode of fifty years earlier, that had been popular at the end of the twenty-first century, when there had been a sweeping revival of twentieth century styles – separate tops and bottoms, with button-style jackets and inane narrow stripes down the trousers. (Even at the time, the style had been derided as *fin-de-siècle* taste.)

"Who are you?" Rina demanded. Her forehead wrinkled in a puzzled frown. It was a long time since she had been in the presence of an actual flesh-and-blood person. "Where did you come from?"

Silently, the man pulled his hands out of his trouser pockets and crossed them in front of him.

"Ah–h—" Rina cried out involuntarily.

A boyish grin flashed across the man's face. "Remember?" he said, laughing.

Rina was not even aware that she nodded in agreement. Almost hypnotically, she took two or three steps toward the man; then her face reddened as she became aware of the vulgarity of her behavior.

"Ah – you're still just the same!" The pleasant baritone voice was teasing. "One moment, detached, imperturbable, cold as marble – the next as impulsive as a twentieth century person – and then blushing crimson when you realize what you're doing—"

"Well! Old times – really old times: it must be fifty years by now, Minoru!"

"Oh? You've been kind enough to remember my name—"

"Frankly, I just remembered. For a long time, I forgot... I mean, it's practically ancient history, isn't it? – When we were together?"

"And even then, it was only half a year," he said bleakly.

The words leapfrogged almost fifty years to penetrate her heart with surprising freshness.

The way it had been – when they were considering whether to renew their short-term marriage contract for another six months, or possibly even a year – it was Minoru who spoke out. Might they not, perhaps, renew on a permanent contract instead? And it was Rina who could not make up her mind, and who put off giving an answer until the very last moment.

It was certainly not due to any lack of affection for Minoru: on the contrary, she was very much in love with him. To be together was joyful; to be separated, very painful. It was, in fact, just because of this that she delayed her reply – why, actually, she could not come to a decision right up to the last moment.

In the end it was her youth that decided the issue. Rina wanted to enjoy life to the full; she was barely in her twenties and not prepared to tie herself down before she had completed even one-fifth of her normal lifespan. She wanted to experiment with many different kinds of experience, with physical and emotional adventures. The times, the mores of society, were changing at a dazzling pace; she wanted to live these changes personally, in the flesh. She felt that a permanent-marriage contract would cut her off from that kind of life. So—

So when she left him it was almost like making an escape.

She made several short-term marriages afterwards, and some were even more pleasant, meaningful, and productive than her married life with Minoru. But somehow, there was always something oddly missing in these relationships – something fresh and strong and vital.

And, right up to the present time, she had never been able to make a firm decision for permanent-marriage – perhaps, come to think of it, because of this kind of latent conflict between desire and discontent that she had continued to allow to live at the bottom of her heart?

"You… now…" Rina began, and stopped short. She had been about to ask if he was involved in a long-term or permanent marriage, but—

Minoru silently shook his head from left to right.

"All alone!"

"Alone… you mean…?"

"Absolutely alone. Precisely, single."

It was almost a rhythmic chanting, the way he said it.

"Liar!"

"True!"

Rina felt the beginning of a cold anger stiffening inside her.

"Where are you staying now?"

"Right here."

"What are you doing?"

"Just staying here, standing like this."

"Don't play games with me!"

She was actually shouting; Rina was horrified at the shrillness of her own voice – but it was bursting out in an uncontrollable flood of emotion.

No other way to heal this pain in her heart... a last chance to decide for permanent marriage...

She did not want to let Minoru leave again.

Then, suddenly, as if reading her thoughts, he laughed.

Rina exploded with furious anger. Rage flashed murderously from her eyes.

"What did you come for, Minoru?"

"I just came to see – you!"

"Why should there be any need to see someone like me at this late date?"

"Is a need necessary? I wanted to see you, so I came to see you."

"Why? To blame me? To complain about fifty years ago? To enjoy tormenting me?"

Rina strode over to him. The physical closeness made her legs wobbly. Minoru turned pale.

"Stop! Don't!"

"What!?"

"Don't come any closer!"

Rina could not check her compulsive movement: she threw herself onto his chest – and lurched heavily, almost falling, as her body met only empty air. Struggling to regain her balance, she stared wide-eyed.

Minoru's shape was fading.

Astonishment overwhelmed her, and then a great emptiness, as if the very bottom of her soul had torn apart.

So that was it. She should have understood...

Minoru's shape was a phantom manifested by her own elaborate electronic flower-arranging machine.

Perhaps, over a period of several months, when she had been absent-mindedly playing on the keys of the electronic instrument, her fingertips had unconsciously – automatically – impressed her memories of Minoru on the memory-bank of the electronic brain. Of course! And then the automatic – unconscious – operation of her fingertips a little while ago, played back the image the same way the flower arrangements were produced.

Astonishment vanished.

But loneliness did not go away. Rather, she was helplessly in the grip of a meaningless yearning, and suffocating futility gnawed at her heart like acid.

Life was much longer than it used to be, but even then she had already lived half her lifetime. She could hear the sound of her heart breaking apart, a rustling like dead leaves—

At my age – perhaps even the heart begins to get tired.

Perhaps if she agreed to start work at the school, it would not feel altogether unbearable.

– *First publication:* Hayakawa SF Magazine, *October 1967*

Girl

Translated by Alfred Birnbaum

THE CITY was an overripe fruit about to drop. Rotting outward from deep in the core, its putrid flesh was held by only the barest shell.

Once the City fell, no one knew what would become of it. If things degenerated any further, even hell would close its borders. For the City's inhabitants, there was no escape.

GIL PROBED a long tongue into the bottom of the Venetian cut-glass stemware for the last of the nectarine pulp. Sitting with his platinum-mink-encased genitals exposed, he could sense the attention he was drawing. Every nerve ending in his body tingled, almost painfully, from the repeated caresses of staring eyes.

Gil knew his own charms better than anyone. The smooth, honey-colored curve of his back from his shoulders on down, his wisp-cinched queen bee waist, his wind-teased shock of straight blond hair, and, only slightly darker, his amber-hued eyes.

Even more, he knew, his was a beauty in motion, a fluid grace to his movements that had been there from birth – the same as his mother's.

Ordering another drink, Gil surveyed the premises from his high stool at the bar. The several faces he met fairly dripped with desire. He felt like spewing up the contents of his stomach. Of late, he'd had no appetite, no sex drive, no nothing. All he could do was to keep drinking, like this, bathing his tissues in toxic drams.

153

When he redirected a transparent sigh back toward the counter, a half dozen glasses of the divine nectarine liquor stood before him.

"Curser?" he called the bartender's name feebly.

The drinks, she answered, were from that customer and that one and that one and...

"I don't want 'em."

"That so?" Curser's voice was terribly businesslike. Too cold for the likes of Gil, who had come here lonely, unbearably lonely.

The six glasses, having absorbed the multicolored lights of the bar, were reflected on the polished ebony countertop. A pathetic tableau, simply lovely.

Gil fancied cut glass. It elicited a resonance in his delicate soul. So like him: edgy, hypersensitive, close to the point of breaking.

He drank half his cocktail and drowsily stood up. Sliding off the stool seemed less a rising motion than a slip.

Now even more eyes were trained on him. Not a few of them recognized him as Jill Abel.

He tossed the out-of-sorts Curser a tip, hoping to elicit a smile, but she only relaxed the occupational deadpan for a split-second. Her peachy cheeks barely quivered.

Fighting the undertow that threatened to suck him down into a sludge of despair, Gil forded the dimly lit room through swirls of dirty purple smoke. The drinks had gone to his head. He was a deep-sea fish creeping across the ocean floor. A mild attack of human-detox came over him. Suddenly, reality siphoned off. Everything – people's faces, feet, voices – everything drifted far, far away.

He collapsed.

Someone had tripped him, he knew, intentionally, but he was helpless to do anything about it. His left elbow hit hard, the pain returning him to his senses for a brief instant.

"You okay?"

The John who'd tripped him was lifting him in a gentle embrace, caressing his genitals. Must be slipping, he thought, letting some

154

guy he'd never even seen before climb all over him. Mustn't get too aroused... would be my own fault... my guilt.

"How 'bout it, like now?"

How many times had he surrendered to the momentary rapture of being touched there?

That utterly irresistible shudder of pleasure.

Inadvertently, he pushed the guy's heavy breastplate aside.

The John was disoriented at first, then flew into a rage.

Gil grabbed for the back of a chair and pulled himself up to his feet. With the John clinging fast to his collar, Gil's soul began to flood with tears. Have mercy, have mercy...

Expecting a beating, he braced himself and pleaded.

"Forgive me, I beg of you."

At which, the fists that were pumped up with rage fell limp, sapped of all strength. The John lowered his voice to a deflated whisper of pity.

"Beat it, Jill. Didn't know you were such a wimp."

Denied even the violent side of human relations, Gil once again set his feet lumbering toward the exit.

WHILE he waited for the ancient relic of an elevator, a woman careened out of the bar. Gil was leaning against the cracked wall, eyes closed, but from the scent and sound of her presence, he'd conjured up a full mental picture of her.

"Hey, it's here. You getting in or not?"

"Go on ahead."

Gil cracked open his eyes to confirm his image of the woman. But what he saw made him gasp. It wasn't a woman; it was a girl. No, not simply a girl. Her skin, soft and creamy white. He felt the urge to touch her, ever so gently. Just a little. Just a touch.

"Oh?"

With that, the girl boarded the massive freight lift.

Gil looked on as the door slid shut in slow motion. Always missing the boat. Always too timid, too shy, knocked out of the running, out of sync with the world.

His excitement, far from subsiding, blended into a curiously colloidal state as he waited for the next lift.

The hellhound elevator – floor carpeted, walls and ceiling in burgundy velvet – lurched into descent, carrying him with it.

Depressed, he waited for the door to open, then slinked out. But when he looked up into the acid rain that came pattering down on his head, his heart squealed.

"Evening. We meet again, I see."

And here he'd been thinking she'd gone. A tumult roared through his breast.

"Y–you waited?"

"Sure."

The girl turned abruptly and started walking, her bright toothy smile hovering in view. Gil scrambled after her. His stupor was dissipating posthaste.

"Where'er you going?"

The girl flashed her enamel lovelies to his question.

"Home."

"Where's that?"

"Where I live."

"And someone's waiting for you?"

Gil began to feel frustrated. What did this female mean, leading him on?

"I'm unattached."

Gil caught up with her, to walk alongside her through the black wind. The girl looked angelic in profile. But weren't angels boys? A girl, the image of a boy.

The girl wore skintight black leggings and a black shirt draped over as far as her wrists. Black hair, black pupils, black to the tips of her shoes. What little skin that showed radiated a phosphorescent glow.

Gil detested jerks who designed clothes that showed off a body's lower parts in such graphic detail. And he felt nothing but contempt for himself for having chosen his show gear.

Street level was deserted.

Who, especially this late at night, would be out walking in the cold and wet with no umbrella, no aircar? Nobody on the street, however, also meant no stick-ups, no nick-and-runs.

The hundred-storied buildings glimmered like glitzy chandeliers. Gil loved their cheap sparkle. He loved this rotting city.

Without warning, the girl touched Gil on the arm.

"You... human?"

Gil returned the girl's driven black-eyed stare and thought, So she didn't know, eh? Didn't know he was Jill Abel, the dancer, spent excretus of the City's dazzling decadence, high civilization tottering on the edge of collapse.

"Umm."

"Well, then, you're... male?"

Gil's chest boasted two voluptuous mammalian protuberances. Much bigger than the girl's own budding breasts. And at the same time, he displayed a male organ swaddled root-to-tip in fur.

"Yes. I'm a man." He answered honestly.

"Looks more like a tail."

She smiled as she spoke, then broke right back into stride, so quickly that Gil didn't even notice the vermilion peck planted on his pale cheek. All the same, he walked at a slower pace for a while.

The girl's home was forty-seven floors underground. Tiny, but a cozy enough little hole. An egg-shaped room after the latest fashion, with an oval bed, slightly too big for one person, suspended close to the ceiling.

"How d'you get up there?"

To ask was to be shown: the girl lowered a ladder by remote control. "May I?" The girl laughed.

"Fine by me, but maybe you'd like to shower first?"

Gil nodded humbly, as if he'd had the shit beaten out of him. He stripped off his clothes, received a towel embroidered with the name "Kisa," and stepped into the immaculate bathroom. For a moment, he stood there blankly. There could be no doubt about it. The girl was a whore, named Kisa. A streetwalker. That's why she'd lured him here – that was the whole of it... that and nothing else.

After his shower, the entire bathroom turned into a drier. He watched in the mirror as his golden hair tossed in the whirling gusts of hot air.

His implanted breasts maintained their picture-perfect form. He'd had the cosmetic surgery done that time he'd played the Sphynx. The attributes proved so fabulously popular, it seemed a shame to lop them off.

The Sphynx's mother was half-maiden, half-serpent, known as the Echidna. The Echidna gave birth to all manner of horrible monsters. The Chimera, the Gorgon, the Cerberus, then later the Dragon, and lastly the Sphynx.

Thoughts of "Mother" made him suddenly want to vomit. Beautiful, shapely breasts, never-once intended to nurse a child – well, fair enough. Stepping out of the bathroom, he was surprised by a four-legged white robot, standing by with proffered bath towel.

"Not bad, huh? Built this baby myself." Gil looked Kisa in the face, then gazed back at the robot. "From a kit, a Flexi?"

"Customized. Even speaks. Goes by the name 'Sphynx'."

Gil shivered and covered his breasts with the towel. The two-foot-tall Sphynx looked like a blanched dynosaur skeleton. On voice-command from Kisa, it started to walk, bones rattling, one foot set out in front of the other, barely holding together.

"Excruciating."

"No, really! It's my baby. Tell me how cute it is."

Kisa laughed enchantingly, like a fairy sprite... yes, that was it... Mother was something of an enchantress. Which explained his attraction to the girl. That had to be it. That, and that she was a pro. He had her pinned. Right on the mark.

"Why don't you shower, too?"

"Okay."

There came the slightest rustling as the girl peeled off her slinky black silk shirt. Gil was speechless. Her skin virtually lit up the room – as if her dermis enveloped a white inner luminescence.

The girl slipped, silky as her shirt, into the bathroom. Gil heard the steamy sound of the shower, as he crouched down to the floor.

"Sphynx! Gimme a drink."

Sphynx turned its face composed of a Cyclopean red lens and a single speaker toward Gil.

"Many different beverages are available."

"Anything's fine."

Sphynx's random tables came up Scotch. The robot walked on four legs, the two front limbs serving as arms for manual labor. The hind legs had no fingers, whereas each foreleg had three.

Drinking his liquor down straight, Gil grew sleepy. He tucked a cushion behind the small of his back. The silver-gray walls – affixed with a number of exhausted electrophoto transmissions – were all dreamscapes.

Meadows and ocean and springs and other pedestrian fare. The singular absence of either human or animal figures struck Gil as out of character for a girl. Still, Gil thought the scenes pleasant enough. And then it registered – the girl wanted to escape this world. But for where? For some completely other, secret world. Perhaps the girl possessed such a secret world in her mind.

The girl appeared, newborn fresh, brilliant with life, with a vitality so rich it overwhelmed Gil. Like walking white electricity. Delicate white fingers forever energized.

The girl slipped a white nightgown over her electric body.

Gil did not rouse from where he lay propped by the big cushion. The electric girl drew near. His body tingled. When he reached out

159

to put an arm around her shoulders, the girl gently stayed his hand. Her touch sent an shock coursing down his spine.

"For some reason, lately, I've been thinking... remembering things that happened a long time ago... when I was a child..."

"What sort of things?" Gil half-sighed. Had it been any other female, he probably wouldn't have thought to ask her life story.

"You... an Earthling?"

"Yes."

"I always used to look at Earth from where I lived."

"Oh?" Gil responded. "They say that from far away it looks like a jewel."

The girl betrayed a trace of a smile.

"When I was a child, I often fought with my brother. About who'd be the first to take that blue planet."

"Younger brother?"

"Older."

"Who's still fine, I trust."

"If he was, I wouldn't be talking like this."

Whereupon the girl broke away from him and stood up.

Gil had no idea what was going on, but he knew he'd said the wrong thing. He sat up.

"No, that's a lie," said the girl.

Feeling hurt for no reason he could understand, Gil trained his eyes on her.

"Will you leave?"

This wasn't a question; it was an order. Untangling his legs, he managed to get to his feet. The blood vessels in his head throbbed as if squeezed.

"I get it. You're expecting some stud."

That came out nastier than he'd intended.

Kisa froze into a statue. But now her marble hands were opening the door and pointing the way out.

"My roommate's a woman, thank you."

Gil felt ripped asunder. This girl had come here all alone from some poorer outworld. She looked pure and innocent, but surely she'd been hurt – badly – deep down inside. People like her spatter their poisonous lies everywhere. Trip you up, betray you, beat you so bad you can't get up again... Gil flashed back on his own battle-scarred past and cringed. The thought of going through all that again gave him the chills.

"I get the picture. I'm leaving."

As he stepped out from the comfort of that womb-like interior, the girl called out to him.

"Wait. What's your name?"

"Jill Abel."

The girl's expression told him the thread of recognition had connected.

IT WAS nearly dawn by the time he got home, but his cohabitant Remora was still awake, watching the news on the wall-sized screen.

Remora was genetically male, the proof being that the fingers of his left hand, all six of them, had been remodeled into cocks. When asked, "Why the left hand?" his only reply was that if it had been his right hand, he wouldn't have been able to hold his chopsticks.

"Lookit lookit! A sideswipe spaceship collision!" Remora shouted at the top of his lungs. "Lookit lookit look! Bad meanness or what! It's Sirius!"

On the screen in the black oceanic depths of space, a half-crushed silver hull drifted "shipwrecked." Disemboweled scraps of sheared metal glinted in the light of a distant sun.

"Dirty outworlders! Bet it's some 'droid plot!"

In spite of himself, Gil's expression lightened at this irrepressible outburst – yes, there were good folk on this planet, even if they had no education, no refinement, no table manners, even if they were bigots to the core. Telling the most blatant lies, only to find himself deceived in the end, Remora remained tough through it all. Remora might have been a fool, but wasn't everyone a fool?

Floating useless in the void, the half-dismembered corpse looked strangely erotic.

The darkened room gave them the illusion that they themselves were lost in space.

"Hey, you heard the latest sex rave 'mong them outworlders?"

Gil took a seat next to Remora, who placed a hand, the right one, on Gil's knee. Remora was squirming with delight, dying to fill Gil in on the gossip. Come what may, Remora was the man who knew all the latest dirt.

"Haven't the foggiest."

It was the invitation Remora was hoping for. His face lit up, his gorilla's bulk shaking.

"They swim out in the zero-G and jack sperm globules all over 'emselves just like fish."

Cheap thrills. Gross, but the idea did get him off, Gil had to admit.

"Sort of a urological partita, hmm?"

"Huh? Howzat?"

Remora's vocabulary didn't extend that far.

"Kinda like a golden shower spree."

Remora chortled with pleasure. His face was illuminated by the twinkling afterglow of the spaceship debris on the screen.

Then, looking straight at Gil, Remora said, "What gives? You don't usually get excited like this."

Gil blushed.

"Well? C'mon now! Something happen to you out there tonight?"

As he spoke, Remora slowly eased Gil into a reclining position. They hadn't been like this in so long. Remora trembled in his skin.

"*Girl,* I thought you'd never get it up. That's better... and here I was thinking it was time for my tide to be going out."

"Don't go."

Gil's pretty face distorted in a grimace. He couldn't help pitying a guy so insensitive it'd be *sayonara* once the physical part had gone. Yet he knew that if Remora really did leave, Gil would be the one to grieve; it made him desolate. And so the two lovers tumbled deep into the cosmic sea.

Later, as they were falling asleep, Gil told him about the girl.

"Means she's got a thing for you, is what. Pretended not to know you so's to get close, I bet."

"Then why'd she give me the brush-off?"

"To sink the hook," snapped Remora. "Within a week she'll surface. Have confidence."

Confidence? That wasn't it at all! How could he hope to explain to him?

"But anyway," Remora went on, "C'mon, an outworlder? Not your style. Do yourself a favor – throw this one back."

Remora was a die-hard outworld-hater. Probably got dumped real hard by some bitch when he shipped out on the interplanetary routes. Or else, maybe he was hiding a past – maybe he'd been an outworlder himself until his twenties, and so he hated his own origins. Just like Gil detested being a dancer.

Resting in Remora's massive arms, Gil confessed, "I don't know. I'm not sure."

"'Bout what?"

Remora sounded gruff. He hadn't expected Gil to unearth what he'd already taken for a dead issue.

"I don't know… what she's up to – what sort of female she is…"

"Whether she gets it on with her roommate?" taunted Remora, grinning. "Like us?"

Gil wrestled out of Remora's embrace. Gil's mouth seemed to fill with disdain.

Heedless, Remora only drove home his hard feelings with a dare.

"How 'bout a bet then? A thou' sez you blip her within the month."

What was this ape saying? That wasn't what he meant, not at all... Gil rose, hands over his mouth, to go vomit out the acid disgust stinking in the pit of his stomach. While Gil barfed, Remora regaled him with details of his own exploits with women.

Gil realized he'd broken their rules, betrayed their understanding: he'd brought his outside affairs back home. Remora may have been crude and blunt and just plain dumb, he may have conducted himself badly, but at least here – within the confines of these walls – they had to keep a trust, or some semblance of it.

The following day, Gil woke up past noon to find Remora gone. His precious spaceship crewman's helmet was missing. Gil gazed at the shelves of cut-glass trinkets that covered one entire wall. His head throbbed, the glare pierced both his eyes.

He couldn't hold back. He cried, which made his head ache more. Only afterward did a silent, long, fine sleep come over him.

DRUGGED out of his skull, Gil commuted to the Rox Star Club every night.

Except for when he was on stage dancing, he always had someone around, whom he slept with later. Always someone different. For eight months he had no want for anything, and yet he had nothing but need; it was as if a dam had burst.

Physically, he ought to have been exhausted, but dancing gave him a mysteriously sharp clarity. He would usually find himself in a private craft, hard at it with some woman he didn't know. Today Gil noticed that the craft was driven by a real human, not a robodroid, so for appearance's sake he tried to make conversation.

"Y'know, every time I pass here I wonder. What do you think they're building there?"

The lot next to the Rox Star Club had been under construction for some time. They were actually building something – something new was surfacing in the midst of this festering, sore-scarred city.

"Really wouldn't know." The driver obviously didn't want to talk.

The aircar came down for a smooth landing on the Club roof. Totally blasé, Gil pushed aside the woman's paws and climbed out first. The woman was furious. She was pretty enough, but compared to the girl whom he couldn't forget, women like her didn't rate.

Nauseous, he downed a handful of pills without water. A few minutes later, his brain began to decompose, and everything dissolved into the far, far distance – the stone-faced driver, that embarrassing socialite glitterbox of an aircar, the night town atmosphere laid out before him, the gleaming skyscrapers blocking out the miniature planetarium dome of the heavens, the woman screaming like a hysterical mother. Everything retreated, the whole scene intact, out of reach, safe and inviolate.

Gil kept dredging up thoughts from his murky consciousness – Remora's prediction that the girl would show within a week, that within a month he'd have her. But when Gil had gone back to her apartment, she'd already moved.

Time passed. Seasons blurred one into the next. He'd worked his way through a parade of partners. After all this, he was sick of himself – and yet the filthy, sinful image did become him. Still, something in him, some effluent that foamed up from his silted heart, yearned to be saved, if only for one faint, glimmering moment.

Have to find her... have to find her... The urge grew and grew, as day after day his ragged body was grounded into the din. His gray matter was melting. Only his physical movements sparked with electricity – like the City.

Gil advances to stage center and bends in a deep bow. A full house showers him with applause.

Costumed in golden feathers, he crawls out of his mother's womb. His mother is an insect, an enormous spheroid eggcase covered in honey-colored fuzz. The genetically engineered freak wiggles its giant abdomen, and Gil half-emerges. Smeared with emulsion, Gil's golden plumage glistens. The insect suffers. It rages, beating Gil, the cause of its suffering, against the ground with primitive spite. Gil is knocked nearly unconscious. Gil and the insect explode with equal fury, bolts of pure hatred arc and collide.

Writhing and squirming, his torso freed at last, hands flat upon the slime-plastered stage, Gil saw her. His heart forced its way up into his throat.

That face! Out of an audience of thousands, he spotted her in an instant. That face – radiant, electric, white!

Gil extracts his legs from the insect womb. Too quickly, in fact, for huge quantities of blood spill out over the stage. The insect writhes and spreads its paraffin wings. The wires that hold them in place begin to cut into the thorax.

Soaked and sticky with blood, Gil leaps from the stage and runs. Hundreds of hands reach out to touch him as he sweeps past. Gil simply knocks them aside. He isn't a violent person – not ordinarily – but at the moment, anything in his way is his enemy. He is a golden beast charging through fields of shoulder-high grass.

Meanwhile, on stage, the mother insect, body severed in two, losing cascades of blue plasma, screams in its last throes of death.

The audience rises to its feet, thrilling to the new direction of the performance. Rochster, the theater owner, peers into his closed-circuit display, calculating the cost of repairing the blood-soaked stage.

Gil latched onto the girl. Gripping her by the shoulder, without a word, he proceeded to lead her outside.

Only then does the audience suspect that something is amiss. The crowd shouts. The guards fight them back. The woman next to Gil tears at his costume, railing at him insanely. A guard moves in to protect the star, but women batter him down. Gil's only thought is to shield the girl – and to dash for the nearest exit. When hordes of women rush after Gil and the girl, the security crew slams the heavy doors, letting the two escape.

Gil grasped the girl's beautiful electric hand.

"At last…"

Kisa smiled, running apace.

"You're sopping wet."

"Keep running. It'll dry."

"You stink of blood."

"I was just born, after all."

The girl led Gil into the construction site next to the Rox Star. The frame of the building was all that had been erected. Hushing their breath, they looked up to see the night sky. The chandelier heavens.

Inside the skeletal structure were several rows of benches. Sitting down, the two of them locked gazes, audibly, golden eyes to black eyes.

"Do you... what *do* you feel toward me?"

His voice trembled and caught. Never in his life had he asked such a mawkish question. Kisa laughed.

"These two months passed clear for me."

And prior to that? Gil swallowed the question. But what about himself? What the fuck had he done these last two months?

Clothed all in white, the girl looked even whiter. Had her birthplace never seen a sun?

"Unless I purged myself, I didn't think I could see you."

Gil's heart ached. *For someone the likes of me?* How defiled could she have been before? What hell had she been involved in?

"You see, I..."

"Don't tell me."

Gil commanded the girl to turn and face him. He didn't care: so she was a prostitute, a lesbian, a swindler, someone who hurt people so bad they'd never right themselves again. Maybe she'd plummeted into despair, laboring under misery that had been with her since birth.

Kisa wound her long black hair around Gil's neck as she held him. This was good. Perhaps this is what a mother's embrace was like.

"I must tell you, I..."

"Yes?"

"My roommate threw me out."

"But why? No, I don't care," Gil cautiously withheld his words. "Have you no place to go?"

Kisa shook her head on Gil's shoulder.

"Come home with me, then," he offered, giving thanks that Remora had chosen to leave.

Suddenly, a large shadow fell over them. Looking up in alarm, they saw a gigantic pterodon glide across the night sky. An idiot had let out his pet to roam the City.

A breeze wafted through the skeletal structure. It tussled Gil's hair, which was now completely dry. Kisa gave Gil a squeeze.

"Know what this is, where we are here?"

"No."

The girl grinned. "It's a church."

"A what?"

"The M/F On-Call Network Church."

The Mothers and Fathers Church? Gill had heard of it – supposedly it was run by an organization of psychics. They homed in on souls in crisis, places in need of love, wounded hearts, battlefields of all kinds and they came forth to heal. To treat, sometimes to scold. Materialized from millions of light-years beyond...

So this is what it was. An actual old-fashioned church, with rows of pews, a crucifix, and altar.

What in this city had they sensed calling out for parental love?

Gil left Kisa, made his way over to the unfinished statue of Mary, and bared his chest. A face – the girl's face – burrowed into the fullness of Gil's breasts. He heard Kisa's voice asking, could he really give milk? He didn't know. Why didn't she just suck?

Thirteen years later, the City in all its decadence was destroyed by two filth bombs, sending two hundred million inhabitants to hell.

Gil and Kisa had long since parted ways. Yet the Mothers and Fathers worked to save as many people as they could in the years before the City breathed its last. The light they provided was small, but certainly it was there, shining deep in the shadows of the City.

A light made visible by the dark.

– First published in Hayakawa SF Magazine, *June 1985*

Defamiliarize.

Q what kind of the world is this?

TSUTSUI YASUTAKA

Standing Woman
Translated by Dana Lewis

I stayed up all night and finally finished a forty-page short story. It was a trivial entertainment piece, capable of neither harm nor good.

"These days you can't write stories that might do harm or good; it can't be helped." That's what I told myself while I fastened the manuscript with a paper clip and put it into an envelope.

As to whether I have it in me to write stories that might do harm or good, I do my best not to think about that. I might want to try.

The morning sunlight hurt my eyes as I slipped on my wooden clogs and left the house with the envelope. Since there was still time before the first mail truck would come, I turned my feet toward the park. In the morning no children come to this park, a mere sixty-six square meters in the middle of a cramped residential district. It's quiet here. So I always include the park in my morning walk. Nowadays even the scanty green provided by the ten or so trees is priceless in the megalopolis.

I should have brought some bread, I thought. My favorite dogpillar stands next to the park bench. It's an affable dogpillar, large for a mongrel, with buff-colored fur.

The liquid-fertilizer truck had just left when I reached the park; the ground was damp and there was a faint smell of chlorine. The elderly gentleman I often saw there was sitting on the bench next to the dogpillar, feeding the buff post what seemed to be meat dumplings. Dogpillars usually have excellent appetites. Maybe the liquid fertilizer, absorbed by the roots sunk deep in the ground and passed on up through the legs, leaves something to be desired.

They'll eat just about anything you give them.

"You brought him something? I slipped up today. I forgot to bring my bread," I said to the elderly man.

He turned gentle eyes on me and smiled softly.

"Ah, you like this fellow, too?"

"Yes," I replied, sitting down beside him. "He looks like the dog I used to have."

The dogpillar looked up at me with large, black eyes and wagged its tail.

"Actually, I kept a dog like this fellow myself," the man said, scratching the ruff of the dogpillar's neck. "He was made into a dogpillar when he was three. Haven't you seen him? Between the haberdashery and the film shop on the coast road. Isn't there a dogpillar there that looks like this fellow?"

I nodded, adding, "Then that one was yours?"

"Yes, he was our pet. His name was Hachi. Now he's completely vegetized. A beautiful dogtree."

"Ah yes. That turned out to be a splendid shrub." I nodded repeatedly. "Now that you mention it, he does look a lot like this fellow. Maybe they came from the same stock."

"And the dog you kept?" the elderly man asked. "Where is he planted?"

"Our dog was named Buff," I answered, shaking my head. "He was planted beside the entrance to the park-cemetery on the edge of town when he was four. Poor thing, he died right after he was planted. The fertilizer trucks don't get out that way very often, and it was so far I couldn't take him food every day. Maybe they planted him badly. He died before becoming a tree."

"Then he was removed?"

"No. Fortunately, it didn't much matter there if he smelled or not, so he was left there and dried out. Now he's a bonepillar. He makes fine material for the neighborhood elementary school science classes, I hear."

"That's wonderful."

The elderly man stroked the dogpillar's head. "This fellow here, I wonder what he was called before he became a dogpillar."

"No calling a dogpillar by its original name," I said. "Isn't that a strange law?"

The man gave me a quick glance, then replied casually. "Didn't they just extend the laws concerning people to dogs? That's why they lose their names when they become dogpillars." He nodded while scratching the dogpillar's jaw. "Not only the old names, but you can't give them new names, either. That's because there are no proper nouns for plants."

Why, of course, I thought.

He looked at my envelope with MANUSCRIPT ENCLOSED written on it.

"Excuse me," he said. "Are you a writer?"

I was a little embarrassed.

"Well, yes. Just trivial little things."

After looking at me closely, the man returned to stroking the dogpillar's head. "I also used to write things."

He managed to suppress a smile.

"How many years is it now since I stopped writing? It feels like a long time."

I stared at the man's profile. Now that he said so, it was a face I seemed to have seen somewhere before. I started to ask his name, hesitated, and fell silent.

The elderly man said abruptly, "It's become a hard world to write in."

I lowered my eyes, ashamed of myself, who still continued to write in such a world.

The man apologized hurriedly at my sudden depression.

"That was rude. I'm not criticizing you. I'm the one who should feel ashamed."

"No," I told him, after looking quickly around us, "I can't give up writing because I haven't the courage. Giving up writing! Why, after all, that would be a gesture against society."

The elderly man continued stroking the dogpillar. After a long while he spoke.

"It's painful, suddenly giving up writing. Now that it's come to this, I would have been better off if I'd gone on boldly writing social criticism and had been arrested. There are even times when I think that. But I was just a dilettante, never knowing poverty, craving peaceful dreams. I wanted to live a comfortable life. As a person strong in self-respect, I couldn't endure being exposed to the eyes of the world, ridiculed. So I quit writing. A sorry tale."

He smiled and shook his head. "No, no, let's not talk about it. You never know who might be listening, even here on the street."

I changed the subject. "Do you live near here?"

"Do you know the beauty parlor on the main street? You turn in there. My name is Hiyama." He nodded at me. "Come over sometime. I'm married, but..."

"Thank you very much."

I gave him my own name.

I didn't remember any writer named Hiyama. No doubt he wrote under a pen name. I had no intention of visiting his house. This is a world where even two or three writers getting together is considered illegal assembly.

"It's time for the mail truck to come."

Talking pains to look at my watch, I stood up.

"I'm afraid I'd better go," I said.

He turned a sadly smiling face toward me and bowed slightly. After stroking the dogpillar's head a little, I left the park.

I came out on the main street, but there were only a ridiculous number of passing cars: pedestrians were few. A cattree, about thirty to forty centimeters high, was planted next to the side-walk.

Sometimes I come across a catpillar that has just been planted and still hasn't become a cattree. New catpillars look at my face and meow or cry, but the ones where all four limbs planted in the ground have vegetized, with their greenish faces stiffly set and their eyes shut tight, only move their ears now and then. Then there are catpillars that grow branches from their bodies and put out hand-fuls of leaves. The mental condition of these seems to be completely vegetized – they don't even move their ears. Even if you can still make out a cat's face, it may be better to call these cattrees.

Maybe. I thought, *it's better to make dogs into dogpillars. When their food runs out, they get vicious and even turn on people. But why did they have to turn cats into catpillars? Too many strays? To improve the food situation, even by a little? Or perhaps for the greening of the city...*

Next to the big hospital on the corner where the highways inter-sect are two mantrees, and ranged alongside these trees is a man-pillar. This manpillar wears a postman's uniform, and you can't tell how far its legs have vegetized because of its trousers. It is male, thirty-five or thirty-six years old, tall, with a bit of a stoop.

I approached him and held out my envelope as always.

"Registered mail, special delivery, please."

The manpillar, nodding silently, accepted the envelope and took stamps and a registered mail slip from his pocket.

I looked around quickly after paying the postage. There was no one else there. I decided to try speaking to him. I had been giving him mail every three days, but I still hadn't had a chance for a leisurely talk.

"What did you do?" I asked in a low voice.

The manpillar looked at me in surprise. Then, after running his eyes around the area, he answered with a sour look, "Won't do to go saying unnecessary things to me. Even me, I'm not supposed to answer."

"I know that," I said, looking into his eyes.

When I wouldn't leave, he took a deep breath. "I just said the pay's low. What's more, I got heard by my boss. Because a postman's pay is really low." With a dark look, he jerked his jaw at the two mantrees next to him. "These guys were the same. Just for letting slip some complaints about low pay. Do you know them?" he asked me.

I pointed at one of the mantrees. "I remember this one, because I gave him a lot of mail. I don't know the other one. He was already a mantree when we moved here."

"That one was my friend," he said.

"Wasn't that other one a chief clerk or section head?"

He nodded. "That's right. Chief clerk."

"Don't you get hungry or cold?"

"You don't feel it that much," he replied, still expressionless. Anyone who's made into a manpillar soon becomes expression-less. "Even I think I've gotten pretty plantlike. Not only in how I feel things, but in the way I think, too. At first, I was sad, but now it doesn't matter. I used to get really hungry, but they say the veget-izing goes faster when you don't eat."

He stared at me with lightless eyes. He was probably hoping he could become a mantree soon.

"Talk says they give people with radical ideas a lobotomy before making them into manpillars, but I didn't get that done, either. Even so, a month after I was planted I didn't get angry anymore."

He glanced at my wristwatch. "Well, you better go now. It's almost time for the mail truck to come."

"Yes." But still I couldn't leave, and I hesitated uneasily.

"You," the manpillar said. "Someone you know didn't recently get done into a manpillar, did they?"

Cut to the quick. I stared at his face for a moment, then nodded slowly.

"Actually, my wife."

"Hmm, your wife, is it?" For a few moments he regarded me with deep interest. "I wondered whether it wasn't something like that.

Otherwise nobody ever bothers to talk to me. Then what did she do, your wife?"

"She complained that prices were high at a housewives' get-together. Had that been all, fine, but she criticized the government, too. I'm starting to make it big as a writer, and I think that the eagerness of being that writer's wife made her say it. One of the women there informed on her. Anyway, it seems my wife has a pretty good idea who it was that did it. She was planted on the left side of the road looking from the station toward the assembly hall, next to that hardware store."

"Ah, that place." He closed his eyes a little, as if recollecting the appearance of the buildings and the stores in that area. "It's a fairly peaceful street. Isn't that for the better?" He opened his eyes and looked at me searchingly. "You aren't going to see her, are you? It's better not to see her too often. Both for her and you. That way you both forget faster."

"I know that."

I hung my head.

"Your wife?" he asked, his voice turning slightly sympathetic. "Has anyone done anything to her?"

"No. So far nothing. She's just standing, but even so—"

"Hey." The manpillar serving as a postbox raised his jaw to attract my attention. "It's come. The mail truck. You'd better go."

"You're right."

Taking a few wavering steps, as if pushed by his voice, I stopped and looked back. "Isn't there anything you want done?"

He brought a hard smile to his cheeks and shook his head.

The red mail truck stopped beside him.

I moved on past the hospital.

THINKING I'd check in at my favorite bookstore, I entered a street of crowded shops. My new book was supposed to be out any day now, but that kind of thing no longer made me the slightest bit happy.

A little before the bookstore in the same row is a small, cheap, candy store, and on the edge of the road in front of it is a manpillar on the verge of becoming a mantree. A young male, it is already a year since it was planted. The face has become a brownish color tinged with green, and the eyes are tightly shut. Tall back slightly bent, the posture slouching a little forward. The legs, torso, and arms, visible through clothes reduced to rags by exposure to wind and rain, are already vegetized, and branches sprout here and there. Young leaves bud from the ends of the arms, raised above the shoulders like beating wings. The body, which has become a tree, and even the face no longer move at all. The heart has sunk into the tranquil world of plants.

I imagined the day when my wife would reach this state, and again my heart winced with pain. It was the anguish of trying to forget.

If I turn the corner at this candy store and go straight, I thought, *I can go to where my wife is standing. I can see my wife. But it won't do to go,* I told myself. *There's no telling who might see you; if the women who informed on her questioned you, you'd really be in trouble.* I came to a halt in front of the candy store and peered down the road. Pedestrian traffic was the same as always. *It's all right. Anyone would overlook it if you just stand and talk a bit. You'll just have a word or two.* Defying my own voice screaming, *"Don't go!"* I went briskly down the street.

Her face pale, my wife was standing by the road in front of the hardware store. Her legs were unchanged, and it only seemed as if her feet from the ankles down were buried in the earth. Expressionlessly, as if striving to see nothing, feel nothing, she stared steadily ahead. Compared with two days before, her cheeks seemed a bit hollow. Two passing factory workers pointed at her, made some vulgar joke, and passed on, guffawing uproariously. I went up to her and raised my voice.

"Michiko!" I yelled right in her ear.

My wife looked at me, and blood rushed to her cheeks. She brushed one hand through her tangled hair.

"You've come again? Really, you mustn't."

"I can't help coming."

The hardware-store mistress, tending shop, saw me. With an air of feigned indifference, she averted her eyes and retired to the back of the store. Full of gratitude for her consideration, I drew a few steps closer to Michiko and faced her.

"You've gotten pretty used to it?"

With all her might she formed a bright smile on her stiffened face. "Mmm. I'm used to it."

"Last night it rained a little."

Still gazing at me with large, dark eyes, she nodded lightly. "Please don't worry. I hardly feel anything."

"When I think about you, I can't sleep." I hung my head. "You're always standing out here. When I think of that, I can't possibly sleep. Last night I even thought I should bring you an umbrella."

"Please don't do anything like that!" My wife frowned just a little. "It would be terrible if you did something like that."

A large truck drove past behind me. White dust thinly veiled my wife's hair and shoulders, but she didn't seem bothered.

"Standing isn't really all that bad." She spoke with deliberate lightness, working to keep me from worrying.

I perceived a subtle change in my wife's expressions and speech from two days before. It seemed that her words had lost a shade of delicacy, and the range of her emotions had become somewhat impoverished. *Watching from the sidelines like this, seeing her gradually grow more expressionless, it's all the more desolating for having known her as she was before – those keen responses, the bright vivacity, the rich, full expressions.*

"These people," I asked her, running my eyes over the hardware store, "are they good to you?"

"Well, of course. They're kind at heart. Just once they told me to ask if there's anything I want done. But they still haven't done anything for me."

"Don't you get hungry?"

She shook her head.

"It's better not to eat."

So. Unable to endure being a manpillar, she was hoping to become a mantree even so much as a single day faster.

"So please don't bring me food." She stared at me. "Please forget about me. I think, certainly, even without making any particular effort, I'm going to forget about you. I'm happy that you come to see me, but then the sadness drags on that much longer. For both of us."

"Of course you're right, but—" Despising this self that could do nothing for his own wife, I hung my head again. "But I won't forget you." I nodded. The tears came. "I won't forget. Ever."

When I raised my head and looked at her again, she was gazing steadily at me with eyes that had lost a little of their luster, her whole face beaming in a faint smile like a carved image of Buddha. It was the first time I had ever seen her smile like that.

I felt I was having a nightmare. *No*, I told myself. *This isn't your wife anymore.*

The suit she had been wearing when she was arrested had become terribly dirty and filled with wrinkles. But of course I wouldn't be allowed to bring a change of clothes. My eyes rested on a dark stain on her skirt.

"Is that blood? What happened?"

"Oh, this," she spoke falteringly, looking down at her skirt with a confused air. "Last night two drunks played a prank on me."

"The bastards!" I felt a furious rage at their inhumanity. If you put it to them, they would say that since my wife was no longer human, it didn't matter what they did.

"They can't do that kind of thing! It's against the law!"

"That's right. But I can hardly appeal."

And of course I couldn't go to the police and appeal, either. If I did, I'd be looked on as even more of a problem person.

"The bastards! What did they—" I bit my lip. My heart hurt enough to break. "Did it bleed a lot?"

"Mmm, a little."

"Does it hurt?"

"It doesn't hurt anymore."

Michiko, who had been so proud before, now showed just a little sadness in her face. I was shocked by the change in her. A group of young men and women, penetratingly comparing me and my wife, passed behind me.

"You'll be seen," my wife said anxiously. "I beg of you, don't throw yourself away."

"Don't worry." I smiled thinly for her in self-contempt. "I don't have the courage."

"You should go now."

"When you're a mantree," I said in parting, "I'll petition. I'll get them to transplant you to our garden."

"Can you do that?"

"I should be able to." I nodded liberally. "Yes, I should be able to."

"I'd be happy if you could," my wife said expressionlessly.

"Well, see you later."

"It'd be better if you didn't come again," she said in a murmur, looking down.

"I know. That's my intention. But I'll probably come anyway."

For a few minutes we were silent.

Then my wife spoke abruptly.

"Good-bye."

"Umm."

I began walking.

When I looked back as I rounded the corner, Michiko was following me with her eyes, still smiling like a graven Buddha.

Embracing a heart that seemed ready to split apart, I walked. I noticed suddenly that I had come out in front of the station. Unconsciously, I had returned to my usual walking course.

OPPOSITE the station is a small coffee shop I always go to called Punch. I went in and sat down in a corner booth. I ordered coffee, drinking it black. Until then I had always had it with sugar. The bitterness of sugarless, creamless coffee pierced my body, and I savored it masochistically. *From now on I'll always drink it black.* That was what I resolved.

Three students in the next booth were talking about a critic who had just been arrested and made into a manpillar.

"I hear he was planted smack in the middle of the Ginza."

"He loved the country. He always lived in the country. That's why they set him up in a place like that."

"Seems they gave him a lobotomy."

"And the students who tried to use force at the Diet, protesting his arrest – they've all been arrested and will be made into manpillars, too."

"Weren't there almost thirty of them? Where'll they plant them all?"

"They say they'll be planted in front of their own university, down both sides of a street called Students Road."

"They'll have to change the name now. Violence Grove, or something."

The three snickered.

"Hey, let's not talk about it. We don't want someone to hear."

The three shut up.

When I left the coffee shop and headed home, I realized that I had begun to feel as if I was already a manpillar myself. Murmuring the words of a popular song to myself – with the keywords changed – I walked on.

I am a wayside manpillar. You, too, are a wayside manpillar. What the hell, the two of us, in this world. Dried grasses that never flower.

– *First publication:* Shōsetsu Gendai *(Modern Fiction), May 1974*

HANMURA RYŌ

Cardboard Box
Translated by Dana Lewis

Suddenly, I perceived myself.

If that's what you call birth, it was pretty disappointing. Then my body, bent and folded flat, was quickly unfolded, and in the next instant I was overturned and enraptured with the sensation of my bottom being fitted together and closed.

To tell the truth, I came into the world without having any idea of what was happening to me.

Even so, I still remember how strong and dependable I felt myself to be when that wide tape, sucking tight against my skin, crisscrossed my bottom. But that was only for the shortest of moments. Again I was spun round, and turned right side up. When I think back on it, I realize that by then I was already on the conveyor belt, but at the time I was completely absorbed in sensing the white fluorescent light that filled my surroundings, and I didn't even notice that I was moving, swaying as I went.

My comrades... perhaps I should say my brothers? In any case, it was when we were riding that belt conveyor that I first realized that they and I were separate entities. They were swaying in front of me and behind me, and I thought to myself that I, too, was swaying just like them.

They had the same markings on their bodies as I had on mine. We were exactly the same size. In fact, it was at that time that I first realized I had markings on my own body as well.

I was feeling a bit forlorn. I had just been born and didn't understand things clearly, but I couldn't help feeling that I wasn't closely attached to them. I was born and, thus separated from my brothers, began to exist. Perhaps I felt forlorn because I wasn't used to an independent existence.

I spoke to the comrade closest to me to drive away the loneliness.

"I wonder why we're swaying?"

My comrades, well mannered, were all queued up, swaying from side to side. The one I spoke to was directly in front of me in the queue.

"How should I know?" he answered.

"We're moving. We're being transported someplace," said the one behind me.

"I wonder where we're going?"

"How should I know?" he answered. He spoke exactly like the one in front of me.

"In any case, we're going to be filled. Isn't that good enough?"

The comrade behind me was suddenly overjoyed.

"We'll be filled! Hey, everybody! From now on we're going to be filled!"

Pleasure spread through all my queued-up comrades when he cried out.

"We'll be filled! We'll be filled! We'll all be filled!"

A chorus began, and before I knew it I, too, had joined in. I thought, In a few moments I'd be filled. This body of mine would be filled completely. That was my vindication for living. That was my purpose in life.

My body shook, not just because of the conveyor belt, but with joy. The expectation that in a moment I would be filled left me on Cloud Nine. But suddenly I heard a thin, whooshing sound, and we were given an even more violent shaking. I had a sense of falling forward, and was on the verge of tumbling dangerously from the conveyor belt.

"What happened?" asked a worried voice from behind. "We're not going anywhere."

"Good Lord! Surely they're not going to tell us to stay as we are! This isn't funny. Hurry up and fill us!"

Unease spread to everybody the moment the conveyor belt stopped. Of course I also waited nervously for the movement to resume. If I had to spend my whole life like this with an empty body... Just thinking of it made me cry out, abandoning all propriety.

"Move! Don't leave us like this!"

That stoppage was agony. Not only had we yet to be filled, we still didn't have anything at all in our bodies.

How long did that uneasy time continue? I have a feeling it was a very long time. By the time the conveyor began, with a thudding impact, to move again, we were at our wits' end, not even caring if we weren't filled, just so long as something, anything was put into our bodies.

"Anything'll do; I want something put in fast!" Writhing with base desires, I was transported to the end of the conveyor belt before I knew it.

Ecstasy came suddenly.

A round, flexible something rushed into a corner of my square body.

...I shivered.

For the first time since my birth I was numb with the pleasure driven into my body. The round, pliable objects lithely and accurately began to fill me. My pleasure mounted as the accumulated weight of the objects increased. I will never forget the pleasure of that moment, mounting higher and higher, leaving me no time even to breathe. My bottom was buried without a gap, and the objects climbed steadily higher and higher.

Then at last I was full. I had been completely filled!

Even then my body was being moved. When I was completely full and quivering with the pleasure of it, the top of my body was suddenly bent and folded again, and that tape that sucked tight against my skin sealed my body tight.

I felt myself powerful with a strength ten times more than I had felt before. My adequately filled self slid down an incline, was pulled around, heaved and piled, but even that violence was not painful, as though somewhere within it was a gentle consideration.

I came to rest. No sooner had I come to rest than the weight of my comrades came down on top of me. I myself was positioned on top of more of my comrades. In the end, in front, in back, to right and left, I was tight against the bodies of my comrades, filled and quivering with joy.

"It's wonderful! I'm completely full!"

That shout could be heard from somewhere among my piled-up companions. I, too, was lucky like the owner of that voice. I felt I had been born for pleasure.

It appeared that, still piled up, we had begun to move again. But this time it was in darkness. In the midst of ceaseless small vibrations and occasional leisurely swaying, I felt completely satisfied.

However, from far away towards the edge of our pile, a voice started up, filled with sarcasm.

"You all seem pretty smug, don't you now."

The voice was hoarse as though tired.

"Well, it's something to be satisfied about. But it's not going to last for long."

"Who's talking like that?" asked one of my comrades cheerily.

"Heh, heh," returned the sarcastic hoarse voice. "Right now we're being taken to town in a truck. When we get there, you'll all have your lids cut open, and you'll have to cough up all those things you've got in your bodies."

"Liar! Who could think of emptying us so soon, now that we've finally been filled…"

"You're still a lot of babies," ridiculed Hoarse Voice. "First off, you probably don't even know what you've got in your bodies."

"I don't know," admitted another voice from the back. "What are those round things, tell us!"

"Oh, I'll tell you all right," said Hoarse Voice. "They're tangerines. The things you got stuffed in your bodies are tangerines. When tangerines get to town they're divided up and sent to stores, piled up and sold. That's why you're all going to get your lids cut open and be emptied."

We, the load of a truck, were returned to silence.

"That's okay. Maybe it can't be helped," said one of my companions who seemed to be near Hoarse Voice. "We're filled with tangerines. No doubt it's true. Tangerines are transported to town and sold in stores. Probably that's true, too. That's why we've been filled with tangerines and are being taken to town. And then, probably, when we reach the town, our lids will be cut and we'll cough up our tangerines—"

A voice that was not quite a shriek and not quite a sigh filled the truck.

"But that's not the end, right? We're a species born to have our bodies filled!"

"With something more than air, that is," said Hoarse Voice nastily.

"That's right," continued the second voice with strong self-control, not rising to Hoarse Voice's challenge. "We are boxes. Cardboard boxes. We can do more than just hold tangerines. Even after we've had our tangerines taken out we can still hold other things."

"That's right, all right," laughed Hoarse Voice. "In my body right now there's a cotton jacket and a dirty towel and a lunch box and a pair of old shoes. They belong to the driver of this truck. But that's not what it was like before.

"I was a box full of writing materials. Writing materials like kids use at school. Writing materials, each bugger wrapped up proper, filling me to the brim. I was filled! Even I wasn't like this in the beginning."

For some reason Hoarse Voice began to get angry.

"You can put anything in a box. But even so, you guys, the world is like that. You were made to put tangerines in. They stuff tangerines into your bodies, and after they've all been taken out, not one left behind, nobody cares what'll happen to you."

"No!"

"It's true! No mistake about it. After the tangerines are gone you guys are just empty boxes. Bothersome, troublesome empty cardboard boxes. Even the guys who made you never thought about what happens after that."

"That's terrible..." Somebody began to cry. "You mean when these tangerines reach their destination, that's the end?"

Hoarse Voice began to laugh crazily.

"That's right! That's right! You all get the can!"

"What happens then?"

"If your luck's bad, you'll be burned right off and turned into ash. If it goes like usual, you'll have your bottom tape yanked off. You'll be folded up flat, piled and left somewhere. In a while you'll be gathered together and taken away someplace, and that's the end of it."

"After I've been emptied of tangerines, my body will never be filled again?"

"After that, it's fate. It's up to fate. If your luck's good they may put in something else. Like me, an oily cotton jacket, dirty towels, old shoes..."

"Anything's fine. I want to be filled! I want to live!"

"It's better to resign yourself. A box you put tangerines in is a tangerine box. A tangerine box with its tangerines gone is garbage. Then you guys, you've got 'tangerine box' written all over you. Even if you get, like, bundles of money stuffed into you, a tangerine box is still a tangerine box."

"On that body of yours..." the comrade right next to Hoarse Voice seemed to be looking over his companion's body. "You've got 'pencil box' written on you, don't you. Were you a box for putting pencils in?"

Hoarse Voice laughed crazily again.

"I'm a box for putting pencil boxes in! I told you. There's good luck and bad luck. I'm not lucky, not me. In this cardboard box called me, pencil boxes like elementary school kids use... You get that? Even a pencil box is a box!"

Hoarse Voice had begun to cry.

"A box for putting boxes in! I was a box for putting boxes in! There's nothing inside a pencil box before it's sold. It's an empty box! And those were stuffed into me...

"Can you understand that feeling? Filled in form only. It's not like you've really been filled. You're filled with empty boxes! You guys here worrying about what happens after you get to town and have your tangerines taken out, that's a luxury! Aren't you filled and happy enough to shiver!"

"Hey, Mr. Pencil Box, don't cry."

"I'm not a pencil box! I'm a box for pencil boxes!"

"But even after you were emptied aren't you still alive? Cheer up!"

My comrades all joined in, trying to encourage the old cardboard box with the hoarse voice. But even then we were approaching the town that was to be our final destination.

Lowered from the truck, we were scattered far and wide. It was a bustling vegetable and fruit market, and there I had no choice but to observe a most blood-curdling scene.

Right next to where I and two or three of my comrades had been placed together in a clump, a big bonfire was blazing. People gathered around that fire, rubbing their cold hands together. Now and then they fed the fire scraps of wood and empty cardboard boxes from among my comrades.

I had to sit there and stare at what my end would be. A sense of helplessness welled up within me. My sole salvation was the tangerines still stuffed within my body.

However, as I gazed upon my comrades burning up one after the other, I suddenly awoke to the truth that I was not really full. Considerable gaps remained between the round tangerines. Every time

I thought of the dark road ahead, my heart grew wilder with the thought that my present half-filled state was not enough.

Consumed with lust, I forgot myself. "Put more in! Even fuller!" I screamed, even though I was already tightly closed with tape.

"Hey! Calm down!" My comrades rebuked me, unable to contain themselves, but I continued to scream.

"Put more in! Even fuller!"

For a tangerine box, I enjoyed the greatest of luck. Right after being transported from the market to the town's fruit store, the other two boxes with me were opened and the tangerines inside them piled up in front of the store by shop attendants. But I was placed, untouched, in the back of the store. Two, three days passed, but I stayed put on the concrete floor. Until the second day I had my two empty comrades beside me, but on the third day they were folded up roughly by the shopkeeper and taken away.

Just before being folded, one of them shouted in my direction.

"Farewell! It was an empty life!"

I tried to say something in return, but he had already ceased to exist as a box.

A box is for putting things in. It is in having things put into them that boxes find pleasure in life. When things are packed in lightly, a box's body can shiver with insurmountable gratification.

Yet people make boxes just to put tangerines in, and once that duty is finished, even if a box can still be used, they abandon it without a care. I have no way of knowing what happened to my forsaken comrades, but no doubt every one of them had their lives as boxes closed out.

Fortunately for me, I was chanced upon by a customer who wanted to buy a whole box of tangerines and was taken to his house by one of the fruit store attendants. There I was pushed onto a warm dark shelf in the kitchen and had the tangerines inside me taken out little by little.

Only at that time was I unable to complain that I was empty, that I was not filled. Instead, I prayed desperately that I could buy even a little more time before the last tangerine was taken away.

But that did not take long. My emptied self was dragged out to a bright place and was cast away. Then, in a short while, people began, little by little, to fill me again.

Beer bottle caps and thick plastic bags, padding used for packing, all kinds of nonflammable garbage was tossed inside me.

Even with that, I was satisfied. It doesn't matter what's inside. Just so long as its body is filled, a box is satisfied.

And at last, I was filled. It was the second climax of my life. Filled with nonflammable garbage, I was left alone for more than half a year.

My good luck continued. One day, my nonflammable friends quickly left my body. By all rights, my own life should have ended there as well, but for some reason only my contents were thrown away and I was left in the street outside the house. Then, the children came, one getting inside my body and two others pushing and pulling the two of us around. I was worn threadbare on the concrete road, but I was enraptured with being filled by human children.

The children took the game to heart. They carried me to a nearby park with a pond, and played there over and over again every day. In just a few days I was worn out, but I was still alive. Perhaps I was able to last longer because I had the dirt of the path beneath me instead of concrete.

But as far as having anything put into me again, it was hopeless. My corners were split. I was full of holes. Never again would I be able to perform my role as a box.

Then the children tired of their game. One windy night I was blown over, and drew closer to the pond.

To a cardboard box, water is an object of terror. The wind maliciously pushed me toward the water's edge.

"This is the end..."

I resigned myself to my fate. The wind blew stronger, and at last

I was blown over and fell onto the water. Fallen, but still floating. I was blown by the wind like a sailing ship, and moved toward the center of the pond.

A cardboard box fears the water. And that water soaked steadily into my body. I began to sink, unable to move even when blown by the wind. The water infiltrated me, making my body ridiculously heavy.

Sinking. I was sinking.

The park where I had passed the hours playing with the children was lost to my sight. The sky, the wind, both passed from my consciousness.

"Here my life has come to an end." So thinking, I gave myself up. Slowly, slowly, I sank toward the bottom of the pond.

...What ecstasy...

I was enraptured. I was filled! For the first time in my life I was completely filled! The water, with perfect, even density, was filling my body!

It was an ecstasy like melting. Indeed, my body would no doubt dissolve in the water. Yet wasn't that the same as dissolving in the ecstasy of being filled?

As I quietly submerged, my body swamped with water, I was numb with joy.

"It no longer matters if I die," I whispered. Could there ever have been another cardboard box so perfectly filled? Could there ever have been another cardboard box who ended his life in such ecstasy...?

I no longer have a need for the concept of time. Adequately filled at last and gently dissolving, I am the embodiment of joy.

– First publication: The All-Yomimono, *July 1975*

The Legend of the
Paper Spaceship

Translated by Gene van Troyer and Ōshiro Tomoko

H ALFWAY *through the Pacific War, I was sent
from my unit to a village in the heart of the mountains, and there I lived
for some months. I still recall clearly the road leading into that village;
and in the grove of bamboo trees beside the road, the endless flight of
a paper airplane and a beautiful naked woman running after it. Now,
long years later, I cannot shake the feeling that what she was always
folding out of paper stood for no earthly airplane, but for a spaceship.
Some time long ago, deep in those mountain recesses...*

1

THE PAPER airplane glides gracefully above the earth; and weaving
between the sprouts of new bamboo, stealing over the deep-piled
humus of fallen and decaying leaves, a white mist comes blowing,
eddying and dancing up high on the back of a subtle breeze, moving
on and on.

In the bamboo grove the flowing mist gathers in thick and brood-
ing pools. Twilight comes quickly to this mountain valley. Like
a ship sailing a sea of clouds, the paper airplane flies on and on
through the mist.

*One – a stone stairway to the sky
Two – if it doesn't fly
Three – if it does fly, open...*

A woman's voice, singing through the mist. As if pushed onward by that voice, the paper airplane lifts in never-ending flight. A naked woman owns the voice, and white in her nudity she slips quickly between the swaying bamboo of the grove.

(*Kill them! Kill them!*)

Alarm sirens wove screaming patterns around shrieking voices.

(*Kill everyone! That's an order!*)

(*Don't let any get to the ship! One's escaped!*)

(*Beamers! Fire, fire!*)

A crowd of voices resounding in this mist, but no one else can hear them. These voices echo only in the woman's head.

Tall and leafy and standing like images of charcoal gray against a pale ash background, the bamboo trees appear and disappear and reappear among the gauzy veils of the always folding rolling mist. The fallen leaves whisper as the woman's feet rustle over them. Mist streams around her like something alive as she walks, then flows apart before her to allow the dim shape of what might be a small lake to peek through.

Endworld Mere: the *uba-iri-no-numa.* After they had laughed and danced through the promises and passions of living youth, it had once been common for old people to come to this place to end the misery of their old age by throwing themselves into the swamp's murky waters.

Superstition holds that Endworld Mere swarms with the spirits of the dead. To placate any of the lingering dead, therefore, these valley folk had heaped numerous mounds of stones in a small open space near the mere. This place they named the *Sai no Kawara,* the earthly shore where the journey over the Great Waters began. They gathered here once a year for memorial services, when they burnt incense and clapped hands and sent their prayers across the Wide Waters to the shore of the nether world.

No matter how many stone towers you erect on the earthly shore of the River of Three Crossings, the myths tell us that demons will destroy them. Whether physical or spectral, here too the "demons" had been about the tireless task of destruction. In the very beginning there had probably been but a few mounds of tombstones to consecrate the unknown dead; but over the years, hundreds of stones had been heaped, and now lay scattered. Throughout most of the year, the place was now little more than a last rest stop where the infrequent person bound on the one-way trip to Endworld Mere paused for a short time before moving on. Because of its deserted silence, men and women seeking a little more excitement in life found the place ideal for secret rendez-vous.

Secret meetings were often a singular concern for these simple village folk. They could think of little else but pleasure. "Endworld Mere" is a name that suggests even the old go there with stealth, and possibly the dreadful legends surrounding the place were fabricated by anxious lovers who wished to make it a place more secure for their trysts.

Owing to these frightening stories, the village children gave the mere a wide berth. Round lichen-covered stones, rain-soaked and rotting paper dolls, creaking wooden signs with mysterious, indecipherable characters inscribed on them: for children these things all bespoke the presence of ghosts and ogres and night-mare encounters with demons.

Sometimes, however, the children would unintentionally come close enough to glimpse the dank mere, and on one such occa-sion they were chasing the madwoman Ōsen, who was flying a paper airplane.

"Say, guys! Ōsen's still runnin' aroun' naked!"

"*Hey*, Ōsen! Doncha wan' any *clothes?*"

All the children jeered at Ōsen. For adult and child alike she was a handy plaything.

But Ōsen had a toy, too: a paper airplane, as thin, as sharp-pointed as a spear.

One, a white star
Two, a red star…

In the mist she sings, and dreams: the reason she flies her paper airplane, the hatred that in her burns for human beings.

Ōsen, whose body is ageless, steps lightly over the grass, reaches the mere where the enfeebled old cast themselves away to die. The paper airplane flies on against the mist before her. No one knows what keeps the plane flying so long. Once Ōsen lets go of it, the "airplane" flies on seemingly forever. That's all there is to it…

A madwoman, is Ōsen, going about naked in summer, and in the winter wearing only one thin robe.

2

THERE IS a traditional song that the village children sang while playing ball, of which I vaguely recall one part:

I'll wait if it flies,
if it doesn't I won't –
I alone will keep waiting here.
I wonder if I'll ever climb
those weed-grown stairs someday –
One star far and two stars near…

Naked in the summer, and in the winter she wears one thin robe.

Most adults ignored the children who jeered at Ōsen, but there were a few who scolded them.

"Shame on you! Stop it! You should *pity* poor Ōsen."

The children just back-talked, often redoubling their jeers to the tune of a local rope-skipping song, or else throwing catcalls back and forth.

"Hey, *Gen!* Ya fall in *love* with Ōsen? Ya *sleep* with her last night?"

"Don't be an idiot!"

Even if adults reprimanded them like this, the kids kept up exactly the same sort of raillery. After all, everyone knew that last night, or the night before, or the night before that, at least *one* of the village men had made love to Ōsen.

Ōsen: She must have been close to her forties. Some villagers claimed she was much, *much* older than that, but one look at Ōsen put the lie to their claims: She was youthful freshness incarnate, her body that of a woman not even twenty.

Ōsen: community property, harlot to all who came for it, the butt of randy male superiority. Coming to know the secrets of her body was a kind of "rite of passage" for all the young men of the village.

Ōsen: the village idiot. This was the other reason why the villagers sheltered her.

Ōsen was the only daughter and survivor of the village's most ancient family. Among those who live deep in the mountains and still pay homage to the Wolf God, the status of a household was regarded as supremely important. That such an imbecile should be the sole survivor of so exalted a household gave everyone a limitless sense of superiority – Ōsen! Plaything for the village sports!

Her house stood on a knoll, from where you could look down on Endworld Mere. Perhaps it's better to say where her house was *left*, rather than stood. At the bottom of the stone stairs leading up to her door, the openwork gate to her yard didn't know whether to fall down or not. Tiles were ready to drop from the gate roof, and tangled weeds and grass overgrew the ruins of the small room where long ago a servant would hold a brazier for the gatekeeper's warmth in winter.

A step inside the gate and the stone stairs leading up were choked with moss and weeds. The curious thing was that the center of the stairway had not been worn down; rather, both sides were. Nobody ever walked in the middle, say the old stories. According to the oldest man in the village, on New Year's Eve they used to welcome in the new year and send off the old with a Shinto ritual, and in one line of the chant there was a passage about a Gate protected by the Center of a Stone Stairway built by a forgotten Brotherhood; and since no one knew the meaning of *that*, the old man said, people felt it best to avoid the center of *this* stone stairway whenever they passed up or down it.

The stairway climbed a short way beyond Ōsen's house to where the ground flattened and widened out and was covered with a profusion of black stones. An old crumbling well with a collapsing roof propped up by four posts was there. Sunk into the summit of this hill, one of the highest points in the valley, the well had never gone dry: Fathoms of water always filled it. If any high mountains had been massed nearby this would have explained such vast quantities of water; but there were no such mountains, and this well defied physical law. Sinner's Hole, they called it. When the men were finished with Ōsen they came to this wellside to wash.

Once, when a shrill group of cackling old women had gathered at the well to hold the yearly memorial services and pray to the Wolf God, one of them was suddenly stricken with a divination and proclaimed that if Ōsen were soaked in the well, her madness would abate. This cheered up those who envied Ōsen's great beauty, so on that day twelve years ago poor Ōsen was stripped to the raw before the eyes of the assembled women and dunked into the winter-frigid well water. An hour later, her body flushed a livid purple, Ōsen fainted and was finally hauled out. Sadly her idiocy was not cured. The story has it that the old crone who blurted the augury was drunk on the millet wine being served at the memorial service, and that afterward she fell into Endworld Mere and drowned. Because of the wine?

From then on, once someone undressed her, Ōsen stayed that way. If someone draped a robe over her, she kept it on. Since someone undressed her nearly every night and left her as she was in the morning, Ōsen most often went around naked.

Beautiful as the men might find Ōsen's body, others thought it best to keep the children from seeing her. Therefore, each morning a village woman came around to see that she was dressed. Ōsen stayed stone still when being dressed, though sometimes she smiled happily. She went on singing her songs –

Folding one, dah-dum
fold a second one, tah-tum
a third one fold, tra-lah!
Fly on, I say fly! Fly ever on to my star!

– folding her paper airplanes while she murmured and sang. And one day soon, to the stunned amazement of the villagers and eventual focus of their great uproar, Ōsen's stomach began growing larger.

No one had ever stopped to think that Ōsen might someday be gotten with child.

The village hens got together and clucked about it, fumbling in their brains for hours to find some way to keep Ōsen from having the child. Finally they moved en masse to the ramshackle house where Ōsen lived her isolated life, and they confronted her with their will.

The idiot Ōsen, however, shocked everyone when for the first time in living memory she explicitly stated her *own* will; she would have this baby.

"Ōsen! No arguments. We're taking you to the city, and you'll see a doctor!"

"Don't be ridiculous, Ōsen. Why, you couldn't raise it if you had it. The poor thing would lead a *pathetic* life!"

Large tears welled in Ōsen's eyes and spilled down her cheeks. None of the village women had ever seen Ōsen weep before.

"Ōsen... baby... I *want it born...*" said Ōsen. She held her swollen stomach, and the tears kept streaming down her face.

How high in spirit and firm in resolve they had been when they had come to drag Ōsen away! Why it all evaporated so swiftly they would never know. Captured now by the pathos, they, too, could only weep.

Ōsen soon dried her tears, and began folding a paper airplane.

"Plane, plane, fly off!" she cried. "Fly off to my father's home!"

The women exchanged glances. Might having a baby put an end to Ōsen's madness?

And then the paper airplane left Ōsen's hand. It flew from the parlor and out into the garden, and then came back again. When Ōsen stood up the airplane circled once around her and flew again into the yard. Ōsen followed it, singing as she gingerly stepped down the stone stairs, and her figure disappeared in the direction of the bamboo grove.

One old crone, with a gloomy, crestfallen face, took up a sheet of the paper and folded it; but when she gave the plane a toss it dipped, and fell to the polished planking of the open-air hallway.

"Why does *Ōsen's* fly so well?" she grumbled.

Another slightly younger old woman said with a sage nod and her best knowing look, "Even a stupid idiot can do *some* things well, you know."

3

First month – red snapper!
    hitotsuki – tai
Second month – then it's shells!
    futatsuki – kai
Third, we have reserve, and
    mittsu – enryode
Fourth – shall we offer shelter?
    yottsu – tomeru ka
If we offer shelter, well then,
    tomereba itcho

Shall we fold up Sixth Day?
   itsuyo kasanete muika
Sixth Day's star was seen –
   muika no hoshi wa mieta
Seventh Day's star was too!
   nanatsu no hoshi mo mieta
Eighth – a mountain cabin daughter
   yattsu yamaga no musume
Ninth – left crying in her longing
   kokonotsu koishiku naitesōrō
Tenth at last she settled in the tiny cabin!
   toto yamaga ni sumitsukisōrō

– Rope-skipping song

ÔSEN kept flying her airplanes, the village men kept up their nightly visits to her bower, the village women never ceased their fretting over her delivery... and one moonlit night a village lad came running down her stone stairs yelling: "She's *having* it! Ōsen's baby's on the way!"

A boy was born and they named him Emon. When he was nearly named Tomo – "common" – because Ōsen was passed round and round among the village men, the old midwife quickly intervened.

"As the baby was comin' out, Ōsen cried *'ei-mon,'*" the old woman reported. "That's what she said. I wonder what she meant?"

"Emon. Hmmm..." said one of the other women gathered there.

"Well, try asking."

Addressing the new mother, the midwife said, "Ōsen, which do you prefer as a name for the baby – Tomo, or Emon?"

"Emon," Ōsen answered clearly.

"That's better, it's related to Ōsen's entry gate," said an old woman who had memorized the chants for the Year End Rites.

"How do you mean?" a fourth woman said.

"Emon means *ei-mon,* the Guardian Gates," said the old woman.

"I've heard that in the old days the New Year's Eve rituals were recited only here, at Ōsen's house. *Ei-mon* is part of the indecipherable lines... let's see... ah, yes, 'You must go up the center of Heaven's Stairs, the stone stairs protected by *Ei-mon*, Emon's Gate.'"

At this a fifth woman nodded.

"Yes, that's right," she said, adding, "It's also in one of the songs we sing at the New Year's Eve Festival. Here... 'Emon came and died – Emon came and died – Wherever did he come from? – He came from a far-off land – Drink, eat, get high on the wine – You'll think you're flying in the sky...'"

"Hmmm, I see now," said the fourth woman. "I was thinking of the *emon* cloth one wears when they die. But a man named Emon came and died? And protects the gate? I wonder what it all means... "

The women took pity on Ōsen's child and everyone resolved to lend a hand in raising him. But... Emon never responded to it: he had given only that first vigorous cry of the newborn, then remained silent, and would stay so for a long time to come.

"Ah, what a shame," one woman said. "I expect the poor deaf-mute's been cursed by the Wolf God. What else for the child of an idiot?"

"We said she shouldn't have it," another replied with a nod.

Indifferent to the sympathy of these women, Ōsen crooned a lullaby.

Escaped with Emon, who doesn't know, flow, flow...

"Why it's a *Heaven Song*," one of the women said suddenly. "She just changed the name at the beginning to Emon."

Moved to tears by the madwoman's lullaby, the women spontaneously began to sing along.

Escaped with Emon, who doesn't know,
     shiranu Emon to nigesōrō

flow, flow, and grow old
    nagare nagarete oisōrō
all hopes dashed in this mountainous land.
    kono yama no chide kitai mo koware
No fuel for the Pilgrim's fires –
    abura mo nakute kochu shimoyake
no swaying Heaven's Way.
    seikankoko obekkanashi
Emon has died, alone so alone,
    Emon shinimoshi hitori sabishiku
wept in longing for his distant home.
    furusato koishi to nakisōrō

Everyone so pitied Emon, but as he grew he in no way acknowledged their gestures of concern, and because of this everyone came to think the mother's madness circulated in her silent child's blood.

Not so. When he was awake Emon could hear everyone's voices, though they weren't voices in the usual sense. He heard them in his head. "Voice" is a vibration passing through the air, sound spoken with a will. What Emon heard was always accompanied by *shapes*. When someone uttered the word "mountain" the syllables *moun-tain* resounded in the air; the shape projected into Emon's mind with the word would differ depending on who spoke it, but always the hazy mirage of a mountain would appear. Listen as you will to the words *Go to the mountain,* it is possible to distinguish five syllables. But in young Emon's case, overlapping the sound waves he could sense some one thing, a stirring, a *motion* that swept into a dim, mountainous shape.

For the tabula rasa mind of the infant this is an enormous burden. Emon's tiny head was always filled with pain and tremendous commotion. The minds and voices of the people around him tangled like kaleidoscopic shapes, scattering through his head like voices and images on the screen of a continuously jammed television set. It's a miracle Emon did *not* go mad.

No one knew Emon had this ability, and men kept calling on Ōsen as usual. In his mind Emon soon began walking with tottering, tentative steps: along with, oh, say, Sakuzō's or Jimbei's shadowy thoughts would come crystal-clear images, and with them came meanings far beyond those attached to the spoken words.

"Hey there, Emon," they might say. "If you go out 'n' play I'll give you some candy." Or they would say something like: "A *big whale* just came swimmin' up the river, Emon!"

But Emon's mind was an unseen mirror reflecting what these men were really thinking. It differed only slightly with each man.

And then one day when he was five years old, Emon suddenly spoke to a village woman.

"Why does everyone want to sleep with Ōsen?" he asked.

Ōsen, he said; not *Mother.* Perhaps because he kept seeing things through the villagers' minds, Emon was unable to know Ōsen as anything more than just a woman.

"E-emon-boy, you can *talk?*" the woman replied, eyes wide with surprise.

Shocking. Once Emon's power of speech was known, they couldn't have the poor boy living in the same house with that common whore Ōsen... So the men hastily convened a general meeting, and it was concluded that Emon should be placed in the care of "the General Store" – the only store in the village.

This automatically meant that Emon must mix with the children's society; but as he knew so many words and their meanings at the same time, the other children were little more than dolts in comparison and could never really be his playmates. And not to be forgotten: since he was Ōsen's child the other boys and girls considered him irredeemably inferior, and held him in the utmost contempt. So it was that reading books and other people's minds soon became Emon's only pleasure.

4

I ONCE spoke to Ōsen while gazing into her beautiful clear eyes. "You're pretending," I told her. "You're crazy like a fox, right?" Instead of answering, Ōsen sang a song, the one she always sang when she flew the paper airplanes, the ballad of a madwoman:

Escaped with Emon, who doesn't know, flow, flow, and grow old...

The "Heaven Song," of course. Now, if I substitute some words based on the theory I'm trying to develop, why, what it suggests becomes something far grander:

Shilan and Emon fled together,
    Shiranu to Emon to nigesōrō
Fly, fly, and they crashed,
    nagare, nagarete ochisōrō
the ship's hull dashed in this mountainous land.
    kono yama no chide kitai mo koware
No fuel – the star maps have burned,
    abura mo nakute kōchuzū mo yake
interstellar navigation is not possible.
    seikankōkō obotsukanashi
Emon has died, alone so alone,
Wept in longing for his distant home.

The last two lines of this song remain the same as in the version recorded earlier, but all of the preceding lines have subtly changed. For example: in line one, *shiranu* would normally be taken to mean "doesn't know," but in my reinterpretation it is now seen as the Japanization of a similar-sounding alien name – *Shilan*. In the second line, I am supposing that *oisōrō* (meaning "grow old") is a corruption of the word *ochisōrō* (meaning "fall" or "crash"); and I am further assuming that *kochu shimoyake* ("Pilgrim's fires") in line four is a corruption of *kōchūzu mo yake* ("star charts also burned"). In lines three, four, and five, three words have double meanings:

> *kitai* = hope/ship's hull
> *kōchū* = pilgrim/space flight
> *seikankōkō* = heavenly way/interstellar navigation

In the above manner, line three changes its meaning from "all hopes dashed in this mountainous land" to "the ship's hull dashed in this mountainous land," and so forth. There is more of this sort of thing...

Once a week an ancient truck rattled and wheezed up the steep mountain roads on the forty-kilometer run between the village and the town far below, bearing a load of rice sent up by the prefectural government's wartime Office of Food Rationing. This truck was the village's only physical contact with the outside world. The truck always parked in front of the General Store.

Next door to the store was a small lodging house where the young men and women of the village always congregated. The master of the house was Old Lady Také, a huge figure of a woman, swarthy-skinned and well into her sixties, who was rumored to have once plied her trade in the pleasure quarters of a distant metropolis. She welcomed all the young people to her lodge.

On summer evenings the place was usually a hive of chatter and activity. Even small children managed for a short time to mingle in the company of their youthful elders, dangling their legs from the edge of the open-air hallway. Rope-skipping and the bouncing of balls passed with the dusking day, and the generations changed. Small children were shooed home and girls aged from twelve or thirteen to widows of thirty-five or thirty-six began arriving, hiding in the pooling shadows. They all came seeking the night's promise of excitement and pleasure.

It was an unwritten law that married men and women stayed away from the lodge, though the nature of their children's night-play was an open secret. And how marvelously different this play was from the play in larger towns and cities: the people who gathered at Old Lady Také's lodge doused the lights and immediately explored each other's bodies. This, it must be said, was the only leisure activity they had. In the mountains, where you seldom find other diversions, this is the only amusement. The muffled laughter of young girls as hands slipped beneath their sweat-dampened robes, their coy resistance... And the heady fragrance that soon filled the room drew everyone on to higher delights.

Occasionally one of the local wags would amble by the lodge, and from a safe distance flash a startling light on the activities. Girls squealed, clutching frantically at their bodices, draping their drenched clothes over their thighs. In order to salvage this particular night's mood, someone asked in a loud voice:

"Say, Osato, your son's gonna be coming around here any day now, isn't he?"

"What?" said the widow.

"Yeah – he finally made it, I think!"

"Ho!" she laughed. "Ho! You're being nasty, kid. He's *only* twelve..."

"Well, if he hasn't, he'll find out how to pretty soon," the voice continued. "So maybe you should ask Ōsen as soon as possible...?"

"Hmmm... You might be right. Maybe tomorrow. I could get him spruced up, take him over in his best kimono..."

A young man's voice replying from deep within the room said, "Naw, you're too late, Osato!"

"And just what is *that* supposed to mean?"

"For Gen-boy it's too late. He beat you to it. It's been a month already." Laughter. "His mother's the last to know!"

"But he never... Oh, that *boy!*"

As ever, Emon was near them all and listened to their banter. And sometimes, as everyone moved in the dark, he searched their minds.

(There'll be trouble if she gets pregnant...)

(Ohhh, *big*. It'll *hurt*. What should I do if I'm forced too far?)

(I wonder who took my boy to Ōsen's place? I *know* he didn't go alone. Yard work for that boy tomorrow, lots. I'll teach *him*. And I was waiting so patiently...)

Emon's mind-reading powers intensified among them as he roved over their thoughts night after night. He could see so clearly into their thoughts that it was like focusing on bright scenes in a collage. He was therefore all the more puzzled by his mother, Ōsen. She was different. Didn't the thoughts of a human being exist in the mind of an idiot? The thoughts of the villagers were like clouds drifting in the blue sky, and what they thought was so transparent. But in Ōsen's mind thick white mist flowed always, hiding everything.

No words, no shapes, just emotion close to fear turning there...

As Emon kept peering into the mist, he began to feel that Ōsen let the men take her so that she might escape her fear. Emon gave up the search for his mother's mind and returned to the days of his endless reading.

His prodigious appetite for books impressed the villagers.

"What a bookworm!" one of them remarked. "That kid's *crazy* about books."

"You're telling me," another said. "He read all ours, too. Imagine, from Ōsen, a kid who likes *books*."

"Wonder who taught him to read..."

Visiting all the houses in the village, Emon would borrow books, and on the way he tried to piece together a picture of his mother's past by looking into everyone's minds. *Was Ōsen an idiot from the time she was born?* he wanted to know. But no one knew about Ōsen in any detail, and the only thoughts men entertained were for her beautiful face and body. Her body, perhaps ageless because of her imbecility, was a strangely narcotic necessity for the men.

A plaything for all the men of the village, was Ōsen, even for the youngest: for all who wished to know her body. Their dark lust Emon could not understand, but this emotion seemed to be all that kept the people living and moving in this lonesome place – a power that kept the village from splitting asunder.

Ōsen – madwoman, whore; she seized the men, and kept them from deserting the village for the enchantments of far-off cities.

5

A memory from when I was stationed in the village: in front of Old Lady Také's Youth Lodge some children are skipping rope. In my thoughts I hear:

First month – red snapper!
    hitotsuki – tai
Second month – then it's shells!
    futatsuki – kai
Third, we have reserve, and
    mittsu – enryode
Fourth – shall we offer shelter?
    yottsu – tomeru ka

The rope-skipping song I recorded earlier in this tale. A little more theory: with only a shift in syllabic division the song now seems to mean:

hitotsu	*kitai*
ONE	SHIP'S HULL

futatsu	*kikai*
TWO	MACHINES

And with but a single change of consonants we have:

mittsu	*nenryode*
THREE	FUEL

Almost like a checklist...

Eventually the day came when Emon entered school. He was given a new uniform and school bag, purchased with money from the village Confraternity of Heaven Special Fund, which had been created long ago to provide for Ōsen's house and living. Emon went happily to the Extension School, which was at the far end of the village. There, in the school's library, he could read to his heart's content.

Miss Yoshimura, the schoolteacher, was an ugly woman, long years past thirty, who had given up all hope of marriage almost from the time she was old enough to seriously consider it. Skinny as a withered sapling and gifted with a face that couldn't have been funnier, yet she was a kindhearted soul, and of all those in the village she had the richest imagination and most fascinating mind. Having read so many books, she knew about much more than anyone else; and the plots of the uncountable stories she had read and remembered! They merged like twisting roots in her imagination, until they seemed to be the real world, and "reality" a dream. Most important, though, where everyone else never let Emon forget his inferiority, only Miss Yoshimura cared about him as equal to the others. Emon readily became attached to her, and was with her from morning until evening.

One day the old master of the General Store came to Miss Yoshimura.

"Ma'am," he began, "Emon's smart as a whip, but there's gonna be trouble if he becomes, you know, grows up too early."

"Ahm, oh, well... " Miss Yoshimura said, flustered.

"Since he's got Ōsen's blood and what not," the old man went on assuringly, "and watches the youngsters get together at Old Lady Také's place... well, if he gets like Ōsen, there'll be trouble. Some girl'll wind up gettin' stuffed by him, sure enough."

Embarrassed, Miss Yoshimura said, "Well, what do you think it best to do then?"

"Now as to that, we was thinkin' since he dotes on you so, it might be better for him to stay at your lodgin' house. Of course, the Confraternity Fund'll pay all his board."

"All right, I don't mind at all," said Miss Yoshimura, perhaps a bit too quickly. "Of course, only if he *wants* to do it.... How I *do* pity the poor child..."

And in her thoughts an imaginary future flashed into existence, pulsing with hope – *no I could never marry but now I have a child whom I will raise as my own and days will come when we hesitate to bathe together oh Emon yes I'll be with you as you grow to manhood* – Her face reddened at her thoughts.

Emon came to live in her house, then, and happy days and months passed. Most happily, the other children ceased to make so much fun of him. And the men never came around to sleep with Miss Yoshimura as they did with Ōsen.

She avoided all men. Her mind shrieked rejection, that all men were nothing more than filthy beasts. Emon quite agreed. But what went on in her mind?

As much as she must hate and avoid men, Miss Yoshimura's thoughts were as burdened as any other's by a dark spinning shadow of lust, and come the night it would often explode, like furnace-hot winds out of hell.

Squeezing little Emon and tasting pain like strange bitter wine, Miss Yoshimura would curl up tightly on the floor with sharp, stifled gasps. The entangled bodies of men and women floated hugely through her thoughts, and while she tried to drive them away with one part of her mind, another part reached greedily for something else, grabbed, embraced, and caressed. Every word she knew related to sex melted throughout her mind.

Miss Yoshimura always sighed long and sadly, and delirious voices chuckled softly in her mind.

(*Oh, this will never do...*)

Denouements like this were quickly undone, usurped by their opposites, images flocking in her head, expanding like balloons filled with galaxies of sex words that flew to Ōsen's house. Miss Yoshimura fantasized herself as Ōsen, and grew sultry holding one of Ōsen's lovers. Then the lines of her dream converged on Old Lady Také's lodge, and she cried out desperately in the darkness:

"I'm a woman!"

Male and female shapes moved in the night around her...

She returned to her room, where moonlight came in shining against her body. She moaned and hugged Emon fiercely.

"*Sensei,* you're killing me!"

At the sound of Emon's voice, Miss Yoshimura momentarily regained herself – only to tumble yet again into the world of her fantasies.

(Emon, Emon, why don't you grow up...?)

Conviction grew in Emon's mind as the days turned:

In everyone's heart, including his dear *sensei's,* there lurked this ugly thing, this abnormal desire to possess another's body. *Why?* Emon did not realize that he saw only what he wished to see.

Everyone's desire. From desire are children born. I already know that. But who's my father?

He kept up his watch on the villager's minds, that he might unravel that mystery, and he continued to gather what scraps of knowledge that remained about his mother. More and more it appeared that she had escaped into her mad world to flee something unspeakably horrible.

In the mind of the General Store's proprietor he found this: (Ōsen's house... People say it was a ghost house in the old days, and then Ōsen was always cryin'. No, come to think about it, weren't it her mother? *Her* grandfather was killed or passed on. That's why she went crazy...)

Old Lady Také's thoughts once whispered:

(My dead grandmother used to say that they were hiding some crazy foreign man there, and he abused Ōsen, so they killed him, or something like that...)

And the murmuring thoughts of Toku the woodcutter gave forth a startling image:

(Granddad saw it. Ōsen's house was full of blood and everyone was dead, murdered. That household was crazy for generations, anyway. Ōsen's father – or was it her brother? – was terrible insane. An' in the middle a' all them hacked bodies, Ōsen was playin' with a ball.)

Old Genji knew part of the story, too:

(Heard tell it was a *long* time ago on the hill where the house is that the fiery column fell from the sky. Since around then all the beautiful girls were born in that family, generation after generation, an' couldn't one of 'em speak. That's the legend.)

Long ago, in days forgotten, something terrible happened. Ōsen alone of the family survived and went mad, and became the village harlot. This was all that was clear to Emon.

6

THEY SAY that time weathers memory away: in truth the weight of years bears down on memory, compressing it into hard, jewel-like clarity. A mystery slept in that village, and sleeps there still. Over the years my thoughts have annealed around these puzzling events, but the mystery will remain forever uncovered – unless I go there and investigate in earnest.

I have tried to return many times. A year ago I came to within fifty kilometers of the village and then, for no rational reason I can summon up, I turned aside, went to another, more *amenable* place. Before embarking on these journeys I am always overcome by an unshakable reluctance, almost as if I were under a hypnotic compulsion to stay clear of the place.

Another curious fact:

In all the time I was stationed there, I recall no else from the "outside" ever staying in the village more than a few hours; and according to the villagers, I was the first outsider to be seen at all in ten years. The only villagers who had lived outside those isolated reaches were Old Lady Také and Miss Yoshimura, who left to attend Teacher's College.

If, in going there, I actually managed to come near the village proper, unless the military backed me I feel certain the locals would somehow block my return.

Is there something, some power at work that governs these affairs?

Such a power would have a long, strong reach, to the effect that this village of fewer than two hundred people may exist outside the administration of the Japanese government. I say this because during the Pacific War no man from that village was ever inducted into the Armed Forces.

And who might wield such power? Who mesmerized everyone? Old Lady Také, or the Teacher? And if both of them left the village under another's direction, who then is the person central to the mystery?

The madwoman, Ōsen?

When summer evenings come, my memories are crowded with the numerous songs the village children sang. It was so queer that everything about those songs was at complete variance with the historical roots that those villagers claimed to have: that the village had been founded centuries earlier by fugitive retainers deserting the Heike Family during their final wars with the Genji in the Heian

Period, and that since that time no one had left the village. Yet none of the old stories lingering there were of Heike legends. It is almost as if the village slept in the cradle of its terraced fields, an island in the stream of history, divorced from the world.

Is something still hidden beneath the stone stairs leading up to Ōsen's house? "Unknown Emon" gave up in despair and abandoned something there. A pump to send water up to the well at Sinner's Hole, or something hinted at in the children's handball song:

I wonder if I'll ever climb
those weed-grown stairs someday
One – a stone stairway in the sky
Two – if it doesn't fly, if it never flies open...

When the day of flight comes, will the stairs open? Or must you open them in order to fly? – Questions, questions: it may be that the mystery of "unknown Emon" will sleep forever in that place.

And what became of Ōsen's child?

After a time Emon once again attempted what he long ago had given up on – a search of his mother's mind. The strange white mist shrouding Ōsen's thoughts was as thick as ever.

(*Begone!*)

Emon's thoughts thundered at the mist in a shock wave of telepathic power.

Perhaps the sending of a psychic command and the discharge of its meaning in the receiver's mind can be expressed in terms of physics, vectors of force; then again, it may just be that Emon's telepathic control had improved, and he was far more adept at plucking meaning out of confused backgrounds. Whatever: with his command, the mist in Ōsen's mind parted as if blown aside by a wind, and Emon peered within for the first time.

Her mind was like immensities of sky. Emon dipped quickly in and out many times, snatching at the fragmented leavings of his mother's past. The quantity was small, with no connecting threads of history: everything scenes in a shattered mosaic.

There was only one coherent vision among it all: a vast machine – or a building – was disintegrating around her, and a mixture of terrible pain and pleasure blazed from her as she was held in a man's embrace.

And that was *odd:* that out of all her many encounters with all the men of the village, only this one experience had been so powerful as to burn itself indelibly into her memory.

The age and face of this man were unclear. His image was like seaweed undulating in currents at the bottom of the sea. The event had occurred on a night when the moon or some other light was shining, for his body was bathed in a glittering blue radiance. All the other men Ōsen had known, lost forever in the white mist that filled her mind and robbed her will, and only *this* man whom Emon had never seen existed with a force of will and fervency. Joy flooded from the memory, and with it great sorrow.

Why this should be was beyond Emon's understanding.

A vague thought stirred: *This man Ōsen is remembering is my father...*

While Emon poked tirelessly through the flotsam in the minds of his mother and the villagers, Miss Yoshimura played in a fantasy world where her curiosity focused always on Ōsen. It was now customary for her to hold Emon at night as they lay down to sleep, and one night her heart was so swollen with the desire to be Ōsen and lay with any man that it seemed ready to burst.

How could she know that Emon understood her every thought?

How could anyone realize the terrible wealth of pure *fact* that Emon had amassed about their hidden lives?

But his constant buffeting in this storm of venery took its awful toll. Excluding the smallest of children, Emon was of the unswayable opinion that all the villagers were obscene beyond the powers of any description. Especially Ōsen and himself – they were the worst offenders. Through the minds of the men he was constantly privy to Ōsen's ceaseless, wanton rut, and the pain that he was Ōsen's child was heavy upon him. Ever she bared her body to the men, and...

Emon hated her. He hated the men who came to her, and in his superlative nine-year-old mind this wretched emotion was transformed into a seething hatred for all the human race.

It was on one of his infrequent visits to his mother that he at last vented his anger, and struck an approaching man with a hurled stone.

"Drop dead, you little bastard!" the man raged. "Don't go makin' any trouble, if you know what's good for you. Who d'ya think's keepin' you *alive!*"

Emon returned to the parlor after the man left and gazed at his silent mother's dazzling, naked body. He shook with unconcealed fury.

(I want to *kill* him! I *will* kill him! *Everybody!*)

Ōsen reached out to him then.

"My son, try to love them," she murmured. "You *must,* if you are to live..."

Stunned, Emon fell into her arms and clung to her.

For the first time in his life he wept, unable to control the flow of tears.

Moments later Ōsen ended it all by releasing him and standing aimlessly, and that was when Emon began to suspect – to hope! – that her madness might only be a consummate impersonation. But it may have only been one clear moment shining through the chaos. There was no sign that the madness roiling Ōsen's brain had in the least abated.

Emon little cared to think deeply about the meaning of Ōsen's words, and his hatred toward the human race still filled his heart. But now he visited his mother far more often. It was during one of these visits, as he sat on the porch beside Ōsen some days or weeks later, that Emon *heard* a strange voice.

The voice did not come as sound in the air, or as a voice reaching into his mind with shapes and contexts. It was a *calling*, and it was for Emon alone – a tautness to drag him to its source, a thrown rope pulling. Unusually garbed in a neat, plain cotton robe, Ōsen was staring down the long valley, her mind empty as always.

"Who is it?" Emon called.

Ōsen turned her head to watch Emon as he scrambled to his feet and shouted the question. The vacuous expression on her face suddenly blanched, frozen for an instant in a look of dread.

"Where are you!" Emon shouted.

As if pulled up by Emon's voice, Ōsen got slowly to her feet and pointed to the mountains massed on the horizon.

"It's over there," she said. "That way..."

Emon hardly glanced at her as he started down the stone stairs, and then he was gone. He didn't even try to look back.

Time froze in yellow sunlight for the madwoman, and then melted again. Ōsen wandered blindly about, wracked with sobs, at some point arriving at the small waterwheel shack that housed the village millstone. The violence of her weeping resounded against the boards. She may have lost her capacity for thought, but she could still feel the agony of this final parting from her only child.

One of the villagers, catching sight of her trembling figure as he passed by, approached her with a broad grin, reached for her body with calloused hands.

"Now, now, don't cry, Ōsen," he said. "Here, you'll feel lots better..."

The look she fixed him with was so hard and venom-filled, the first of its like he had ever seen from her. For a moment he felt a faint rousing of fear shake his heart, then slapped his work clothes with gusto and laughed at his own stupidity.

"Now what in hell..." And cursing Ōsen, he grabbed to force her to the grassy earth.

Ōsen slapped his hands away.

"Human *filth!*" she shouted clearly, commandingly. Her words echoed and re-echoed in the stony hollows around the water mill: "Be gone and *die!*"

As Emon hurried far off down the road, the witless villager walked placidly into Endworld Mere, a dreamy look transfixing his face as he sank unknown beneath the dark and secret waters.

In the bamboo grove white mist danced again on the back of the air, and a white naked woman-figure ran lightly, lightly, chasing a paper airplane that flew on and on forever.

At the *Sai no Kawara,* the earthly shore where children come to bewail the passing of those who have crossed over the Great Waters, there is a weather-beaten sign of wood inscribed with characters that can only be spottily read:

It seems so easy to wait one thousand – nay, ten thousand years... driven mad with longing for the Star of my native home...

– *First publication:* Hayakawa SF Magazine, *February 1975*

KAJIO SHINJI

Reiko's Universe Box
Translated by Toyoda Takashi and Gene van Troyer

"I WONDER who gave this to us?" Reiko, still wearing her coat, turned the gift in her hands.

The box, a forty-centimeter square, was so light that she thought it might well be empty. A myriad sparkling galaxies patterned the creamy wrapping paper and a satin ribbon with an elaborate bow like a star's corona bound it. Among the many wedding gifts, it really seemed out of place.

"Could it be a mistake? There's no card on it."

"Let's put it off till tomorrow," Ikutarō grumbled from the armchair. "I never imagined that a honeymoon would be this tiring."

"But... Just this one, dear. I'd like to see what's inside."

Giving up, he nodded. She smiled to him and started undoing the ribbon. "You should take off your coat, at least," he told his bride, then rose and went into the kitchen.

Inside the wrapping paper was a white carton. Embossed golden letters on it said: *The Universe Box... Presented by Fessenden & Co.*

"Isn't it strange? There're no names inside, either."

Ikutarō brought two cups of coffee and placed one in front of her.

"Have a coffee break. I guess they forgot to identify themselves in their haste."

He picked up a bundle of telegrams from their wedding well-wishers. Reiko opened the carton without finishing her coffee. A transparent cube came out, packed in Styrofoam pads.

At first she could see only absolute darkness in the cube. But, as her eyes focused, she began to make out small specks of light.

"Look! There's a universe inside!"

She set the universe box on the coffee table in front of her husband.

"Well, it must be a new type of decoration," he said drolly. "Did you know there are similar fantastic ornaments, using optical fiber or transparent bubbles of wax? Maybe this is just the latest variation. Anyway, I'm afraid we can't enjoy its beauty in this dinky apartment. We'll have to stash it in the closet till we can move into a bigger place."

Ikutarō's indifference couldn't have been plainer. His eyes quickly went back to the telegrams.

He paid more attention to what I said before we got married, Reiko thought.

A sheet of paper was still in the carton.

HOW TO USE THE UNIVERSE BOX

This box contains a real universe. You can use it for interior decoration. Furthermore, there is no need to worry about supplying energy as the box is powered by its own internal stellar processes. CAUTION: *Do not reset the dial on the lower part of the box. It controls the progression of time within the box.*

In case of product defect, we are ready to replace the whole box free of charge. Please send it back to our research and development department, postage collect.

FESSENDEN & CO.

How can I send it back when you don't give your address? she thought.

"Hey, I have a good idea." Ikutarō, a little irritated by his wife's divided attention, took the box and wrote something with a white marker pen along the black base: *In memory of our wedding... Ikutarō & Reiko* – "Now it'll remind us of our happiest moment whenever we see this note."

He showed her his inscription, his contented smile somewhat smug.

"Now that your curiosity about this gift is satisfied, you'd better put it away. We have to visit relatives and other people tomorrow, you know, to thank them. It's about time we hit the sack, since we have an early day tomorrow."

Reiko had yet to take off her coat. She nodded absently to him, still gazing into the compelling universe.

IKUTARÔ worked in the business section of a large trading company and often visited the office where Reiko had clerked and done secretarial duties – which, on his initiative, was how they met. He had that high-energy, push-forward spirit that every capable sales executive should have. Also, he had a sense of humor that always made her laugh loudly, even during office hours. His gentle eyes and tanned skin glowed, and he would hold his head higher to show his thick neck and chest when he talked about his university days as a soccer player.

He must be a good guy, she would tell herself, so she said "yes" without reservation when he asked her out – her first date ever, actually: not that she was too shy or selective, just that none of the guys until then had interested her enough. That's all. That, and she wasn't the kind of girl who went man hunting. She was a patient girl who could wait for Prince Charming on his white charger. And there he had been.

Their first date: a movie, a melodrama, her choice. He compromised, and it was a yawner even for her. *Once upon a time boy met girl – they had to overcome mediocre and stereotyped hardships to get together – they lived happily ever after. The End.* Reiko glanced at Ikutarō. He wasn't sleeping, but his glassy-eyed gaze fixed on the screen seemed absent-minded enough to suggest he had mastered sleeping with his eyes open.

After the movie they had tried to have a meaningful conversation for about an hour over drinks at a cocktail lounge. Only at the end did a common topic miraculously emerge: both of them had seen the Disney movie *Dumbo the Flying Elephant* when they were children. Talking about that movie kept them going for another half hour.

They parted after promising a second date. On their fifth date, two months later, Ikutarō took her hand and suddenly, naively but clearly, said: "Reiko, please give me your hand in marriage."

It was perhaps the most clichéd proposal imaginable – somehow that made it endearing – but she wasn't even sure she loved him. Maybe she did, because he must love her enough to propose – and even if she didn't, love might grow in her because of his evident love for her. Still, she wasn't sure and her uncertainty irritated her. She said she'd have to think it over, and when he phoned two fretful days later – days she had spent castigating herself for her indecisiveness – she accepted his proposal over the telephone.

She was a flexible girl, after all.

"Before I marry you, I have to tell you one thing," Ikutarō said as if he were laying out the ground rules for brokering a business deal. "I won't be coming home early or regularly. I'm a salesman with executive responsibilities, and I often have to entertain customers until late at night. Sometimes, I have to drink with them, sometimes play mahjong with them. But I think you can understand why I have to serve them this way – it's all for your happiness."

He said the same thing again just before, then just after, the wedding. To make her happy, he had to get more money. He had to work harder and longer than any of the other sales staff.

For three months after the wedding he would regularly call her to let her know what time he would be home. After that it became every other time. Then, it became once every three times. Nevertheless, every night she would prepare dinner and wait for his return.

"When I'm late, you don't have to wait up, Reiko," he told her, but not only did she not feel like going to bed alone, he wanted a baby – every night when he came home, he would ask for the signs – and they worked at bringing them about – and if she went to bed, she would sleep and not be in the most receptive mood for love-making.

On the other hand, while waiting for him she didn't feel like watching TV or reading books or magazines. She did housework, rearranged the contents of the refrigerator and the cupboards, and tinkered with the meals she prepared for him. You could say it was a form of meditation for her.

One night the weather was rather balmy, so she went out onto the veranda. Their rooms were on the third floor of an apartment tower, and from the veranda she could see the road to the bus stop. It was already past midnight. Reiko put her elbows on the dewing rail and placed her chin on her palms, waiting for Ikutarō's return without expectation.

"All this overtime might kill him, I'm afraid," she murmured to herself. "He works too hard. He must be completely exhausted."

Traffic below was sparse; only after long intervals would a lone car pass by. Soon, a taxi stopped beside their apartment. She could tell it was her husband even from this distance and in the dark. She noticed the heavy smell of alcohol about him when he came through the door.

"Oh, you're still up, are you?" That was all that he said. Then he went to bed – or maybe it's more accurate to say he collapsed into it – somewhat guiltily, she thought.

He was sound asleep – passed out probably – before his head hit the pillow.

Reiko thought that his mental fatigue must be almost unbearable. Anxious for his health, she put away the dinner dishes and the uneaten meal.

Such was life, though sometimes he ate the meals.

THE NEXT week, he came home unusually late. Reiko made not a single grumble about it, which might have made him uncomfortable.

"I'm trying hard to land a new customer right now," he said a little defensively before leaving for work the next morning. "The manager of the purchasing department at his trading company. He wants me to play mahjong with him every night."

That night, too, she waited for him out on the veranda. Tears sprang unexpectedly from her eyes, though she could not understand the reason at first. Then it came to her.

She was lonely.

She looked up at the night sky to stop her tears.

"There are no stars at all!" she said in a small surprised voice.

It had been a long time since last she had looked up at the stars. Smog blanketed the sky and hid the stars, which she had not realized until then. She felt a strange awe because she could not see them. Quietly, she went back into her room, wiping her tears.

And she remembered the universe box. There had been stars in that, she recalled, and with another jolt of surprise, realized that was the last time she had seen stars. *Where is it?* she wondered. She at last found the package in a corner of the closet, covered with a film of dust.

She hastily took it out of the carton.

Now she could see the details of the gift that she had looked over so closely that night so many months ago. There was a real universe enclosed within a transparent cube. Regardless of the bright light in her room, there was absolute darkness in the cube.

She looked closer.

Since the depth of the cube appeared to be only forty centimeters, she should have been able to see the opposite side of her living room through the cube. But all she could see was the seemingly impenetrable darkness in the box.

Is it a hologram? she wondered.

A star floated at the apparent center of the cube, by far the largest one. About seven centimeters in diameter, it was a white star around which she could see ten or more tinier points of light moving almost imperceptibly.

"Fascinating!" She sighed with wonder. Looking into the cube made her calm and peaceful. She sat there peering into the universe box until her husband returned. She barely noticed when he came in.

The next day she went shopping downtown, which was not usual for her. Ordinarily, she went to nearby supermarkets to shop for groceries and commodities. But this time she wanted books, and there were no comprehensive bookstores in the neighborhood. The multi-storey national chain bookstore on Chūo Boulevard, just down from the train station, was the place to go.

Reiko bought a book titled *Mysteries of Universe: A Practical Guide*. The universe box had aroused her curiosity, and this book struck her as elementary and easy enough to understand. Maybe she'd get a good idea of what was going on inside the universe box. At home, she poured over the book. The world of stars, until now almost completely unknown to her, seemed to blossom like a garden of colorful flowers before her eyes. She was hooked.

That night, waiting for Ikutarō, she watched the universe box on the kitchen table.

The largest star must be a "fixed" star, like our Sun, the book told her. *I wonder if it's a white giant, since it shines white,* she mused. *Anyway, it must be older than the Sun. So, all of these small bodies going around it are planets like the Earth.*

Little-by-little, the universe in the box showed changes. She could see the motion of the rice-grain-sized planets, though it was almost imperceptibly slow.

"Do these planets have moons?" she wondered. She observed closely, but could not tell for sure.

"Oh, I'd like to see a shooting star!"

At the time, she had yet to learn that a shooting star was actually a meteor entering the atmosphere that burns from air friction. But she wanted to make a wish that she would be able to have a good life with Ikutarō.

Her husband finally came home and had dinner with her. She was distracted by the universe box, and failed to respond to his questions a couple of times. He smiled bitterly, feeling guilty about her absentmindedness because his late night homecomings might be what made her this way – enchanted by the magic of the universe box.

One night, as she gazed into the universe box with her chin resting on her palms, she had an idea. She got up and turned off the lights. With the curtains drawn, there was only the light of the universe box shining thinly into the room.

She sat down again before the cube within the darkness. There were no sounds; only the light from the star was there. She felt as if she were somehow entering the miniature universe when she kept looking at it.

No, she thought, *this is not a miniature universe but my private universe.*

Then, it happened. Something gaseous with a white tail passed before her eyes.

"It's a comet!"

The comet in the universe box moved toward the star, maybe covering a millimeter a minute, trailing a long incandescent tail. Over the next few hours it seemed to grow in size, blazing spectacularly, and then it plunged into the star's corona and died with a brief flare. It was the first dramatic scene she had witnessed in the universe box. Appreciation – no, glee – filled her.

"This universe is really alive!"

If Reiko had been wondering why this small box attracted her so much, she stopped: she no longer felt the least lonely. For the first time she thought of giving the star and its family of planets names.

The central star should be Ikunōsuke, using part of her husband's name. Then, the planets came: they should be Tarō, Jirō, Saburō, and so on, following the traditional Japanese way of naming boys. Of the planets, Tarō was the largest, almost one third of the size of the central star, Ikunōsuke. She could tell the size of the planets by observing their day and night sides.

She didn't notice that her husband had entered the apartment.

"What on Earth are you doing without the lights!?" he demanded irritably. He smelled like whiskey.

She winced when he turned on the lights, feeling like she'd been yanked back into reality. *Is this real?* she wondered.

"That damned universe box again? You're still hooked?" He sounded even more annoyed. Reiko did not answer.

"I'm hungry. Do we have anything to eat?"

He was rummaging in the refrigerator. She hadn't prepared dinner. The clock struck ten o'clock. The resonance of the dry sound seemed to linger in the kitchen.

"Okay," Ikutarō said in disgust. "I'll go to bed. No dinner." He glanced sharply at her and added, "You'd better get to bed early. I'm leaving early tomorrow morning, too. I want breakfast."

She stared into the universe box for almost half an hour after he fell asleep.

SHE HAD already read more than ten books to learn about the universe: *Creation of the Universe, Development of the Stars, Types of the Galaxies, Types of the Stars, Neutron Stars, Black Holes, Quasars, Double Stars.* Many a word she had not known even existed before was now as familiar to her as mundane items on the grocery lists she less and less frequently wrote.

"Was it a Big Bang that started this universe in the box?" she asked herself while reading one of the books.

The phone rang persistently. Reiko idly picked up the receiver. It was a woman she didn't know.

"Give me Ikutarō, please." The husky female voice referred to her husband by his first name. Reiko absently told her that he wasn't home yet.

"Is this the wife, Reiko-san?" the mystery woman asked in a challenging tone.

"Yes, that's right," Reiko confirmed nonchalantly.

"Oh, it's nothing important." She hung up with a violent click. Reiko also hung up, glad to get back to the astronomy book, and promptly forgot the call. The sultry-voiced woman had been correct.

Ikutarō came home very late that night. When he found his wife sitting in the dark, staring as if hypnotized into the universe box, he said nothing to her. She thought vaguely that although she and her husband sat together, their minds were far apart. With her thoughts in the universe box, they might as well be farther away than the width of the infinite universe. To Ikutarō, the universe box was less than useless: it was ridiculous. He couldn't see the glorious auroral sheets of galaxies, starfields, nebulae, and solar systems flocking in his wife's mind. She just looked like some slack-faced drug addict.

Still in his Burberry mac, he smoked a few cigarettes, not bothering to hide his irritation and contempt. Maybe he had something to say. But, in the end, he went to bed without saying a word. They talked about nothing that night. Reiko was not angry. She cared nothing about the girl on the telephone. She just made it clear to herself that she was not depending on anybody.

It was just because she had nothing that she wanted to talk about with her husband. That night there was only silence in their universe box.

SUNDAY morning.

"What're you doing every day!?" Ikutarō cried out in angry surprise. He was looking in the refrigerator. "It's empty!"

Oh, I haven't been cooking lately, she thought. She'd been eating whatever breads and pastries she could buy in the convenience store on the ground floor of their apartment tower.

"You haven't done the laundry in days, and I can see cobwebs and dust bunnies everywhere! What are you *doing* at home!?" he shouted.

Reiko didn't answer or face her husband. She just gazed into the universe box. Her husband only sounded like a dog barking in the distance.

He had put on his Burberry mac and was standing behind her.

"I'm going out for a walk," he growled, and slammed the door on the way out.

Within the universe box, all the planets were about to line up.

With Ikunōsuke as the leader, the planets were moving into a straight line, Tarō, Jirō, Saburō, and the others, extending to her right from the near side of the box. A solar conjunction. Reiko sighed with awe. This fascinating dance of the many-colored, jewel-like planets in this tiny universe was only for her to appreciate.

It was a breathtaking view!

Reiko stood up to close the curtains for more darkness. This way, the illusion that she was floating in the universe box was more complete. As she sat watching the lined-up planets, a curious thought came to her.

Do any of the planets around Ikunōsuke have inhabitants like on Earth? It was a naive question, but... Maybe. And maybe there are some intelligent creatures there like the human race?

There should be, she concluded.

Then, maybe there's someone like me who is gazing into her own universe box, within which there may be a planet like the Earth, on which someone may be looking into her universe, within which... Maybe I'm in someone else's universe box and she's wondering about me and whether I might be here...!

She went on mumbling about the infinite regression of universe boxes wheeling through her head.

Ikutarō came home very late that night. His rage exploded when he found Reiko still at the universe box. He threw a matchbook on the table in front of her, which showed the name of a notorious hotel.

"I've been there until just a little while ago," he said ominously. Reiko contemplated the multiple universe boxes that seemed to have expanded all about her. Ikutarō thundered, *"Don't you* FEEL *anything?"*

She felt nothing at all. Everything was remote from her. What was that noise coming from the funny cartoon character confronting her?

"You've been like this for months! That freaking universe box is more important to you than me, isn't it!? Why don't you fight me? How can you be so indifferent to me when I'm screwing another woman!? Wanna hear the details? God! I should have thrown that box away that first night!"

She showed no sign that she'd heard a word he'd said.

"Look at me when I talk to you!" he shrieked.

Nothing.

"To hell with this!" Hysterically, Ikutarō hammered the universe box with a single blow from the side of his fist. It flew off the table, banged onto the floor, and skidded almost to the wall. There was an actinic flash from the box like a camera strobe going off.

This was the first time he had ever shown any violence to her. What was that all about? Reiko calmly picked up the box and held it closely, without noticing that the dial on the box had been turned during the incident. The flow of time in the universe box had accelerated drastically. As if caring for her own baby, she looked closely into the universe.

Ikunōsuke, the white giant, was not shining or rather, it had dimmed to the point of invisibility.

"The universe box seems to be broken," Reiko observed tonelessly.

"*Good!*" Ikutarō roared.

"Everything is over," she said without emotion. She knew it. Everything around her had fractured into disconnected frames of images like jostling panes of glass.

Ikutarō didn't say a word. He dropped heavily into the other chair with a huff, and they just sat there wordlessly, facing each other across the kitchen table.

He chain-smoked several cigarettes with quick puffs. Reiko looked into the dead darkness in the universe box. All the planets around Ikunōsuke were somewhere within that darkness. This universe box that she and Ikutarō lived in was in its own darkness.

Then, a slight change took place. She thought she saw one of the planets that used to orbit the star disappear into the darkness where the star used to be. The darkness guttered like a dim ember. She could see the other planets speeding towards the dark spot, which began to glow redly, and then some nearby stars appeared that were clearly moving towards the spot. She set the box on the table to get a clearer look.

"The universe box is still alive!" she joyously exclaimed. "It's just that Ikunōsuke became a black hole! The star must have shrunk smaller than the Schwarzschild radius!"

"Oh, for God's sake!" Ikutarō groaned. And began to look dangerous.

Reiko remembered this topic from the book about black holes. Normally, such a process would take a vast amount of time, but in this universe box, where time had been accelerated by the turned dial, planets, asteroids, comets, and even some nearby stars were attracted to it with amazing speed. Hundreds of thousands of years seemed to be passing with each instant.

Ikutarō looked like he was about to do something violent again, when the hotel matchbook on the kitchen table went skittering into the box through the transparent panel with a gush of air. *Whoosh!*

"Hey, what are you doing?" he cried out in surprise.

The cigarette he was smoking jerked from his fingers and shot after the matchbook. The kitchen table started to tremble. Small articles like the newspaper, towels, and clock went into the box as if by magic. *Woosh, woosh, whoosh!*

With the progress of time accelerated, Ikunōsuke, the white giant, had turned into a major black hole in nearly no time relative to their universe. With its tremendous mass, it started to attract nearby stars, gaining more mass and attraction. Now, the black hole had begun to attract articles outside the cube. Ikutarō was clinging to the table leg, crying.

He had no understanding of was happening, and his eyes were wide with terror. Now, larger items like the TV set, stereo, and toaster oven went into the small cube. Ikutarō finally lost his grip and his throat-ripping cry of terror was cut off as he was sucked head first into the cube. Bones cracked like he was being munched.

Reiko was not frightened at all. She felt like she was outside it all, looking in. Maybe she was. She'd been in there for a long time anyway, but outside looking in at the same time, and wondering if someone were watching her. Maybe that someone was her, and maybe this was the revenge of the universe box against her husband. Her universe, collapsing on them both. Her gaze fell on the inscription Ikutarō had scrawled so many months ago on the base with such irritation – almost like a prediction, now – *"In memory of our wedding... Ikutarō & Reiko –"*

That's the way she took it. Her universe box, her revenge.

With a joyful shriek, she dived after her husband.

– *First publication:* Hayakawa SF Magazine, *February 1981*

KAWAKAMI HIROMI

Mogera Wogura
Translated by Michael Emmerich

LET ME tell you about my mornings.

I'm an early riser. Most days, I wake up even earlier than my wife.

If the sun has risen, thin rays of light filter down through the cracks in the ceiling. I just lie there for a while, gazing up at all those rays of light trickling in.

No light appears on days when it's cloudy or raining, even if I wait. On the rare occasions when it snows, the room seems faintly bright even before dawn.

It's warm inside my futon, but the tip of my nose is cold. I want to rush into the bathroom right away, but I have a hard time making myself leave the futon.

After a while, my wife wakes up. She goes off to the toilet before I can manage to get up. My wife is a good riser; no sooner is she up than she's cleaning the house and setting the pot on the fire, humming all the while.

Eventually I get myself ready, and by the time I start making the rounds, checking up on the humans I picked up the previous day or the day before that or even earlier, a bright red fire is blazing in the fireplace, water is boiling away in the whistling kettle, and the whole room is fragrant with the wonderful scent of toast. My wife works fast.

The humans I've collected are in the next room.

Most of them are sprawled on the floor. There are tons of futons and blankets and pillows in there. Very few of the humans ask us if it's all right to use them. Some burrow down into the heaped-up blankets as soon as we take them into the room. Some push aside the humans who are already stretched out on the floor and snuggle up inside their nice, warm futons. Some keep wheeling around the room, stepping on the humans who are lying down. That's what these humans are like.

Even so, after half a day or so everyone settles down into his or her own place or territory or what have you, and silence descends on the room.

Every morning, I go around and give each human a few soft pats on the shoulder. First, this allows me to make sure they're still alive. Second, it gives me a chance to find out if they want to leave immediately, or if they'd prefer to stay a little longer.

I drag the dead ones out of the house and drop them down a hole that has been dug outside, even deeper into the earth. The hole extends more than a hundred meters below the surface. I didn't dig the hole. Neither did my wife. It took our ancestors generations to dig it, working at their own pace.

Originally, the hole was intended to be a place where our clan could drop its dead. But as time passed, our numbers dwindled; now, we have no one left in the world but our parents and our siblings, of which we each have two.

Our parents and siblings live even further south than Kyushu, in a place fairly deep down under the ground. They live quiet lives, free from interactions with humans. Every so often my wife's mother sends us letters, but all she says in them is that we ought to hurry up and get out of Tokyo, and come join them where they are. She seems to worry that my brother-in-law and sister-in-law might get the itch to move to Tokyo, too.

I can always tell which humans are likely to want to leave immediately because they respond when I touch their shoulders, lifting their faces to look up. The humans all have this forlorn look on their faces then. They keep their eyes locked on mine, perfectly still, and mutter things under their breath.

I give each human another soft pat on the shoulder, smiling warmly. Then I return to the main room, where my wife is, and have a few slices of crispy fried bacon, and yogurt with peach jam on top.

When I finish eating, my wife and I carry the big pot of gruel that she has cooked into the next room to give to the humans. My wife ladles the gruel into bowls; I get the humans to line up. Of course, you can't expect too much from these humans: before you know it they're cutting the line, or if they find it too much of a hassle to line up they just grab other people's bowls. They're all like that. Whenever they do something bad, I tell them to stop, and if they still don't stop I give them a swat with my claws and force them to listen. That's how I maintain order.

After all the gruel has been eaten, the room falls silent again. I start getting ready to go to work. My wife polishes the kitchen sink, then starts the washing machine, which moans as it spins. She comes to see me off; I throw open the trap door and go out into the street. I take my time walking to the station. I've got on my cashmere coat and my muffler. And I'm wearing my leather gloves. I get cold easily. I change trains twice on my way to work; the commute takes a little under an hour.

Arriving at work, I punch my timecard. While I'm waiting for one of the office girls to make tea I glance over the faxes that have been left on my desk. When I first came to work at this company, people sometimes threw rocks at me or pelted me with rotten vegetables and things, but over the years both my colleagues and my superiors seem to have grown accustomed to my presence.

The young humans who have joined the company in recent years don't even seem to notice how different I look. I don't think they consciously decide not to wonder about me, why my form is so unlike theirs; they simply can't be bothered. People sometimes make comments – "You're pretty hairy, aren't you?" – but no one openly stares at me anymore, or presses me for information about my background. Until a decade or so ago, people really gossiped a lot.

I sit at my computer until lunchtime, mostly dealing with statistics. Sometimes a young woman comes from general affairs and asks me to write out an address on an envelope in calligraphy, using a brush. I'm a good calligrapher. Everyone says I write sharper-looking characters than anyone else in the company.

I sit there quietly plowing through my assigned tasks until the time comes to open the box lunch that my wife has made me. I get cold even though the office is heated, so I put disposable heating pads on my stomach and lower back. Lunchtime rolls around right about the time the pads begin to lose their heat.

LET ME tell you about my lunch break.

When I finish eating my lunch, I carefully wrap up the empty box again and go give my hands a good washing. I wash off my face while I'm at it. I eat with chopsticks, but I also make good use of my claws and the palms of my hands. My hands get sticky from the oil, and little bits of food get stuck on the fur on my cheeks and around my mouth.

I don't know if it's because no one can stand the sight of me eating or because people see no reason to spend even their lunch breaks in the office, but either way the young woman manning the phones and I are the only two left in our section. There isn't a sound in the whole office, and it gets a little chilly.

I start feeling so cold that I go out to spend what remains of the lunch break in the park in front of the station.

There are lots of humans over in the park, holed up in cardboard shacks; I make it my practice to accept the hospitality of whoever's shack looks the warmest.

"Hey, you're not human, are you?" says the drifter, who has been scrutinizing my hands and feet and face as I crawl inside. These drifters look much more closely at me than the young humans at the office.

"Human? I should say not!" I say, puffing out my chest.

"Don't be so hoity-toity," the drifter chuckles. "You're just an animal."

"What do you mean by that! Humans are animals, too, aren't they?"

"Well, yeah. You've got a point there."

Our exchange typically comes to an end around then. These drifters aren't too talkative. The humans I collect aren't too talkative, either. Generally speaking, the humans in Tokyo have all become pretty closemouthed of late.

As I sit there with my back pressed up against the drifter's, I gradually start to feel warm. It's much warmer pressing up against a human back than it is in the office, even when it's raining – even, in fact, when it's snowing. And yet humans don't seem to huddle together very often. Sometimes I wonder why humans are so distant with one another.

I never pick up drifters. The humans I collect are more unstable than them.

I leave the drifter's cardboard shack and walk around for a while in the alleys that run behind the buildings near the station. There aren't any unstable humans there, not in the alleys. Strange though it may seem, they tend to appear in brighter, more open spaces. Around the kiosks in the station, for instance, or in well-lit coffee shops with wide glass windows, or in department stores.

There are cats in the alleys. Whenever they see me, their hair stands on end and they yowl at me. They say: *Giyaa!* Humans like cats, so they look displeased when cats cry *Giyaa!* at them. I try to steer clear of cats when I walk in the alleys.

Sometimes there's a hole near the end of an alley; when I scrunch up and burrow down inside, I find that the soil there is nice and soft. I dig into the soft soil with my claws, deeper and deeper. Sometimes I get carried away and end up tunneling all the way home. My wife bristles when she sees my wonderful cashmere coat all covered with dirt. I give her a kiss and make my way back through the tunnel.

Above ground, the sunlight is blinding. Even on cloudy days it takes a while after I emerge from the earth for my eyes to get used to the light; I have to wait a bit before I can even open them. I stand there for a moment, feeling the brightness through my tightly closed eyelids. The light feels cold. Even though it comes from the sun, it feels cold. My wife says this is because the sun is just too far away from the earth. Down inside the earth it's much warmer than above ground, because there you're closer to the lowest reaches of the earth, where the magma is. Even the humans I collect look much warmer sprawled out in the second room of our house than they did when they were above ground.

Eventually my eyes grow accustomed to the light, and I am able to open them. I brush the dirt from my coat, wrap my disheveled muffler around my neck again, and return to the office. By the time the lunch break draws to an end, the office is completely filled with humans. I switch on the monitor of my computer and call up rows and rows of figures from inside the hard drive. A young woman makes me some hot tea. I take sips of it, holding the teacup between my claws.

Sometimes my claws slip, and I drop the teacup on the floor. The young women rush right over and, without a word, begin sweeping up the fragments. The young women won't look me in the eye. None of the humans at work ever look me in the eye. They never try to talk to me, either.

I sit at my computer, tapping away on the keyboard with my claws.

LET ME tell you about my afternoons.

In the afternoon, sunlight gushes into the office and it gets a little warmer. There are three potted rubber plants lined up alongside the reception desk. On the way to the toilet, I sometimes blow off a bit of the dust that has accumulated on their leaves. Dust accumulates very quickly on the leaves of rubber plants. By the time the day is half done, they're already thinly coated with dust stirred up by passing humans.

In the toilet, I enter a stall. I'm smaller than humans are, so I can't quite reach an ordinary urinal. I'm about two-thirds as tall as a full-grown man. Once I went ahead and tried to urinate in the urinal anyway, with the predictable result: I couldn't really aim high enough, so I made a mess.

On the way to the toilet, I always talk a bit with the humans who do the cleaning in our building. In the afternoon, they can usually be found on the emergency stairs between the third and second floors. They lean against the wall, not speaking.

Sometimes the cleaning humans pass on a tip.

"There was one of *them* outside today."

They are the humans I collect.

"This guy today looked kind of dangerous."

"Oh? How did he look?"

"Like he might jump off a roof or something."

How unpleasant, the cleaning humans say to each other.

I mean, once, there was this guy who actually jumped, you know, and I saw him go. The humans say things like that, and then they laugh. *Aahaha.* I don't understand why they laugh at such moments. I don't laugh. I only laugh at happy times. The humans don't really seem to be laughing because they're happy. I just don't get humans.

I take out my memo pad and note down where they saw "one of *them*."

When I go back to the office and sit down at my computer, a young woman brings me some tea. The tea the young women make in the afternoon is always lukewarm. Maybe humans get tired in the afternoon. If they're tired they ought to go to sleep, but instead they keep their clothes on, nice and neat, and they sit on their chairs and get up and walk around and so on and so forth, tired all the while.

When I get tired, I lie down right away, in the office or the hall or wherever I am. I spread my cashmere coat over my body like a blanket and sink for some time into a profound sleep. The humans cut a wide swath around me when they pass, being careful not to step on me. I always try to lie down near the wall, so they ought to walk straight by without worrying. But they make a big arc, heels clicking on the floor in an especially busy way, coming nowhere near my supine form.

My whole body is cold when I wake up. I've been lying directly on the floor, so it's only natural. I leap up, causing a momentary buzz among the humans. There isn't actually a buzz, just a tremor of energy that shudders through the air. I can sense it.

The humans dislike me. It's been that way for ages. Back in my ancestors' time, no one could have imagined that the day would come when I would live my life like this, among humans. In the old days, humans used to hate our clan, and if they so much as caught sight of one of us they would shoot him with guns or jab him with spades or sprinkle poison all over the place. Boy, was that terrible.

Hardly anyone tries to attack me now. Humans no longer seem so sure of what they hate and what they like. Deep down at the core of their being they feel hatred for me, yet they let me stay on at the company as if everything were just fine. They tell themselves that they let me stay on because they need me. But most of the humans have no need for me at all. Truth be told, for the vast majority of humans, we who inhabit the earth's depths cause nothing but harm.

I walk slowly through the frigid ripples of attention, return to my computer, and wait for the lukewarm tea some young woman will bring. I check my e-mail and find any number of messages from humans writing to tell me that they came across "one of *them*" in such and such a place. I note down in my pad all the places where "one of *them*" was spotted, and when I've finished I erase the e-mails.

Day after day, the number of e-mails keeps rising. The muffled voices of humans who happen to have heard someone, somewhere, talking about me, keep pushing on and on in my direction, grow-ing like the slender roots of a plant working their way through a boulder.

I drink my lukewarm tea, then drop the teacup on the floor. Every so often I drop my teacup like this, on purpose. Their bodies seeth-ing with hatred, but without letting that hatred out, sending deep black waves rippling through the air in every direction, the humans begin sweeping up the fragments of my teacup.

I gaze at the figures on my computer screen, acting as if noth-ing had happened. The dim red light of the setting sun streams in through the glass of the office's wide windows. The sunset has ex-panded until it fills the sky. A raging sunset that occupies the entire sky over Tokyo.

I begin noting down in my pad the order in which I'll go collect *them*.

WHY DON'T I tell you about my evenings?

When I leave work, I always make a deep bow. The walls of the of-fice building are cloaked in a dusky twilight glow that makes things look wet, and it's hard to make out their edges. The lit-up windows are like square pieces of white paper floating in the air. The humans, on their way out of the office, keep their distance from me as I stand there bowing. The humans never turn to look back at the building after they've left. Even though they could die in the night, and then they wouldn't be coming back the next day. The humans just rush out and hurry on home.

Once I feel I've bowed enough, I start walking toward the part of town where all the action is.

The night is young. The darkness that fills the streets is still fairly light.

I go into a bar and order a draft beer. The young guy who comes to take my order shows a flicker of surprise at the hairiness of my body, but he takes the order without changing his expression. He doesn't take much time bringing out a snack to go along with the drink, either; he sets down a small bowl filled with slices of dried daikon.

The young guy only seems startled at first. He quickly gets used to me, and he comes out promptly with the dishes I keep ordering, one after the other. Deep fried tofu in broth, salt-grilled gizzard, yellowtail and daikon in soup, things like that.

"Say, have you seen any of *them* around here?" I ask sometime around the second bottle of warm sake.

"Oh no, *they* wouldn't come to a place like this!" replies the young man.

Looking around the bar, I see two or even three of *them*. One looks terribly tired, and the whites of his eyes are bleary; another is drooped over, his eyes so clear they're almost blue. The young guy hardly seems to notice when *they* order something; he just keeps bustling briskly around the room.

They slide off their chairs, wobble into walls. I stick out a claw and breezily grab hold of one of *them*, hooking him by his back. He dangles there for a while at the end of my claw, then gradually begins to shrink. It's not long before he's only half my size, and eventually he gets so small I can hold him in the palm of my hand.

Pinching him gingerly between two claws, I lower him into one of the pockets of my cashmere coat. He doesn't shout or try to resist, he just quietly slips down into my pocket. Almost as if he had been wanting this all along.

"Comes to thirty-five-hundred yen, sir," says the young guy who works at the bar, bringing the bill.

"There were a bunch of *them* here, you know," I tell him, taking one of *them* from my pocket, holding him gingerly between two fingers.

The young guy's eyes widen as he stares at the shrunken thing.

"I'll be darned! So we had some here too, huh?" he says, shrugging. He peers uneasily at the *thing*, which is flopped over with his eyes closed, and asks me, "What the hell are *they* anyway?"

"Good question. I'd say... I'm not really sure myself."

"But if you had to say more than that..." says the young guy, urging me on. I put the *thing* back in my pocket and think for a few moments. All of a sudden, over the course of the last decade, these *things* have started increasing in number. When my parents began to feel hopeless about things they always used to say they had "no more spirit to live." It strikes me that maybe that's what *they* are: humans who no longer have what my parents called "the spirit to live."

If they are left to their own devices, these *things* become empty. They themselves become empty, and then the places where they are, and then eventually even the areas around the places where they are. *They* make it all unreal.

You might expect them to die once they're empty, but they don't. Evidently it takes real power even to die.

People who don't die, but who don't live, either; who just are wherever they are, eating away at their surroundings. Eating away at themselves, too. When you get right down to it, that's what *they* are.

When was it, I wonder, the first time one of *them* fell underground, down into the place where I live. I heard a big thump, and when I went into the next room to see what had happened there was a human there. A human I'd never seen before. Of course, in those days my wife and I were still living quietly in our underground world, just the two of us, so we never had any interactions with humans.

"*I'm scared,*" said the human.

"What are you scared of?" my wife and I both asked at once.

"*Scared of it all,*" the human replied, still staring into space.

After that, we had a person a week, then one every five days, then one every three days. Little by little the frequency with which the humans came tumbling down increased, until at last one would drop into the next room every day, without fail.

At first, we just waited for the humans to fall. They would stay there in the next room for a while, then go back aboveground.

"Are you going back up?" I'd ask.

And in most cases the humans would reply:

"*I'm going.*"

Apparently the humans just had to stay underground for a while, and then, once they had done that, they were able to go back aboveground.

All kinds of humans dropped down into our house. We had kids with long arms and lanky legs, we had wobbly old folks, we had well-built adults. The humans all kept to themselves; their bodies gave the space around them a wild look.

Early on, my wife and I would dig a separate hole each time one of the humans who dropped into our house died, and we gave each body a careful burial. After a while we remembered the hole our ancestors had dug, and decided to throw the bodies in there. Humans grow cold and stiff when they die. We *Mogera wogura* also become cold and stiff. Humans cry when one of their number dies, but we don't. We cry when we're sad or when we feel hurt and angry. Death is simply a fact of life, so it doesn't make us sad. It doesn't make us feel hurt and angry. But when a human dies, even though the other humans are always so hollow and reticent and uninterested, they all come together and sob and wail, so that the next room resounds with their cries. They cry in such a way that they seem to be enjoying themselves. I just don't get humans.

I only started collecting humans a few years ago. Since I started going around pocketing humans, those who no longer even have the strength to come tumbling down underground, my nights have gotten busy. Following the sequence written out in my pad, I bustle busily along, gathering humans. They just sit there perfectly motionless, so it's easy to hook them with my claws.

I go around without a moment's rest all through the night, picking up humans, collecting more and more in the pockets of my cashmere coat.

I'LL TELL you about the wee hours of the night.

Now that I'm done gathering up the humans, I feel exhausted.

I walk soundlessly along the long black strip of asphalt. My pockets are full of humans. From time to time I pat the outsides of my pockets to make sure none of the humans are in danger of spilling out.

When I come to the entrance to our house, I raise the trapdoor and wriggle down below ground. My wife is waiting up for me. I've told her that she doesn't have to, but she says it's harder for her to get a good night's sleep if she gets up again after she's gone to bed. So she waits for me, wearing a nice thick sweater over her pajamas, sipping a cup of hot chocolate or warm milk.

"Welcome back!" says my wife in her gentle voice. She's a gentle-voiced *Mogera wogura*. All my wife's relatives are like that. My father-in-law and my brother-in-law both have gentle voices, and my mother-in-law's and my sister-in-law's voices sound just like my wife's, though their faces don't really look all that much alike.

Helping me out of my cashmere coat, my wife asks if I'd like a little rice in some tea or something; then, with a single quick gesture, she hangs my coat on the hanger. The pockets are bulging. My wife sticks a claw down into one of the pockets and gingerly extracts a human. One, two, three... She counts aloud as she lines them up on the table.

At first, the humans remain perfectly still. After a while they begin to scrabble about on the table, beginning with the relatively lively ones. As their movements grow more energetic, they gradually return to their original size. My wife and I carry them into the next room before they get to be too big and let them expand to their full size in there.

The humans who are already in the other room gaze on blankly as the little humans go back to being big humans. The humans I've just collected are universally blank. No matter how unnatural and strange something may appear to humans, they never lose their blank looks. Pretty much the only time they ever cry or blow their noses or otherwise express emotion is when one of their number dies.

Once my wife and I have seen that all the humans are back to their normal size, we sit down on either side of the table and drink a hot cup of fragrant, roasted-leaf tea. Sometimes we have a few rice crackers, too. We hardly ever talk about the humans. We don't talk about my work, either. We talk about other things. What was on sale that day at the supermarket. About how Chiro, at the pharmacy, just had puppies. About the fact that ever since she had her puppies, Chiro is always barking at my wife. My wife and I chat about this and that, sipping our fragrant tea.

In the next room, the humans climb down into the futons, under the blankets. Occasionally some of the humans will talk to each other. My wife and I press our ears to the wall that separates the next room from the living room and listen to their voices. The humans' voices are gentle. I'm only talking about the voices of the humans who drop into our house, and of the ones I collect. The humans at work don't have gentle voices at all.

"*Scary, isn't it.*"

"*Yeah, real scary... grass of remembrance... on the ancient eaves.*"

We have no idea what any of it means. Everything the humans say sounds like a broken machine. They just keep repeating *scary scary* or bellowing *oow oow*.

"*Scary*" is the word the humans say most often. I can't imagine what it is that scares them so much. Their faces blank, their voices gentle, the humans keep saying "*scary scary scary*" back and forth to each other, repeating this in a never-ending loop. What on earth do they find so frightening? And if they're so scared, why doesn't it show? I just don't get humans.

Shortly before my wife and I go to bed, we go into the next room, where the humans are.

We walk around saying things to them. Hey, that hat looks really great on you! What's your favorite food? That futon sure looks nice and warm! Little things like that. The humans reply to our questions with surprising alacrity. Though amongst themselves they hardly ever have a conversation worthy of the name. I like fish best, I'm particularly fond of rockfish, so I was sitting on the shore trying to catch myself some rockfish when this cat came up to me, it was a calico cat with white, black, and tea-colored stripes, and once I killed a cat and ate it but it wasn't any good. They come out with things like that, speaking very fluidly, without a pause.

My wife and I go off to bed and fall into a deep sleep.

All night long, cries and sighs come from the next room, where the humans are. At first my wife and I weren't used to those sounds, so we had trouble going to sleep; nowadays we drift off right away.

My wife snores a little. Apparently I snore a lot myself when I'm asleep.

I'LL TELL you about dawn.

Dawn is when we *Mogera wogura* bear our children.

My wife has had fifteen children so far. They were small, lively children, covered all over with soft hair. But they all died soon after they were born. Not a single one of our children survived. We dug a separate hole for each child, and gave each a careful burial.

The humans shed tears when they learned that our children died. Some of them cried even more vociferously than they had after one of their own number died. My wife and I don't cry, even when the death is that of a newborn child, because death is a fact of life. There are people among the humans I've collected who have strangled their own children, and yet they, even more than any of the others, howl and writhe as they cry. I just don't get humans.

It's not only *Mogera wogura*. Humans also tend to have children at dawn.

In the past decade or so, two of the humans have given birth to children. One had a boy, the other a girl. They were small, lively children, covered all over with soft hair. They were human babies, of course, and yet they looked just like baby *Mogera wogura*. None of the humans paid the slightest attention when they were born. The humans cry and generally make a tremendous fuss when one of them dies, but it seemed as if they didn't give a fart when the babies were born.

The moment the mothers laid eyes on their hairy babies, they tossed them away. Then they crawled right down into their futons and went to sleep. Both the mothers went back aboveground about two days after they had their babies, so the children were left to their own devices here underground. The humans didn't show the slightest interest when they saw them, hairy as they were.

My wife and I raised the children that the humans brought into the world. They grew claws and matured so quickly they hardly seemed human; after three years they were fully grown. We set them free aboveground, and they both scampered off somewhere. We haven't had word of them since.

When the sun rises, thin rays of light filter down through the cracks in the ceiling. I just lie there for a while, gazing up at all those rays of light trickling in. No light appears on days when it's cloudy or raining, even if I wait. On the rare occasions when it snows, the room seems faintly bright even before dawn.

It's warm inside my futon, but the tip of my nose is cold. I want to rush into the bathroom right away, but I have a hard time making myself leave the futon. After a while, my wife wakes up. She goes off to the toilet before I can manage to get up. My wife is a good riser; no sooner is she up than she's cleaning the house and setting the pot on the fire, humming all the while.

Eventually I get myself ready, and by the time I start making the rounds, checking up on the humans I picked up the previous day or the day before that or even earlier, a bright red fire is blazing in the fireplace, water is boiling away in the whistling kettle, and the whole room is fragrant with the wonderful scent of toast.

The next room is overflowing with humans. My wife and I drop the dead ones down the hole, separate the ones who are going to go back aboveground immediately from those who aren't, and distribute the gruel.

The humans all look very listless, as if they're dead. But they aren't dead. They keep eating away at their surroundings, eating away at themselves; they stay where they are, perfectly motionless – but they don't die. Here in our hole, unable to become *Mogera wogura* themselves, as human as ever, they wait for the time when they will be able to go back aboveground.

Some humans die before they are able to go back; then all the others shed tears and writhe about wildly on the floor, and for just a moment their faces, otherwise dead, light up.

– *First publication:* Ryūgū *(The Sea King's Palace), April 2002*

YOSHIMASU GŌZŌ

Adrenalin
Translated by the author and Marilyn Mei-Ling Chin

THREE o'clock, thirty-two minutes.
Mother Sun takes off her clothes at the entrance of summer.
Listen to the voice of the Spirit Diary: a righteous government
disappears. Cactus – midnight shower – a nude white body –
Mother Sun. Now, it is time for the first page of the Spirit Diary.

On the right corner of the Spirit Diary, a brook begins
from our southeast room. When you listen carefully, you can
hear a child's cry and a sweetheart's whisper... like
a cormorant that lost its nest. At the entrance of summer,
cries and whispers ride the brook, flow into mysterious sound.

1976, June sixteenth, Land of Fire. We open the first page
to the northeast region. The spirit's wheel quietly
turns. At the mouth of the river, I record the sounds that
will eventually disappear. I pray that someday a boy on
a bicycle will discover these sounds in a fossil.

I did not pass through hell
To you, spirits, I send an immediate telegram
To drink milk
To memorize the names of flowers

The universe twists its lips. When a child cries in the
receptacle of night, I begin to walk on a path leading to

a shrine. I bid farewell to my first lover. The path
was a river of fire. The lover was the daughter of fire.

Reeds sing
za za za za za

A wind blows, through reeds, za za za za za. When they
utter, a boy with faith in the spirits hears the signals of
the universe, places a stethoscope on a noble woman's
chest and listens to her work. Echoes of ancient ballads
subside.

Over the Birth Road, a swamp is a big house. A water oat, a
cut water oat, Mother Sun's lips are double vowels. I
listen carefully. I can listen quietly to the signals of
the universe and write poems. Za za za za za, placing a stethoscope
to an inlet of the swamp and to the noble woman, I take a shower.
There is a phone at the corner of my room, a brook that flows
beneath my legs.

Mother Sun, I am near a scandal. I am existing like a wet
river, water oat, a cut water oat. I write poems to tell
the real things: river for this, danger for that, lies for
this, sacrifices for that; and this, we call a white river bed.
To tell the real things, burn fire, imagine a spiral pagoda, it
is a phantasmal runner.

I did not pass through hell
I will save that until after I die

To you, children of spirits, I send an immediate telegram

To drink milk
To memorize the names of flowers

Some day, I will return
That day, I will start fire

The brook whispers
Hu rrrr lll – a dice

The first page of the Spirit Diary. A pebble – hu rrrr lll,
the brook whispers, we begin the first step. The first page
is the riverbed of hell.

"The Minister for Foreign Affairs of Japan requests all those
whom it may concern to allow the bearer, a Japanese national,
to pass freely and without hindrance and, in case of need, to
afford him or her every possible aid and protection."

Thus
The river whispers

Then
Tokyo is a responsive transmitting station

We are children of cilium and reeds
Yes

Reed's children... Cilium's...
   Stethoscope and shower

Ahhhhh, the echoes of ancient ballads subside
   The subway's go-ro go-ro
   Ka-Ka, the coupling of trains

Machine's hip bone sews
  the curve around Suidobashi

From a medical office to a pharmacy
  An old woman walks
  Like a line of haiku
  On a path of fire
  To the stone tombs

Then
Tokyo is a responsive
  Transmitting station
  Oh children of reeds
  Send a telegram to the Minister of Japan

  Yearn for the post-war
  Korean pork barbecues
The brook whispers

  These are not words from the spiritual world. I do not own a
  membership card. Without passport or ticket, I am all alone
  this sunny day. At the entrance of summer I show my
  hand-made visa. Mother Sun proves her existence. This noble
  woman washes her hair, takes a shower, and floats her
  mysterious love. These are not words from the spiritual world.

From the medical office to the pharmacy
Adrenalin's
River
Is

Crossed

ADRENALIN

From a transmitting station to a receiving station

Prepare one boat, there is an insane person who will cross the equinox PREPARE ONE BOAT

Local post office to the International Telegraph and Telephone:

Prepare a ferryman, give him his passport

Inside the Spirit Diary, a nurse's mysterious voice sings out: one drop of alcohol, surgical knife, adrenalin gauze. I am afraid to breathe; my voice is filled with blood. Continue the operation, alcohol, surgical knife, adrenalin gauze, adrenalin, a, d, r, e, n, a, l, i, n.

Mother Sun. One o'clock, thirty minutes. Standing on a ferry of the River of Fire, my ears cannot hear the phone. The river whispers, trees start to burn, my lungs branch out.

Speaking in a voice that cannot be a voice causes screams

On the left corner of an era, catch a glimpse of the mysterious brook's curve. That is the inlet. I make a raft, sew a soliloquy's echo, scoop gravel with my hand. River within river, the gangplank creaks under my feet.

One o'clock, fourteen minutes. Mother Sun is hairy. She is a peeping silkworm sewing through a spirit's circuit. A larvae walks through Birth Road, I hear its footsteps. Heart is a river of fire, heart is fire's daughter. At the entrance of summer, Mother Sun takes off her clothes. At the moment of birth, with all my strength and concentration, I look into the world. When the entrance of summer gasps, starts vibrating, grasps hair and cracks an egg – There is a white shadow behind a sliding paper door.

Uttering in a voice that is not a voice causes screams

At a quiet movie theater, I park my bicycle to look at the posters. I bought a torn ticket from the lady at the window. Already I hear the audience clapping.

Mother Sun rents out her house
Buys lemonade
Twice, thrice
I send a secret message

To you, Spirit's children, I send an immediate telegram
I did not pass through hell
Please drink milk
And memorize the names of flowers

1976, June twenty-first. Land of Fire, back from the northeast, I open the first page of the Spirit Diary. I saw the great rock. The giant rock vibrates. I walk on. An image of a woman appears from the rock. I walk on.

Wind blows. Inside my brain the wind blows. I can see a tower of burning fire. My ears are the spirits' ears. My eyes are the great pillars of Islam. My lips are wet in the Buddhist way. Christ on the cross comes to me like the wind. I saw the great rock. A boy stands by its side, a round stage extending far back. Soon, the great rock starts to walk.

Man's shadow walks silently
The face of a wall walks silently

The hall silently walks
  It is like a lake
The giant rock takes a step with its left leg
  The boy lags behind
Joins hands with the rock
  walks the lake

I feel an unmentionable deepness. For a moment, I completely
lose myself. There is the giant rock, there is the land of roots,
there is the soft universe vibrating quietly. The world twists
its lips. When a child cries in the receptacle of night, I begin
to walk on Birth Road, bid farewell to my first lover.

I write a letter, and make a fair copy. I write a love letter,
wind and reeds. To the sound of the giant rock's footsteps, I
write a love letter.

1976, August first, a window. The spirit's Diary has many limbs
like the Asura. Hu rrrr lll – hu rrrr lll, somewhere the voice
of the train conductor calls out. Oh intense heat of August, am
I hearing an auditory hallucination?

A righteous government disappears. I listen to the premonition –
cactus, midnight, shower, a nude white body.

Last night, I passed through hell
To you, children of spirits, I send an immediate telegram
To drink milk
To memorize the names of flowers

This message is the last of the Spirit Diary. Children of Summer,
did you write about the fine sky in your own diaries? I disappear,
leaving behind me a mysterious white cloud.

I did not pass through hell
But
I was born

   Speech finished
   Yours sincerely...

One drop of alcohol.

– First publication: Gendaishi Techō
(*Modern Poetry Notebook*)
September 1976

ASAKURA HISASHI

From Vertical to Horizontal

JAPANESE science fiction was reborn after World War II.

Uchūjin (Cosmic Dust) – a fanzine created by Shibano Takumi – started in 1957, and *SF Magazine* under the editorship of Fukushima Masami (published by Hayakawa Shobō) appeared at the end of 1960. Both magazines started to feature original Japanese stories as well as the translations of foreign language ones. Writers began to try their hands at this new type of fiction: Hoshi Shin'ichi, Komatsu Sakyō, Mitsuse Ryū, Mayumura Taku, Tsutsui Yasutaka, Hirai Kazumasa, Toyota Aritsune, Hanmura Ryō, and many, many others.

Before long, a short story titled "Bokko-chan" appeared in the June, 1963 issue of *Fantasy and Science Fiction.*

Editor Avram Davidson's notes to the story said: "The existence of a flourishing Japanese Science Fiction has been largely unnoticed in the United States... 'Bokko-chan' is the first Japanese SF story to appear here – and, so far as we know, to appear in any English language magazine. The author is a thirty-six year old retired Tokyo pharmacological manufacturer who now devotes all his time to writing Science Fiction, and his stories have been collected in three volumes... Noriyoshi Saitō, the translator, works for the Civil Aviation Bureau of the Ministry of Transportation, conducts a proprietorial school for students of English, and translates to and from both languages."

Even now I can remember my wonder and admiration when I heard this news in 1963. At that time I was an SF fan hoping to become a translator of English language SF, but this man was miles ahead of me, and moreover, an angle of ninety degrees apart. He had accomplished the feat of translating from vertical Japanese to horizontal English!

The next stage began with the International Science Fiction Symposium held in the summer of 1970. Under the leadership of Komatsu Sakyō, Science Fiction Writers of Japan invited foreign authors to the conference. Arthur C. Clarke, Brian W. Aldiss (Britain), Judith Merril (Canada), Frederik Pohl (U.S.A.), Vasilij Bereznoj, Eremei Parnov, Jurij Kagarlitskij, and Vasilij Zaharchenko (U.S.S.R.) accepted the invitation, and came to Japan. Three Japanese were in charge of interpretation: Yano Tetsu, pioneering writer and translator, Fukami Dan, translator of Russian SF, and Saitō-san of "Bokko-chan" fame. The five-day session was a great success, and its finale was a previewing of EXPO 70 in Osaka (Komatsu-san was a committeeman of EXPO too.)

And it was at this conference that Judith Merril suggested a Japanese science fiction translating project, and she volunteered for the job.

Next year, Yano-san visited Toronto, and worked with her. During his three months stay, the translation of Mitsuse Ryu's "The Sunset, 2217 AD" was completed. This story was later included in *Best Science Fiction for 1972* edited by Frederik Pohl. Merril translated one more story, this time with Prof. Tsuruta Kinya: Kita Morio's "The Empty Field."

Next spring, in 1972, Merril re-visited Japan, and stayed for six months. Publisher Hayakawa Shobō supplied her an apartment in Higashi-Koganei, a town near Tokyo. An assistance team was organized under Yano-san: Mori Yu, the editor of Hayakawa Shobo, and Itoh Norio and I, both translators of English language SF. At first I was awed to talk with this famous writer-anthologist, but she was a very sociable person, and soon I felt at ease.

The team visited Judy's apartment frequently, and one day, after the main work was done, we accompanied her shopping for supper. She was full of curiosity and asked us the names of vegetables or fish that seemed very alien to her. All we could answer were the Japanese names. Next time, we were armed with a pocket-sized Japanese–English dictionary.

Judy's translating method was very unorthodox. First, Japanese assistants typed a whole Japanese text in roman letters, then handwrote under every word their meanings in English. After a question-and-answer session, she began to work. After a time, smooth and coherent sentences miraculously started to appear. Her second visit produced the translations of Ishikawa Takashi's "The Road to the Sea," and Komatsu Sakyō's "The Savage Mouth."

After Judy went back to Canada, Yano-san started the Honyaku-Benkyō-kai (Translation Study Meeting) according to Judy's advice. The purpose of it was to improve the quality of our translations (horizontal-to-vertical type) with the aid of native speakers. In the beginning, Judy's team of assistants became the students, and the teacher was David Aylward, Judy's co-worker at the Spaced-Out Library in Toronto, who was staying in Japan then.

These meetings were held at Yano-san's house at first, but as the members increased, the problem of accommodation arose, and the meetings turned into overnight trips to various *minshuku* (guest houses). After David went back to Canada, many teachers joined our group through the network of Yano-san, Shibano-san, and the teachers themselves. We visited, on a monthly or bi-monthly basis, various scenic places and hot springs around the Tokyo area. In its heyday, twenty to thirty people attended these meetings. After the discussion and question-and-answer sessions came the most wonderful hours. We ate and drank, talked and laughed till late at night. These meetings continued to the middle of the 1990s – more than two decades. Moreover, the teachers, bless them, began translating Japanese SF into the English language!

Years passed, and here comes this new anthology. It's a great joy to find that many new stories are included, and that the former Benkyō-kai teachers – Dana Lewis, co-editors Grania Davis and Gene van Troyer, and the publisher of the book, Edward Lipsett of Kurodahan Press – played very important parts in this publication. One more big and happy surprise for me is to find that Judy had continued to work on the translations with David Aylward after she went back to Canada.

It is sad that Judy, Yano-san, Fukami-san and Saitō-san are no longer with us, but I hope they would be very delighted with this publication in heaven!

Translator as Hero
By Grania Davis

Wʜᴀᴛ ɪs the meaning of love? Most people, when asked that question, will first describe intense romantic feelings. But what about translating the phrase "I love a parade"? Does the parade-lover experience intense romantic feelings towards masks and marching music? More likely, our parade-lover simply enjoys a parade, and the correct translation would be "I enjoy a parade." This is the sort of challenge that translators face, every working day. And this is why the humble translator has become my hero in the twenty-first century global village, where language is often the Great Wall that separates peoples and cultures. The translator is by definition a humble hero, an egoless figure, who cannot replace an author's murky words with brighter, clearer words, yet must produce clarity. In my Tibetan-themed novel *The Rainbow Annals* (Avon, 1980; rpt. Wildside Press) a magical shaman often reappears in human form as "the old translator." I chose this metaphor because both the shaman and the translator act as a bridge between worlds.

How would you translate "Sierra Club" or "keep the X in Xmas?" These questions, and countless more, were the focus of intense discussions at the monthly meetings of the Japanese science fiction translators' group, the Honyaku Benkyō-kai, where Japanese translators and western guests gathered to sort out the precise meanings of words. I am no linguist, nor fluent in any foreign tongue, so this is where I was first introduced to the wonders and frustrations of translation.

Consider the complexities of translating science fiction and fantasy from Japanese to English, and the reverse. The nuances of language and culture are often very subtle, and Japanese uses three interchangeable alphabets! How many people are fluent in both languages, familiar with the SF&F genres, and able to capture the elusive "soul" of a story? Of course the Japanese translators have similar complaints about English, as they struggle with our slang-laden prose. That's why the best results can occur when Japanese and English-speaking translators work together in teams, to create a "group-mind" with the author.

I first visited Japan as a tourist in 1972. Judith Merril, the trail-blazing author and anthologist, was sojourning near Tokyo, and pioneering the method of group-translation. The work proceeded slowly, literally word-by-word, and by the time Judy Merril left Japan, a number of outstanding stories had been translated. Some appear in this anthology, *Speculative Japan*.

But more stories were needed to fill a collection. I returned to live with my family in Japan in 1979, in Zama, near neon-lit Tokyo, where I worked as a military historian for the U.S. Army Corps of Engineers. The translators of the Honyaku Benkyō-kai greeted me and my husband warmly. "We are crazy alcoholics and workaholics!" beamed the brilliant late SF author and translator, Yano Tetsu, who was the patriarch of the group, and whose haunting novella "The Legend of the Paper Spaceship" (heroically translated by Gene van Troyer and Ōshiro Tomoko) appears in this book.

Yano-san spoke the truth. The group worked and partied at a fast-forward Tokyo pace, with a keen sense of fun, humor, and creative energy. The translators' weekends became the highlight of our life in Japan. Each month we met at a train station on Saturday afternoon, and traveled together to a scenic spot – for spring blossoms or autumn leaf viewing on the slopes of Mt. Fuji, iris viewing in early summer, or perhaps a hot-spring resort or publisher's seaside villa. We stayed in charming Japanese inns, feasted on banquets of local

AFTERWORD

specialties – and talked and drank, laughed and talked far into the night. In the mornings, over our artfully arranged Japanese breakfast trays, we had serious discussions of hangovers. The weekend ended with Sunday sightseeing, more talk and laughter, and the long train ride home.

We worked hard too. Translations of English-language SF are popular in Japan, and the translators must meet strict deadlines. My husband, Dr. Stephen Davis, and I tried to explain complex and obscure English phrases, and the group helped me polish translations of intriguing Japanese stories. The work was full of wonder and excitement. It was a cross-cultural meeting of group-minds. We developed a keen appreciation for their dry wit, and their fine dry sake.

When I left Japan in 1980, there were enough stories, translated by Judy Merril and others, to fill an anthology. But Judy's original publisher had dropped the long-delayed project. Some of the stories were published individually in magazines, and these were reprinted by Martin H. Greenberg and John L. Apostolou in a collection titled *The Best Japanese Science Fiction Stories* (Dembner, 1989). That anthology has long been out of print, so a few of the very best, knock-out stories are reprinted again here. Many more stories remained unpublished, and new stories were being translated by hero-translators like Dana Lewis.

The World Science Fiction Convention in Yokohama, Japan in 2007 has brought new interest in translated Japanese SF&F. It was the right time for translator-author-co-editor-hero Gene van Troyer, and me, to dust off some extraordinary older stories, and track down some mind-bending newer stories, and create an entirely new anthology of outstanding Japanese science fiction and fantasy. Publisher-hero Edward Lipsett, and his esteemed colleagues at Kurodahan Press, shared this vision, and the result you hold is *Speculative Japan*.

The book includes an informative essay by Worldcon 2007 Fan

Guest of Honor, Mr. Japanese SF-hero, Shibano Takumi; and the weirdest story I have ever read in any language, "The Savage Mouth" by famed Worldcon 2007 Author Guest of Honor, Komatsu Sakyō.

One of the very first post-war Japanese SF stories ever published in English was "Bokko-chan" by renowned and prolific author Hoshi Shin'ichi, in *The Magazine of Fantasy and Science Fiction*, under the editorship of Avram Davidson in 1963. That was almost half a century ago, and since then, translations of Japanese SF&F have been hard for English language readers to find. Why? Perhaps it is because English-language readers are reluctant to look beyond their own linguistic borders. Perhaps it is because the very best Japanese SF&F tends to be mood-driven, instead of action-driven. Compare moody Japanese landscape paintings to life-like English landscapes. Yet Japan isn't all mists and moods. Much of the future seems to originate in Japan, with its micro-electronic and robotic technology, overcrowded and sometimes polluted environment, and the fast-paced energy of group-minds. The problems – and solutions – of the future are often happening in Japan right now.

Japanese science fiction gives us an insight into that future – often shocking, yet a witty and satiric insight. It is the hero-translators, such as Judith Merril and Yano Tetsu, Gene van Troyer (with his wife Ōshiro Tomoko) and Dana Lewis, Asakura Hisashi (who graciously contributed an historic memoir), and the other talented members of the hero-translators' group-mind, who enable us to enjoy these wonderful stories and their haunting insights. It was an honor to know them.

When I lived in Japan, Judy Merril was nicknamed "the demon grandmother," so I was nicknamed "the demon mother." A quarter-century later, I have become a "demon grandmother," and both Judith Merril and Yano Tetsu have passed on. The book you are holding is a rare treasure, and we dedicate it to their immortal memories.

CONTRIBUTORS

Asakura Hisashi
Author (From Vertical to Horizontal)

ASAKURA HISASHI is the pen name of Ōtani Zenji, who derived the "Asakura" portion of his pen name from "Arthur C. Clarke," the renowned British science fiction writer. He was born in Osaka in 1930, graduated from Osaka Foreign Language Institute, and after that worked as a *sarariman* for sixteen years from 1950 to 1966. He started translating Science Fiction in 1962, quit his day job four years later to take up full time translating, and to date has translated about a hundred SF novels and short-story collections (and about forty non-SF books). The first novel he translated was Henry Kuttner's *Mutant*, and the most recent is Ron Goulart's *Ghost Breaker*. Between them, he has translated works by Poul Anderson, Philip K. Dick, William Gibson, Harry Harrison, Fritz Leiber, Alan Lightman, James Tiptree, Jr, Jack Vance, Kurt Vonnegut, and many others. He also translated Judith Merril's "What Do You Mean – Science? / Fiction?" in 1971, and in 2006 Hayakawa Publishing issued his memoirs, *When I Met a Kangaroo* ("Boku ga Kangaloo ni deatta koro"), referring to the kangaroo logo used for many years by Pocketbooks, Inc.

David Aylward
Translator (A Time for Revolution; Another Prince of Wales)

DAVID AYLWARD has been an active participant in the Toronto literary scene since the early 1960s. In 1965 he co-founded Ganglia Press, which became a leading force in the concrete and visual poetry movement in Canada; he was also an editor of the avant-garde poetry magazine *grOnk*. Aylward was a student at Waseda University in the late 1960s and early 1970s, and consulted closely with the many translators in the Honyaku Benkyō-kai. After returning to Toronto, he worked for a time with Judith Merril at the Spaced Out library of Science Fiction and Fantasy. His translations include (with Anthony Liman) *Waves: Two Short Novels* by Ibusé Masuji (Hokuseido Press, 1986), *A Darkening Sea: Poems of Matsuo Bashō* (Maki Press, 1975), and (with Gerry Shikatani), *Paper Doors: An Anthology of Japanese-Canadian Poetry* (Coach House Press, 1981). Aylward's present-day activities are unknown to the editors, and they hope he sees this anthology and gets in touch with them.

Xavier Bensky
Translator ("Collective Reason": A Proposal)

HAVING WRITTEN his East Asian Studies M.A. thesis on *manzai* comedy at McGill University, Xavier Bensky is now completing a Ph.D. on Meiji era science fiction literature at the University of Chicago. In addition to Shibano Takumi's *Shūdan risei no teishō* (Collective Reason: A Proposal), he has also translated Ōshita Udaru's essay *Kagaku shosetsu kenkyu* (A Study on the Scientific Novel) and is currently working on a translation of Meiji SF pioneer Oshikawa Shunro's 1900 novel *Kaitei gunkan* (The Undersea Warship). Born of French and Australian parents, he is fluent in French as well as Japanese and English. He currently lives in Tokyo with his wife, Yuri, and son, Leo, and enjoys *rakugo* in his spare time.

Alfred Birnbaum

Translator (Girl)

ALFRED BIRNBAUM (born 1957 in Washington State) is from America but has lived in Japan since early childhood. He is a graduate of the University of Southern California. He translated Murakami Haruki's first novels, *A Wild Sheep Chase* and *Hardboiled Wonderland and the End of the World*, and short stories beginning with "Hear the Wind Sing," followed by "Dance, Dance, Dance," "Wind-Up," "Bird Chron-
[...] to translating other Japanese authors, [...]is own books, like *Monkey Brain Sushi* [...] *Cats* (Weaterhill, 1993).

[...]ng Chin

[...])

[...]orn in Hong Kong in 1955, where her [...]hild, Chin immigrated to the United [...]nd, Oregon. Chin received her B.A. in [...]iversity of Massachusetts (1977) and [...]f Iowa (1981). Chin is the author of [...]of poetry, including *Dwarf Bamboo* [...]*he Phoenix Gone, the Terrace Empty* [...]ore recently *Rhapsody in Plain Yel-* [...]os, Chin was also a translator for [...]n at the University of Iowa, where [...]*ns of Ai Qing* with Eugene Eoyang

Grania Davis

Editor; Translator (I'll Get Rid of Your Discontent)

GRANIA DAVIS is a respected author and editor of science fiction and fantasy. In addition to her highly-regarded fiction, she has edited the posthumous work of the late, great Avram Davidson. She was introduced to Japanese science fiction in the 1970s by Judith Merril, who welcomed her as a co-editor for a projected anthology of Japanese SF, and during 1979–80 she was resident in Zama, Japan, where she worked with members of the Science Fiction Writers of Japan's Honyaku Benkyō-kai on a number of translations for the anthology. Her novels include *The Rainbow Annals* (1980), *The Great Perpendicular Path* (1980), and *Moonbird* (1986); and in collaboration with her former-late-husband Avram Davidson, *Marco Polo and the Sleeping Beauty* (1988), and *The Boss in the Wall: A Treatise on the House Devil* (1998), She co-edited (with Henry Wessells) Avram Davidson's posthumous Vergil Magus novel, *The Scarlet Fig: Or Slowly Through a Land of Stone* (2005). Her Avram Davidson anthologies include the award winning *The Avram Davidson Treasury* (with Robert Silverberg, 1998), *The Investigations of Avram Davidson* (with Richard A. Lupoff, 1999), *Everybody Has Somebody in Heaven: Essential Jewish Tales of the Spirit* (with Jack Dann, 2000), *The Other 19th Century* (with Henry Wessells, 2001) and *!Limekiller!* (with Henry Wessells, 2003). Her short stories have appeared in numerous science fiction magazines, original anthologies, and best of the year collections. She grew up in Milwaukee and Hollywood, California, and has lived and worked at various times in bustling New York; on the slopes of volcanoes in Amecameca, Mexico and more recently in Rotorua, New Zealand; on a sandbar in Belize; in a Tibetan refugee settlement in the Indian Himalayas; near neon-lit Tokyo, where she worked as a military historian; and at the beach on North Shore, Oahu, Hawaii, where she graduated from the University of Hawaii. She currently lives in San Rafael, Marin County, California, with her family and cats, where she is working on a collection of her own stories, and editing and publishing Avram Davidson's posthumous literary estate.

Michael Emmerich
Translator (Mogera Wogura)

MICHAEL EMMERICH has translated eleven books from Japanese, including Kawabata Yasunari's *First Snow on Fuji*; Takahashi Gen'ichirō's *Sayonara, Gangsters*; Banana Yoshimoto's *Asleep, Goodbye, Tsugumi*, and *Hardboiled/Hardluck*; Akasaka Mari's *Vibrator*; and Yamada Taichi's *In Search of a Distant Voice*. At the time this collection of stories was compiled, he was finishing his Doctoral studies in Japanese literature.

Fukushima Masami
Author (The Flower's Life Is Short)

FUKUSHIMA MASAMI is without a doubt a Grand Master of Japanese science fiction and fantasy. He was born in February, 1929, in Toyohara, Sakhalin Island (now Russian territory). He studied French literature at Meiji University, but left school in midcourse to pursue his calling as a translator, editor, and author of fiction, television dramas, manga and SF&F criticism. He was the founding editor of *Hayakawa SF Magazine* in 1960 and a key figure in the introduction of SF to Japan at a time when it was not yet even recognized as a literary genre, and fostered the development SF writers and translators in Japan as *SF Magazine*'s editor. In short, he was a main force in the spread of SF in Japan. After leaving the publisher Hayakawa Shobō as an editor, he returned to full time writing and played an active part in the field's continuing development in prose, cinema, and manga. His career was cut short when he fell ill in April, 1976 and died at the age of fifty-seven.

Hanmura Ryō
Author (Cardboard Box)

HANMURA RYŌ was a first class original, and is considered one of the three pillars of Japanese SF (with Komatsu Sakyō and Hoshi Shin'ichi). The community suffered a devastating loss in 2002 when he died unexpectedly of pneumonia. Between 1972 and 1973, the former cabaret bartender and radio talk show personality won the Seiun Award for SF, the Izumi Kyoka Prize for literature of the fantastic, the Naoki Prize for best popular fiction, and the Nihon SF Taisho (Japan SF Grand Prize). Born in Tokyo in 1933, he virtually invented alternative history in Japan with novels like 1972's *Ishi no Ketsumyaku* (Bloodline of the Rock) about a clan of vampires shaping the course of Japanese history and modern politics, and 1973's *Sanreizan Hiroku* (Secret Record of Sanrei Mountain) of aliens influencing human history. His ever-popular 1971 novel *Sengoku Jieitai* (Warring States SDF) dropped a small unit of Japan's Self-Defense Force through a time hole into the middle of Japan's Warring States period, where they find that Oda Nobunaga, the great unifier of Japan, doesn't yet exist, and take it upon themselves to unify the nation in his stead. The novel has twice been made into popular movies. A seemingly effortless writer, Hanmura wrote eighteen major novels and series, and scores upon scores of short stories, essays and reviews. His tales ranged from science fiction and fantasy to tales of the bar girls and club mamas plying Tokyo's *mizu shobai* water trade. He is sorely missed.

M. Hattori
Translator (I'll Get Rid of Your Discontent)

M. HATTORI worked on his translation with Grania Davis when Ms. Davis was in Japan in 1979–1980. Unfortunately, they lost touch with each other over the years. The editors hope Mr. Hattori sees this anthology and gets in touch with them.

Hirai Kazumasa
Author (A Time for Revolution)

HIRAI KAZUMASA was born in 1938 in the port city of Yokosuka, near Yokohama. He started writing while still a student in the Chuo University School of Law, and his debut short story, "Homicide Zone," won an honorable mention in *Hayakawa SF Magazine's* first New SF Writer's Story Contest, in 1961. In 1963 he took charge of the TBS television cartoon series "Hachiman" (Eight Men – but also a pun on "eighty-thousand" and "bee men"), which under his direction became a sensational hit with viewers. In 1971 he launched the explosively popular *Wolf Guy* manga series, with the publication of *Harmageddon*. He began serializing Japan's first online novel, *Bohemian-garasu* (Bohemian Glass), in 1994. Since 1997, he has been working on the *New Wolf Guy* series.

Ishikawa Takashi
Author (The Road to the Sea)

ISHIKAWA TAKASHI was born on September 17, 1930, in Ehime Prefecture, and graduated from Tokyo University with a degree in French literature. While holding down his day job as a reporter for Mainichi News, he has produced a respectable body of novels and short story collections. He is a past president of the Japan Mystery Writers Association and is also a member of the International PEN Club of Japan and Science Fiction and Fantasy Writers of Japan. He is a past recipient of the Japan SF Grand Prize, the Edogawa Rampo Prize for mystery writing, the Yokomizo Seishi Prize, and the 31st (1978) Japan Mystery Writers Award for criticism. He is also well known among horse racing aficionados for his occasional commentaries on television.

Kajio Shinji
Author (Reiko's Universe Box)

KAJIO SHINJI was born in 1947. While running his inherited string of gasoline stand franchises, Kajio wrote science fiction stories on the side for decades, managing an exquisite and successful balancing act until 2004, when he finally decided to put the important things first and become a fulltime writer. He has been a part of the science fiction community since middle school, when he began participating in Shibano Takumi's famous *Uchūjin* fanzine. He also made his professional debut through *Uchūjin*, when his "Pearls for Ria" short story published there in 1970 was snapped up to run in Hayakawa's *SF Magazine* the following year. This beautiful and haunting love story remains a favorite of many SF fans in Japan today.

Among other awards, he has won the Japan SF Grand Prize once, and the Seiun Award three times, including one for "Ashibiki Daydream," a story in his *Emanon* cycle. In 1979 he released the first story in this popular cycle, establishing himself as a leader in the Japanese science fiction community and making Emanon a permanent feature in the Japanese SF landscape. He has continued to add to the *Emanon* cycle since, adapting it to cover a staggering range of themes and ideas that still lure and capture new fans. While he is breaking new ground as a mainstream author today, with a film based on a bestseller already in hand, he remains the master of humorous SF in Japan: often emulated but rarely equaled for delightfully imaginative and downright funny twists, seasoning what are still, at the core, seriously thought-provoking tales.

Katō Naoyuki
Cover artist

KATŌ NAOYUKI was born in 1952; he started work as a fan artist in 1971 and made his first professional sale in 1973. His 1974 debut in

SF Magazine, a leading Japanese science fiction monthly, initiated a string of appearances in many important publications, culminating in his receipt of the 18th Seiun Award (the Japanese Hugo) for art in 1979. He has continued to create art for *SF Magazine* and other periodicals, paperbacks (such as the Legend of Galactic Heroes series, for which he also handled mechanical design), games (most of the Traveller series), and posters, as well as a host of models based on his realistic and quasi-organic designs. He has issued three cover collections in Japan, and currently serves as a director of the Japanese Publication Artist League.

Kawakami Hiromi
Author (Mogera Wogura)

KAWAKAMI HIROMI, born in Tokyo in 1958, is the author of more than twenty novels, short stories, and essays. She made her first debut in 1980 as "Yamada Hiromi" in *NW-SF* #16, edited by Yamano Kōichi and Yamada Kazuko, with the story *So-shimoku* ("Diptera"), and also helped edit some early issues of *NW-SF* in the 1970s.

She reinvented herself as a writer and made her second debut in mainstream literature in the 1990s and won a variety of major literary awards, among them the first Pascal Prize for a Short Story by a New Writer in 1994 for her story "Kamisama"; and the prestigious Akutagawa Prize for her novel *Hebi o fumu* (Step on a Snake), which was published in 1996. Kawakami began writing fiction as an undergraduate at Ochanomizu Women's University, where she belonged to the "Science Fiction Study Group." After graduating, she taught science at the high school level until she married and retired to raise her two boys in the mid-1980s.

"Fiction celebrates the wonder and the beauty of the most unassuming things and savors the flavor of the insignificant," she remarked in her commemorative lecture held after receiving the

Tanizaki Jun'ichiro Prize, "and these aspects of the novel engage my interest most at this point in my writing."

Komatsu Sakyō
Author (The Savage Mouth)

KOMATSU SAKYŌ stands shoulder-to-shoulder with Yano Tetsu as a Grand Master pillar of Japanese SF. Where Yano is known as "The Grand Old Man," Komatsu is most often referred to as "The King of Japanese SF," and if comparisons must be sought, he is rather like Isaac Asimov: a renaissance man of encyclopedic knowledge and a near photographic memory. He stormed the scene in 1960, when he entered the first Japanese SF Contest, which was jointly sponsored by Toho Studios, home to *Godzilla* and other films, and Hayakawa Shobō, the publisher of *SF Magazine*. Komatsu's entry received no more than an honorable mention. Toho, being more concerned with ideas for films, made only brief comments on Komatsu's highly literate story, but the assessment of the magazine editors was lengthy, and *SF Magazine* soon asked Komatsu to edit the prize-winning stories: even though the ideas in them were good, the quality of writing was too low to publish them in the magazine as they were. Komatsu is perhaps best known among non-Japanese readers for his novel *Nihon Chinbotsu* (Japan Sinks).

Kōno Tensei
Author (Hikari)

KŌNO TENSEI is a prolific, genre-spanning writer whose forays into science fiction and fantasy have given the field some of its most delicate fables of Everyman meeting the unknown in his own backyard. Born in 1935 on the island of Shikoku, he went to college in Tokyo and stayed on in the capital, writing mysteries, TV dramas, and the fantastical *Machi no Hakubutsukan* (Street Museum) series and

Painting Knife no Gunzō (Images of a Painting Knife) short story collections. Awarded the 17th Mystery Writers of Japan Award in 1963 for his *Satsui to iu Na no Kachiku* (That Animal Called Murderous Intent), he was nominated for the prestigious Naoki Prize for fiction for *Painting Knife* in 1974. When not writing fiction, he has penned numerous books and essays about his other great passions: jazz and ethnomusicology.

Dana Lewis
Translator (Hikari; Where Do the Birds Fly Now?; Standing Woman)

DANA LEWIS was on her second trip to Japan when she went searching for Japanese science fiction in a bookstore in Kobe, and came out with a copy of *SF Magazine* and Yamano Kōichi's *Where Do the Birds Fly Now* short story collection. She chose the book simply because it was the thinnest volume in the shop's small selection, but it was a fortuitous call. It started her on a reading binge and occasional forays into SF translation that continues to this day. Spending some seventeen years in Japan over a series of extended stays, she has also translated thousands of pages of manga. She is a proud survivor (with Gene van Troyer) of the infamous and unforgettable Honyaku Benkyō-kai gatherings presided over by the irascible Yano Tetsu in the 1970s and early '80s. She has slept on the floor at the offices of Yamano's magazine *NW–SF*, and counts herself fortunate to have lent her own living room sofa bed to Judith Merril for a night in Ann Arbor long ago, while they went over early versions of several of the Merril translations in this anthology. She is a regular translator for *The Dirty Pair* series of manga novels.

Mayumura Taku
Author (I'll Get Rid of Your Discontent)

MAYUMURA TAKU is the pen name of Murakami Takuji. Born in

1934, he began making his first appearances in professional fiction magazines in 1961, and he has won numerous awards. He could be regarded in some sense as a "transitional" author – one who bridges "old school" Japanese SF, with its reliance on tropes and themes drawn from Anglo-American SF, and the "newer school" of authors who, in the late 1960s, began exploring a distinctively Japanese SF voice that reflected a Japanese view of the post-industrial world. Drawing on his experience as a *sarariman* (a salaried corporate worker) at a large manufacturer, his stories often feature bureaucracy and depersonalization as central themes. He is also regarded as one of the few early post-WWII Japanese SF authors to work on a consistent "future history theme" in his Administrator (or Governor) Series of stories and novels. A collection of four Administrator novelettes was published in English by Kurodahan Press in 2004 as *Administrator*.

Ōhara Mariko
Author (Girl)

ŌHARA MARIKO says she got into fiction writing at age ten. "I was strongly conscious of myself being a natural liar," she says. "I incorporated my lies into the form of novels; otherwise fiction would have always invaded my life, hurting me and the people around me." Great influences in her writing career have been A.E. van Vogt and Cordwainer Smith. Her first published story, *Hitori de Aruite Itta Neko* (The Cat Who Walked Alone) won second place in the Sixth Hayakawa SF Contest in 1980, and she received a Seiun Award in 1991 for her story *Haiburiddo Chairudo* (Hybrid Child). Since 1997 she has been working on a space opera series, *Archaic States*, for *Hayakawa SF Magazine*, in which galaxies war with each other in the twenty-eighth century. Ōhara also writes for the burgeoning Japanese comics industry, and does scenarios for video games and radio dramas. In addition to this, she writes critical essays and reviews, served as a past president of the Science Fiction and Fantasy Writers of Japan, and has co-edited several volumes of the *SF Baka Bon* series (Collected Slapstick SF Stories).

Judith Merril
Translator (The Savage Mouth; The Road to the Sea; The Flower's Life is Short)

See "Judy-san: Judith Merril, 1923–1997" *starting on page 1.*

Ōshiro Tomoko
Translator (The Legend of the Paper Spaceship)

ŌSHIRO TOMOKO (VAN TROYER) was born in Okinawa in 1948. She is now a professor of Japanese language studies at Okinawa International University and has published numerous academic articles about Japanese language teaching, in addition to language learning textbooks.

Shibano Takumi
Author ("Collective Reason": A Proposal)

SHIBANO TAKUMI is Japan's Mr. Science Fiction. He began writing SF as Rei Kozumi while a high-school mathematics teacher – a job he quit in 1977 to become a full-time translator – and he published his first short story in 1951. Later, 1969–75, he published three SF juveniles, including *Hokkyoku Shi No Hanran* (Revolt in North-Pole City) (1977). But his influence on Japanese SF has been more in his work as editor and publisher of the widely circulated *Uchūjin* (1957–current), the first Japanese fanzine – some would say semi-prozine – in which many stories by later-prominent SF writers – such as Komatsu Sakyō – were published. *Uchūjin* reached issue #190 in 1991 and continues to introduce new writers. Shibano has received many

SF awards; and the "Takumi Shibano Award," given since 1982 to people who have performed generous work in fandom, was named after him. As a translator he has specialized in hard SF: most of Larry Niven's books as well as works by Poul Anderson, Isaac Asimov, Hal Clement, Arthur C. Clarke, James P. Hogan, Andre Norton, Joan Vinge, and many more – about sixty books in all. Shibano has also edited two anthologies of stories from *Uchūjin*, the first in three volumes (1977) and the second in two volumes (1967).

Tatsumi Takayuki
Author (Introduction to "Collective Reason": A Proposal)

TATSUMI TAKAYUKI (born in 1955 in Tokyo) teaches American literature and literary theory at Keio University. He compiled *Nippon SF Ronsoshi* (Science Fiction Controversy in Japan: 1957–1997, Tokyo: Keiso Publishers, 2000), which won the 21st Japan SF Award, and co-edited with Larry McCaffrey a special issue of *Review of Contemporary Fiction* about "New Japanese Fiction" (Dalkey Archive Press, Summer 2002), which will be expanded into an anthology. Recent works include "Literary History on the Road: Transatlantic Crossings and Transpacific Crossovers" (PMLA 119.1 [January 2004]) and the book *Full Metal Apache: Transactions between Cyberpunk Japan and Avant-Pop America* (Duke University Press, 2006).

Toyoda Takashi
Translator (Reiko's Universe Box)

AT THE TIME he worked on this translation, Toyoda Takashi was an electrical engineer at Sharp Electronics and lived in Osaka. He left the world of science fiction and fantasy fandom many years ago, and has not kept in touch with us. We hope he sees this anthology and lets us know where he is.

Toyota Aritsuné
Author (*Another Prince of Wales*)

TOYOTA ARITSUNÉ was born in 1938 in Gunma Prefecture's Maebashi, about a fifty-minute bullet train ride from central Tokyo. He entered Musashi University as a medical student but withdrew mid-course to take up economics. He began writing and publishing imaginative stories early in the development of Japanese SF and is especially noted for his specialty in the Japanese equivalent of Western Military SF with plenty of *bushido* spirit. This is perhaps most well developed in his *Yamatotakeru* Series of novels and stories (Yamatotakeru was a legendary warrior prince of Japan's Kofun Era, fourth century AD). He was also involved in the production and writing of the TBS television cartoon series "Hachiman" (*Eight Men*), *Undersea Boy Marine*, the movie *Space Boy Soran*, and several manga series.

Tsutsui Yasutaka
Author (*Standing Woman*)

TSUTSUI YASUTAKA has been called the "Japanese guru of metafiction," and is a novelist, playwright, literary critic, actor, and musician. He debuted as a writer of detective fiction after being discovered by mystery great Edogawa Rampo, publishing his first story "O-Tasuke" (Help Me) in *Hoseki Mystery Magazine*, but it is in science fiction and fantasy that Tsutsui found his forté and earliest acclaim. His stylistic abilities range from slapstick to fabulism and metafiction, and outside genre SF he is generally viewed as a surrealist. "To me, SF is an approach to deconstruct reality, just as surrealism was," he says. Tsutsui is the recipient of the Izumi Kyoka Prize (1981), the Tanizaki Prize (1987), and the Kawabata Yasunari Prize (1989); and in 1992 he received the Japan SF Grand Prize for *Asa no Gasupāru* (Gaspard of the Morning). In 1987 he was conferred the rank of *Chevalier des Arts et des Lettres* by the French government for his literary achievements.

Gene van Troyer
Editor; Translator (Reiko's Universe Box;
The Legend of the Paper Spaceship)

GENE VAN TROYER was born and raised in Portland, Oregon. He has been writing poetry and science fiction since he was about thirteen years old and began selling it professionally when he was around twenty. He joined Science Fiction Writers of America as an active member in 1971, and has been a member continuously since. In 1973 Fred Pohl helped him connect with Shibano Takumi, and when he came to Japan in 1974 as an exchange student at Waseda University's International Division, Shibano introduced him to the Science Fiction Writers of Japan's Honyaku Benkyō-kai, after which he became a translation consultant to such translators and writers as Yano Tetsu, Shibano, Asakura Hisashi, Itō Norio, Imaoka Kiyōshi (*Hayakawa SF Magazine* editor at that time), Sakō Mariko, Ōtani Jun, Fukami Dan, and many others. From 1975 through 1980 he had a regular critical review column of American science fiction in *SF Magazine*'s "SF Scanner" section, and continued to write reviews for *SF Magazine* through 1994. His own fiction and poetry has appeared in *Eternity*, *Vertex*, *Last Wave*, *Amazing Stories SF*, and *Asimov's SF*. He is a past editor of *Portland Review*, a literary journal published by Portland State University, and *Star*Line*, the journal of the Science Fiction Poetry Association. Most recently, he edited *Collaborations: A Collection of Collaborative Poetry* published by Ravenna Press in Edmonds, Washington (2007). He presently lives in Urasoe City, Okinawa Prefecture, Japan.

Yamano Kōichi
Author (Where Do the Birds Fly Now?)

YAMANO KŌICHI was born in Osaka in 1939, studied in Kobe, but was mainly interested in movies, writing film criticism, and producing some experimental films. One of them was praised by the leading movie and theater avant-gardist Terayama Shūji, who encouraged the young author to write fiction. In Tokyo Yamano moved in theatrical and literary circles, wrote short absurdist plays and short stories, as well as much criticism in newspapers and periodicals, mainly about avant-garde writers such as Gabriel García Marquez, and about SF, which he followed in columns published in leading dailies and weeklies. He was also an editorial consultant to a Japanese SF publisher, introducing many European writers, and he published for a time the iconoclastic *NW–SF* magazine and a series of *NW–SF* trade paperbacks. Judith Merril dubbed him "the Japanese Michael Moorcock," and as Moorcock had done himself with is own influential U.K. new wave journal *New Worlds*, Yamano financed his own *NW–SF*. His books include the short-story collections *Tori wa ima doko o tobu ka* (Where Do the Birds Fly Now?, 1971), *Satsujinsha no sora* (The Murderer's Sky, 1976), *Za Kuraimu* (The Crime, 1978), the novel *Hana to kikai to geshitaruto* (Flowers, Machine, and the Gestalt, 1981), *Revolucion* (linked stories, 1983), *SF no tanjō* (The Progress of SF), and *Thoroughbred no tanjō* (The Progress of the Thoroughbred, 1990, non-fiction; Yamano is a well-known researcher of thoroughbred pedigrees and devotee of horse-racing, keeping and breeding horses himself in Australia). His iconoclastic criticism often set him at odds with established figures in Japanese SF and resulted in semi-exile from some important SF circles for many years. Yamano's other career as a racehorse commentator and owner has overtaken his SF, but at sixty-eight he is still writing screenplays and remains his iconoclastic self.

Yano Tetsu
Author (The Legend of the Paper Spaceship)
& Translator (The Savage Mouth; The Road to the Sea;
The Flower's Life is Short)

YANO TETSU is the first "Grand Old Man" of Japanese science fiction – some might say one of the founders of post-War Japanese SF&F – and was a prolific translator and author of adult and children's fantasy and SF. He began to introduce Japanese readers to the works of U.S. science fiction writers in the late 1940s. "After the war," he recollected to Gene van Troyer, "I made a living collecting trash on U.S. military bases. One day I was told to burn a lot of military editions of popular American fiction, which American soldiers threw away when they were done with them, and some of them had such fantastic and futuristic covers that I rescued them." His plan, he said, was to use these cast-off books to learn English so he could find out what such fabulous covers reflected. He was stunned by their content – a literature he never dreamed could have existed.

Fueled on the works of Robert A. Heinlein, Fredrick Pohl, C.M. Kornbluth, Arthur C. Clarke, Fredrick Brown, Isaac Asimov, and many others, Yano began to translate and find publishers for these works. He was the first Japanese writer of the genre to visit the United States, in 1953, as a guest of Robert A. Heinlein. He soon teamed up with Shibano Takumi to become part of the *Uchūjin* coterie, which published the semi-professional but influential fiction, review, and critical magazine *Uchūjin*; and he took part in founding Science Fiction and Fantasy Writers of Japan in 1963, and served as its president from 1978 to 1979.

Yano was born in Matsuyama, Ehime Prefecture and grew up in Kobe. After studying at Chuo University for three years, he was drafted into the Japanese Army, serving two years and two months. He learned to read English and eventually began translat-

286

ing science fiction. The works of Robert A. Heinlein, Frederik Pohl, Desmond Bagley, and Frank Herbert were among the approximately three hundred and sixty books he translated, and he was a close personal friend of Heinlein's. He also wrote stories of his own, including "The Legend of the Paper Spaceship," which first appeared in English translation in 1984 and has since appeared in several collections. Some of his stories, notably "Kamui no Ken" (The Sword of Kamui) have been adapted to anime and manga.

Yano's dedication bore fruit. The SF he had helped introduce to Japan has inspired a generation of Japanese authors and given rise to a literature that could rival its Anglo-American inspiration. In the late 1960s he helped sponsor Judith Merril's six month stay in Japan with the express purpose of having an American SF writer of renown work on translating Japanese SF&F stories into English. Several of those stories appear in this collection for the first time.

Yano died on October 13, 2004, from cancer of the large intestine.

Yoshimasu Gōzō
Author & Translator (Adrenalin)

YOSHIMASU GŌZŌ is a poet and multimedia art, poetry, and dance performer. While his literary output is not generally considered a part of SF, the spirit and subject matter of his poetry often overlaps the fantastic, the magical realist, and the science fictional. He is a recipient of the Takomi Jun and Rekitai poetry awards in Japan. His is a modern voice from the ancient Japanese bardic tradition that antedates the tanka and haiku conventions. Born in Tokyo in 1939, Yoshimasu has orbited post-war Japanese poetry since the publication of his first book *Departure* in 1964. Moving through unexplored regions with over thirty collections of poetry and prose, which include *Devil's Wind, A Thousand Steps*, and

Osiris, God of Stone, Yoshimasu overturns daily language through the art of *soku-zuke*, a form of *renga* or linked verse. He writes: "My body, was, wrapped, in, a light blood color. / Where, I was, walking, I've, already, forgotten." As one leading literary critic wrote: "To think about Yoshimasu is to think about change."

Kurodahan Press

Bringing the finest in Asian fiction to the English-speaking world, and opening new worlds of the imagination to readers around the globe.

www.kurodahan.com

黒田藩プレスでは、フィクション、学術を中心に選び抜かれたアジアの名作・傑作を英訳編集し、世界に向けて発信しています。古典・名作の翻訳や復刻本を中心に、お求めやすい価格で世界中の読者や専門家に提供していきたいと考えています。

眉村 卓　引き潮のとき　(全五巻)

人類が宇宙に進出し、惑星に植民を開始した時代。司政官制度が設けられ、惑星タトラデンにはキタ・PPK4が赴任を命じられる―。新しい世界を構築した未曾有のSF巨篇、ついに復刊!第27回星雲賞(日本長編部門)受賞作品。

ISBN 4-902075-06-7 (第一巻) ／ ISBN 4-902075-07-5 (第二巻)
価格：2,200円 ／ 表紙：Jim Tetlow

眉村 卓　夕焼けの回転木馬

人生の疲れを感じ始めた中原、会社勤めをしながら小説家をめざす村上。ある夜、小さな飲み屋で出会った二人に、ねじれた記憶と時間を巡る奇妙な現象が始まる―。

戦前、戦後の大阪の街を舞台に、作者自身の体験を織りまぜながら描く眉村ワールドの傑作。日本文芸大賞受賞。

昭和61年に角川文庫から出版された作品に著作者による加筆、訂正を加えて完全版として出版するものです。

ハードカバー版は100冊限定(シリアルナンバー付)、著作者のサイン入りです。

新書判: ISBN 4-902075-02-4 ／ 価格：1,500円
ハードカバー版: ISBN 4-902075-20-2 ／ 価格：4,000円
表紙：ジョニ・ウェルズ

Also from Kurodahan Press…

Lairs of the Hidden Gods

Tales in the Cthulhu Mythos from Japan

volume one: **Night Voices, Night Journeys**
volume two: **Inverted Kingdom**
volume three: **Straight to Darkness**
volume four: **City of the Dreaming God**

Edited by
Asamatsu Ken

Introduced by
Robert M. Price

Chilling, and full of surprises: this four volume anthology of Japanese horror stories is the first collection of its kind to be published in English. Starting with the basic material of H.P. Lovecraft's Cthulhu Mythos tradition, these authors create a world of terror all their own.

"I cannot say enough good things about this book. All of the stories are good with some being fantastic."
*Brian M. Sammons,
in Book of Dark Wisdom*

Each volume features about 300 pages of new translations and expert commentary. Covers are by manga artist Yamada Akihiro. You'll want to collect them all!

Order online (kurodahan.com) or through your local bookseller.

Science Fiction from Kurodahan Press

APHRODITE

YAMADA MASAKI

TRANSLATED BY
DANIEL JACKSON

The floating city

Aphrodite: ever beautiful, ever filled with the limitless energy of creation.

This is the story of Makita Yūichi, a youth who escapes the regimented world of Japanese society for the beauty and freedom of the island city Aphrodite. As the global economy spirals downward, leaving Aphrodite deserted and slated for destruction, only Yūichi can save her…

ISBN 4-902075-01-6 US$15.00 Cover art by Kobayashi Osamu.

Order online (kurodahan.com) or through your local bookseller.

KURODAHAN PRESS